Also available by Eva Gates

Lighthouse Library Mysteries

Read and Buried
Something Read Something Dead
The Spook in the Stacks
Reading Up A Storm
Booked for Trouble
By Book or By Crook

Writing as Vicki Delany

Sherlock Holmes Bookshop Mysteries

There's a Murder Afoot
A Scandal in Scarlet
The Cat of Baskervilles
Body on Baker Street
Elementary, She Read

Year Round Christmas Mysteries

Silent Night, Deadly Night
Hark the Herald Angels Slay
We Wish you a Murderous Christmas
Rest Ye Murdered Gentlemen

Ashley Grant Mysteries

Coral Reef Views
Blue Water Hues
White Sand Blues

Constable Molly Smith Mysteries

Unreasonable Doubt
Under Cold Stone
A Cold White Sun
Among the Departed
Negative Image
Winter of Secrets
Valley of the Lost
In the Shadow of the Glacier

Klondike Gold Rush Mysteries

Gold Web
Gold Mountain
Gold Fever
Gold Digger

Tea by the Sea Mysteries

Tea & Treachery

Also Available by Vicki Delany

More than Sorrow
Murder at Lost Dog Lake
Burden of Memory
Scare the Light Away
Whiteout

A Death
Long
Overdue

A Death Long Overdue

A LIGHTHOUSE LIBRARY MYSTERY

Eva Gates

CROOKED
LANE

NEW YORK

Copyright © 2020 by Vicki Delany

Published in the United States by Crooked Lane Books, an imprint of The Quick Brown Fox & Company LLC.

Crooked Lane Books and its logo are trademarks of The Quick Brown Fox & Company LLC.

Library of Congress Catalog-in-Publication data available upon request.

ISBN (hardcover): 978-1-64385-458-8
ISBN (ebook): 978-1-64385-459-5

Cover illustration by Joe Burleson

Printed in the United States.

www.crookedlanebooks.com

Crooked Lane Books
34 West 27th St., 10th Floor
New York, NY 10001

First Edition: October 2020

10 9 8 7 6 5 4 3 2 1

To: Mom

Chapter One

R eunions can be tricky things. Everyone involved approaches the gathering bursting with excitement and full of high expectations. Sometimes it turns out well: friends reconnect, photos of children and grandchildren are shared and exclaimed over, accomplishments praised, new friends made, and old enemies reconciled. Sometimes—not. Long-buried grievances are given fresh air, friendships doubted, old jealousies and resentments remembered, and new ones discovered.

Everyone goes home miserable and tells their loved ones they had a marvelous time.

Ten years later they do it all again.

I don't actually know this from personal experience. I missed my high school class's tenth reunion because it was the same weekend as my second brother's wedding. I would have preferred to attend the reunion. My brothers and I are not close, but family is family, my mother says when it suits her to think so. Besides, my sister in-law has no sisters or female cousins, so I had to be a bridesmaid. I'll never forgive her for that frilly shocking-pink dress I was forced to wear. I'm short enough that I looked like a cartoon character in it. The humidity had done its work on my curly dark hair, adding to the cartoon aspect, and the color didn't go well with the bad case of sunburn I'd suffered the weekend before.

Last year, I missed my college's tenth reunion because I'd just arrived here, in the Outer Banks, to take up the post of assistant director of the Bodie Island Lighthouse Library. Everyone wrote to tell me they'd had a marvelous time.

Right now, I was sincerely hoping Bertie James's fortieth reunion to mark her class's first day of undergrad studies would turn out to be the success she was expecting.

"Our exhibit might not exactly be worthy of the Bodleian," Charlene Clayton said, referring to the great English library where she'd worked for a few years, "but it's impressive enough."

"Speaking as a North Carolinian," Bertie replied, "I'm mighty impressed."

"Your friends and colleagues will love it." I added under my breath, "I hope."

We stood back and admired the display—the history of libraries in North Carolina. Charlene and I had gathered artifacts from near and far and worked hard over the past few days to put it together. We were proudly showing it off to Bertie James, our boss and the library director.

The idea for the exhibit had been Charlene's, something to show Bertie's college class when they gathered tomorrow evening for the start of their reunion weekend at the Bodie Island Lighthouse Library.

* * *

We'd put the display together in secret, working into the night after Bertie had left for the day, our activities concealed behind old sheets strung across the entrance to the library's alcove, and "Keep Out" signs prominently displayed. When the library was open, we'd stationed Charles, one of our more formidable staff members, at the entrance to keep the curious—Bertie most of all—out.

Now it was time for the big reveal. At closing time on Thursday evening, library staff, board members, invited Friends of the Library, and lingering patrons had gathered to see it. Charlene ripped away the sheets; Charles returned to his favorite wingback chair next to the magazine rack to wash his whiskers and have a snooze; and everyone had suitably oohed and aahed.

"I doubt," Ronald Burkowski, our children's librarian, said, "the Bodleian could have done better with the materials available."

Bertie clapped her hands. "You people are amazing."

"I'll second that," Charlene said modestly.

"Meow," added Charles from his chair.

The exhibit was a collection of old photographs of libraries in North Carolina, as well as items librarian friends had sent us or we'd been able to uncover in the depths of the town hall basement. Stuff was down there that probably hadn't been seen by a human being since the building was first built.

We'd found a real card catalog and displayed it with the narrow drawers open to show the neat rows of little typewriter-printed cards; there was also a selection of photos showing enormous rooms full of row upon row of the neatly labeled wooden cabinets.

Charlene pointed to a sign I'd hung on the back wall next to the window, showing a woman's plump red lips with her index finger pressed to them, and the word "Silence" in loud black print. "I cannot begin to imagine how they kept the kids quiet when story time let out."

"I have a vison of them descending the stairs in a calm, neat little row," Ronald said, "faces scrubbed, hair combed, socks pulled up, shirts tucked in, not saying a word under the stern eye of the children's librarian. *Not.*"

One of the photographs was of two women, in floor-sweeping skirts, high-necked blouses with puffy sleeves, and hair pulled sharply back, organizing a bookshelf, and another showed a woman on horseback, with a jaunty hat and split skirt, cradling a stack of books in her free hand. We laughed over a staff picture from the 1960s of the librarians—all women of course—with their big hair and orange and brown dresses or twin sets with pearls. Photos of patrons showed more big hair, along with flowery orange or checked pants or jeans with wide lower legs they called bell bottoms. A stern-faced librarian, complete with horn-rimmed glasses, hair pulled back into a tight bun, and high-necked blouse, sat behind a huge manual typewriter, her fingers poised above the keys. We'd dragged a similar machine out of storage, dusted it off, and displayed it next to a still-sharp letter opener, a memento of some long-ago Nags Head anniversary.

"I've just noticed," Charlene said, "there isn't one man in any of these pictures. Librarian was a woman's career back then and still largely is"—she acknowledged Ronald with a smile and nod that he returned—"but even the patrons in these pictures are all women."

"Is that Bertie's office in that picture?" Mrs. Fitzgerald, the chair of the library board said. "It must be. The window's the same, and there's a slice of the marsh showing. Look at all those filing cabinets—there's scarcely room for the director's desk. Never mind that hideous broadloom, covering up the marvelous original flooring."

"The floor in my office isn't that old," Bertie said. "The broadloom was pulled up along with layers of plywood and linoleum and some rotting hardwood back in the 1990s, and new wood laid down then."

"I feel so old," my aunt Ellen, one of the Friends of the Library, said. "I remember this stuff like it was yesterday, and now it's ancient history."

A small stack of books had been placed on one side of the desk. I opened the cover of one to show everyone the withdrawal slip. A small cardboard pocket had been glued to the inside of the cover, and a handwritten record of people who checked the book out and a stamp for the day it was due back had been slipped inside. The book was *The Celestine Prophecy* by James Redfield, and the last due date for it was July 11, 1995. The book itself had suffered some damage—a spilled cup of coffee by the look of it—which would be why it had been removed from circulation. All these years later, we still got requests for that book.

"Nineteen ninety-five," Aunt Ellen muttered. "Ancient history."

"At least we've no cuneiform tablets or rolled-up parchment scrolls to show you," Charlene said with what I thought was a tinge of regret.

"The Lighthouse Library," Mrs. Fitzgerald said, "came late to computer cataloguing, as I remember. Not many places were still using record cards like that one by the mid-nineties."

"The things that matter the most," Bertie said, "haven't changed. And that's people reading good books and loving literature and wanting to improve their knowledge of science and history."

"Hear, hear," Mrs. Fitzgerald said, and everyone murmured their agreement.

"I remember that book." Mr. Snyder, one of our regular patrons, pointed to *The Celestine Prophecy*. "It was a huge bestseller. Bunch of made-up nonsense pretending to be a novel."

"Which," Charlene pointed out, "is pretty much the definition of a novel."

"You know what I mean," he said.

"I do," Bertie said. "*The Celestine Prophecy* struck a chord in a lot of people at the time."

"I don't see any pictures of the library cat," fifteen-year-old Charity Peterson said.

Bertie laughed and gave Charles an affectionate glance. "Perish the thought. An animal in a library!"

"Speaking of ancient history," Aunt Ellen said. "Look at that computer. It's huge."

From the depths of the town hall basement, we'd excavated a real, although no longer working, Commodore 64. Charlene had searched the newspaper archives and found an article on the purchase of the machine, along with a picture of the then library director proudly showing it off to wide-eyed children.

"That's a computer?" a pre-teenage boy said. "I thought it was a TV or something." At that moment his phone buzzed. He pulled it out of his pocket and checked the screen. "Mom's here." He hefted his book bag and ran out of the library.

"A computer a child carries around in their pocket," my aunt said. "Whoever would have thought?"

"When you put it like that," Mrs. Fitzgerald said, "we are old, Ellen." Turning to us, she continued, "My congratulations to Charlene and Lucy for honoring Bertie and her class with such a thoughtful gesture." Bertie's class had gone to the University of North Carolina, but after graduation several of the women settled in the eastern part of the state, and those from further afield liked the idea of a summer weekend in the Outer Banks, so they'd decided on Nags Head as the perfect spot at which to gather.

Bertie, normally calm, unflappable, the very picture of the yoga instructor she was, had been excited about the forthcoming reunion for weeks. She was in touch with some of the women regularly, she said, but others she hadn't seen for years.

Our library isn't large: there are plenty of better places for gathering twenty women to laugh about the joys and terrors of their youth; show off pictures of families and pets, homes and holidays; and brag about their careers. But the Lighthouse Library is something very special, and Bertie was proud to offer it as a venue for the kick-off party. And Ronald, Charlene, and I were determined to show it off to its best advantage and to make Bertie proud.

"You've done a splendid job," Mrs. Fitzgerald said.

"Did you really wear your hair like that?" Charity Peterson peered at a photo at the front of the display. Bertie's freshman class: the group of beaming young women, arms around each other, posing on the wide steps of an ivy-covered building. "Ugh."

Her mother poked her in the ribs.

"What?" Charity said. "That sweater? Purple, orange, and brown stripes? Ugh."

I'd been thinking much the same thing, but I didn't say so.

"Which one are you, Ms. James?" Charity asked.

"Second on the left," Bertie said. "In the purple, orange, and brown sweater."

Charity slipped a peek at Bertie and said nothing, clearly thinking that Bertie, today wearing a light flowing dress of pale blue, had changed.

Which she had. That college picture was forty years old. Taken before I was born, never mind Charity.

"The 1980s and '90s," Louise Jane McKaughnan said, "were not known for the elegance of fashion."

"I like it," Theodore Kowalski said. "Everyone looks so young and free."

"Oh yes," Bertie said, "those were the days. We *were* young and free."

"You still are, Bertie," Connor McNeil, mayor of Nags Head, said.

She gave him a big smile.

"You've done a fabulous job with this collection of old junk," Connor said. "Feel free to come around any time and clear out the basement."

I studied the photo of a row of cabinets with neatly printed little labels on them. "Hard to imagine having to do all that on paper."

"We managed," Bertie said, "just fine."

"Some of this stuff's well before your time, isn't it, Bertie?" Connor asked.

"Charlene and I gathered whatever we could find," I said. "This exhibit isn't meant to be only about Bertie's year, but about the history of libraries in general. We thought the women would get a kick out of it."

"When do your friends arrive?" Mrs. Fitzgerald asked.

"Tomorrow," Bertie said. "They'll be dribbling in throughout the day and gathering here tomorrow evening for a welcome reception."

"Which is not," I reminded Mrs. Fitzgerald as well as Connor, who, as the major of Nags Head, was the overall boss of the library, "an official library function. Charlene, Ronald, and I are working it as a favor to Bertie, and the refreshments are being paid for by the attendees themselves."

The three—four including Charles, and one must never forget Charles—employees of the Bodie Island Lighthouse Library were a close group and extremely fond of Bertie. We'd do just about anything for her. Including acting as waitstaff and cleaning crew for her college reunion. We'd been through some tough times together, and Bertie always had our backs.

"You don't have to keep reminding me, Lucy," Connor said.

"She's afraid someone will complain about inappropriate use of library resources," Louise Jane said. "But you needn't worry, Lucy, honey. I'll be here to set them straight."

"Thank you so much LJ," Charlene said. "We can always count on you."

"I would hope so," Louise Jane sniffed.

Connor put his arm loosely around my shoulders. "The town's fully supportive of Bertie hosting her class here. We're happy to have the tourist dollars, if nothing else. Where are they all staying?"

"Most of them are at the Ocean Side," Bertie said, "but a few have friends or family to visit, or are coming with their families to make a vacation out of it. One or two of the women live locally."

We studied the exhibit for a few moments more, and then Bertie turned to us. It might have been a trick of the light, but I thought I saw tears in her eyes. "Thank you so much. Lucy. Charlene. Ronald. This weekend means the world to me."

Louise Jane shifted from one foot to the other and cleared her throat.

"And you as well, Louise Jane," Bertie said. "You've proven yourself to be a valuable member of our library community many times."

Louise Jane waved her hand in the air and sniffed again, but I could tell she was pleased.

"I can't wait to show it to Helena," Bertie said. "She's going to love it."

"Is she in one of these pictures?" Connor pointed to a picture of the 1990s-era library staff.

"I don't see her," Bertie said.

"She wasn't one for the limelight," Aunt Ellen said. "She pretty much stayed inside her office and never came out unless she had something or someone to criticize."

I cast a quick glance at my aunt Ellen, who rarely ever had a bad word to say about anyone. Helena must have rubbed her the wrong way somehow.

Helena Sanchez had been the library director before Bertie. I'd never met her because, on retirement, she moved to Florida, and as far as I knew, she'd never come back before now. It was just a coincidence that she was in the Outer Banks for a visit at the same time as Bertie's reunion, but when Bertie heard about it, she invited her predecessor to come to tonight's party, mainly to see our historical exhibit and talk about the old times in libraries.

Charles leaped off the shelf and landed nimbly at my feet. He rubbed himself against my legs and meowed as though to say, "Enough of this standing around and talking. It's dinner time."

Bertie agreed. "Thank you for coming everyone. It's time to close the library. We have a busy day tomorrow."

"As do we all," Theodore Kowalski said. "I haven't even started the current book club selection yet, and I'm very much looking forward to it. *The Moonstone.* One of my absolute favorites. Are you reading it, Connor?"

"I'm trying," Connor said. "When I can find the time. It's a big book."

"As are most of the great works of literature. Go big or go home—isn't that what young people today say?" asked Teddy who was all of thirty-three years old. He, unlike almost every other person on planet Earth, likes to pretend he's older than he is. He thinks it gives him, and his rare-book-dealing business, a more serious air.

"*The Moonstone?*" Charity asked. "Is it about travel to space? I like those old-timey books about rocket ships and weird aliens."

"The Moonstone of the title," Theodore said, "is a precious jewel with a mysterious past that's stolen during a house party in England. It's a mystery novel. *The* mystery novel, some would say."

The group began to disburse. While Theodore explained the plot of our book club selection to Charity, Mrs. Fitzgerald called good night and walked out with Mrs. Peterson who, as always, had some suggestions for expanding the children's programs at the library. Ronald and Charlene collected their briefcases and left; the remaining patrons gathered their books, and I went behind the desk to check them out. Bertie headed down the hall to her office to gather her things.

Soon only Connor, Louise Jane, and I remained in the library.

"Uh, can I help you Louise Jane?" I asked.

She looked between Connor and me.

"What?" he said.

"Would you mind," she said.

"Mind what?"

She jerked her head toward me.

"Oh," he said. "Right. I'll be outside, Lucy. When you're ready."

I eyed Louise Jane suspiciously as the door closed behind Connor. "What's up?"

She threw a quick glance at the historical exhibit before turning back to face me. "You know I said I'm happy to help here tomorrow night, at Bertie's reunion."

"Yes," I said. "And we appreciate that. Is something wrong?"

She studied my face intently. I studied hers equally intently in return. Louise Jane and I had never exactly been friends. She'd resented me since the moment I first stepped foot in the library to take up the job of Assistant Library Director. Louise Jane had thought the job should be hers, not bothering with the minor fact of her being not at all qualified. As far as she was concerned, being a fierce lover of the library as well as a descendent of long lines of proud Bankers (as natives of the Outer Banks are called) and a storyteller of local renown, should be enough. But it wasn't and I got the job. Louise Jane had made some feeble attempts to frighten me away from the library and back to Boston, but here I was a year later, comfortably settled into my position. She'd saved my life recently, and I was grateful. Extremely grateful. I'd thought we could be friends now. But I still wasn't entirely sure I could trust her.

"Historical items are all well and good, but you need to be careful when dredging them up."

I sighed. Louise Jane was not just a collector of legends and a storyteller. She was a ghost hunter. Although she'd never quite put it that way.

"I don't think we have anything to worry about," I said. "Look at the faces in those old photographs. Everyone's smiling. If they're not smiling, it's because they're so interested in what they're being shown."

"Appearances," Louise Jane said, "can be deceiving."

I didn't have the time, nor the interest, to engage with Louise Jane tonight. Sometimes, pretending to go along with her is the only way to bring things to a conclusion. "You'll be here in case anything untoward happens, right?"

"Yes. Yes, I will be."

I switched off the computer. "Now, if we're finished here, I have a date with the handsomest man in Nags Head, North Carolina."

"And I have a date with a stack of reference books."

I shouldn't have asked, but I never learn. "What are you reading about?"

"The haunting of this library. As you know, between my grandmother, her mother, and me, there's scarcely a story about the ghostly happenings in these parts that remains a secret. But in this case, 'scarcely' is the important word. Great-Gran said something the other night about a librarian who came to an unnatural end, and the story was hushed up."

"Not that again. This building has only been a library for a couple of decades. No ghostly librarian haunts the shelves."

"Your Yankee pragmatism does you credit, Lucy. Sometimes. You worry about what you can find of card catalogues, old photos, and manual typewriters. Let me worry about the spirit world."

If Louise Jane had been wearing a cape, she would have swirled it about her shoulders and made a suitably dramatic exit. Instead, she hoisted her leather satchel over her shoulder and stalked out of the library. That is, she would have stalked had she not had to do a nimble little dance to avoid Charles, who'd slipped unnoticed between her feet.

I shook my head. Charles washed his whiskers.

Chapter Two

Friday evening I dressed in black slacks and a crisp black blouse with a stiff white collar, and twisted my hair into a knot on the top of my head. If I was pretending to be a waitress, I wanted to dress the part.

I posed for Charles, stretched out on my bed. "How do I look?"

He yawned.

I studied myself in the mirror. My mother's a beautiful woman. I've occasionally been called "cute." I'm cursed with a thick mane of out-of-control black curls and round cheeks (more cuteness) that turn red far too easily when I'm embarrassed. Unlike my cousin Josie, who gets her height from her father's side of the family, I get mine from the Wyatt women, meaning not much of it. I like to think I have nice eyes, although I'd never tell anyone that. They're large and round and a soft brown color with green flakes that, Connor tells me, dance when I laugh.

I smiled at the thought and decided I'd do.

"Bertie said you can come down and join the party," I told Charles. "But behave yourself, or I'll bring you back here."

He jumped off the bed and ran to the door.

I have the world's best commute. I live above the library in what I call my Lighthouse Aerie. My apartment is tiny, but perfect for me at this stage of my life, and I don't mind living several miles outside of town. Taking the hundred steps up and down the twisting spiral iron staircase several times a day saves on gym membership.

Charles and I went downstairs to help with the setup for the party. We had an hour between the library closing at six and guests arriving at seven. Charlene and Ronald had brought a change of clothes with them, and they were clearing space in the main room for chairs and refreshment tables. Like me, my colleagues were dressed in black pants. Ronald's shirt was black, and Charlene's blouse white. Ronald had accented his outfit with a huge, yellow polka-dot bow tie. I arrived as my cousin Josie O'Malley came through the doors, laden with bakery boxes. Connor was right behind her, bearing a case of wine.

"I've more in the car," Josie said. I took the first load from her and went into the staff break room while Ronald hurried to help Connor.

I took platters down from the shelf and began arranging the treats. Josie owns Josie's Cozy Bakery, one of the most popular spots in Nags Head. She often provides desserts for library functions, but tonight she'd done canapes as well. I used what little self-control I have to keep myself from diving into the miniature crab cakes, crostini with smoked trout, cucumber roll-ups, and phyllo triangles.

Charles sprang onto the table. Charles has absolutely no self-control. "Not for you," I said as I put him on the floor.

Josie came in with more boxes, and my mouth watered as I helped her arrange the selection of baked goods. I'd had a small salad for lunch and no time for dinner. That, I realized as I studied the treats, might have been a mistake.

"You can have one if you want," Josie said.

"How'd you know that was what I was thinking?"

She grinned at me. "That's what everyone's thinking when they see my food. Try one of those." She pointed to a small chocolate-covered square.

I picked one up and studied it. It consisted of a dark crumbly base, a thick layer of custard, and a topping of chocolate ganache. I took a tentative bite, and I almost swooned as the flavors exploded in my mouth.

"Oh my goodness," I said. "This might well be the best thing I've ever eaten. What is it?"

"It's called a Nanaimo bar. A baker friend of mine moved to Vancouver Island, and she sent me the recipe. Trust me, you might think you want another one now, but don't. They're really filling."

I popped the rest of it in my mouth and chewed happily.

"Mom says this is a party for Bertie's library school crowd," Josie said, referring to my aunt Ellen.

"Yup. The start of a reunion weekend. They'll be doing the usual tourist stuff tomorrow and Sunday."

"Where did Bertie go to college?"

"She did her undergraduate studies at the University of North Carolina. That's close enough that some of her class settled in this area, but far enough many of them didn't. So they don't see each other much. I gather it's the anniversary of the first day of class, when they all met, not their graduation. This is strictly a classmates' weekend, from what Bertie tells me. Meaning, the women didn't bring husbands and families with them, or if they did, said husbands will be left to their own devices."

"Not hard to entertain oneself in the Outer Banks in summer." Josie studied the arrangement of canapes, cookies, squares, and tarts on the trays. "How's that look?"

"Good enough to eat."

She laughed.

"Be sure you have a peek at the historical exhibit Charlene and I put together before you leave. The only non-schoolmate coming tonight will be Helena Sanchez, who was the library director here before Bertie. She also went to North Carolina, but before Bertie and her crowd, so Bertie invited her. Did you ever meet Ms. Sanchez?"

Josie's pretty face twisted. "I've met her, but only once or twice, when I was with Mom."

"Was your mom a Friends of the Library member back then?"

"She was. I vaguely remember hearing her telling Dad she was going to quit. Something about not being able to get along with the director. That was several years ago, and I had plenty of other things on my mind, so my memory of that fleeting conversation might be faulty. Shortly after that, Ms. Sanchez retired, Bertie was hired, and Mom stayed on. If you're okay here, I'm off. Jake's taken the night off work, and we're having a date night."

"Have fun," I said. Josie had married Jake Greenblatt over the winter. She still had that newlywed glow about her. I hoped she always would.

I walked her to the door, and we hugged good night. Then I turned to face into the room. Connor and Ronald had set up the bar, and Charlene was arranging plates and cocktail napkins on the table where we'd put the food. Most of our bookshelves are on rollers, and we'd pushed them back to create a larger space for people to mix and mingle. We were expecting twenty-one guests, which was easily doable even for our small library. We'd had far larger parties before. Somehow the Lighthouse Library seems to be able to stretch at the seams to accommodate everyone who wants to come in.

"I offered Ronald a hand when the guests arrive," Connor said, "but he says the three of you have it all under control."

"We do," I said. "The food's made, so all we have to do is serve, tend bar, and keep things tidy. And then clean up, of course, so we look like a library at opening time tomorrow."

He pulled me into his arms and kissed me lightly on the top of my head. Then, conscious of Ronald and Charlene trying not to watch us, he pulled away. "Good night, Lucy,"

"Good night," I said.

He touched my arm lightly and called, "Break a leg," to Ronald, who had a background in theater before becoming a librarian. On the way out, Connor held the door for Louise Jane.

Ronald and Charlene stopped what they were doing, to stare. I might have stared myself.

"Goodness," Charlene said.

"Where'd you get that?" Ronald asked.

"A little something from the back of your mother's closet?" I asked.

"I always believe in dressing the part." Louise Jane wore a proper maid's uniform circa 1920s. Calf-length black dress buttoned to the throat and down the sleeves, white apron, black stockings, thick-soled black shoes. Her hair was pulled back and tucked under a crisp white cap with lace trim. She surveyed the room. "You seem to have everything under control in here. Has the food arrived?"

"It's in the break room," I said.

"I'll help you bring it out then."

"We're waiting until the guests arrive. Then you and I will circulate with the dishes. Ronald's tending bar, and Charlene will keep an eye out for potential spills or dirty napkins needing to be whisked away, and talk to the guests about our historical display."

One eyebrow rose. "Do you think that's wise, Lucy, honey? The room will get quite crowded. We don't want any accidents."

"Which is the potential spills part of my job, LJ," Charlene said. "It's all been decided. No need to worry your pretty little head about it."

"I'm only providing the benefit of my experience at this sort of thing," Louise Jane said.

Ronald and I exchanged looks. Charlene and Louise Jane never did get on. Charlene is an academic and historical librarian. The history of shipping along the eastern coast of North America is her specialty, and she's so qualified she'd worked for a time at the Bodleian Library at Oxford University in England. Louise Jane, on the other hand, is an enthusiastic amateur. She probably knows as much, if not more, history of the Outer Banks than Charlene, but her knowledge came not from history books, but from family stories and local legends, which are not always completely reliable. If Louise Jane didn't know something, she simply made it up.

A habit not inclined to endear her to the literal-minded Charlene.

It didn't help that Louise Jane had a strong interest in what she calls the paranormal history of the Outer Banks in general and our library in particular. Charlene thought that nothing but rubbish.

"Noted," Charlene said.

"Car pulling up outside," Ronald said. "It's quarter to seven, so probably Bertie."

"Stations everyone," Charlene said. "Let's do her proud."

Louise Jane dropped into a deep curtsy, and we all—even Charlene—laughed.

Charles laid claim to his favorite chair, the comfortable wingback next to the magazine rack.

Three women arrived with Bertie. They were all of an age, all smiling broadly, but the similarities ended there. These three were Bertie's closest friends from her college years, and they'd met for a drink before coming here to join the rest of their class for the party. She introduced us.

Mary-Sue Delamont was short and slight, almost a perfect caricature of a librarian with her beak nose, thick eyeglasses under bushy eyebrows, slate gray hair tied into a stiff bun, and sensible shoes. She wore a brown pantsuit that looked as though it had been plucked directly from one of the photos Bertie had given us of them at college.

Lucinda Lorca towered over her friends, and was as thin as a runway model. She looked about twenty years younger than

Bertie, the result, I thought, of some discreet surgery. She wore a yellow dress with a deeply plunging neckline and tight bodice, a thin belt, and flaring skirt; plenty of good jewelry; and sandals with dangerously high heels.

Ruth McCray was short and round, with pudgy red cheeks, a huge smile, and a mass of frizzy red hair heavily streaked with gray. She wore jeans and a red T-shirt under a blue denim jacket and had hiking boots on her feet.

After we'd been introduced, Ruth threw up her arms and declared, "I cannot believe I've never been to this library before, even when I was working in Manteo. I'm green with envy, Bertie. I saw a boardwalk heading for the marsh as we drove up. Maybe a walk down to the water later?"

"That can be arranged," I said. "It's lovely down there after dark."

"Ooh, a cat!" Mary-Sue exclaimed. "What a darling. What's his name?"

"Charles," I said. "After Mr. Dickens."

"Is he a Himalayan?"

"Yes."

Without another word she charged across the room and scooped Charles up. Charles never minded being scooped. As long as he wasn't eating.

"Can I get you ladies a drink?" Ronald asked. "I have wine, beer, iced tea, and peach juice."

They asked for wine, and Bertie said she'd have juice because she was driving. The guests followed Ronald to the makeshift bar on what was normally our circulation desk.

Cars and taxis began pulling up a few minutes later, and librarians of all shapes and sizes poured into our library. They squealed and hugged and exclaimed how they hadn't changed a bit, and phones were whipped out to show family photographs. Ronald was kept busy behind the bar, and Charlene showed the guests our historical display. The women laughed uproariously over the pictures of themselves and their school, and reminisced while looking at the photos of rows of card cabinets, and the books containing stamped withdrawal notices.

"They say when the wind blows from the south, he wanders the upper floors looking for playmates." Louise Jane was talking to one woman in a low voice. The woman's eyes were wide, and she leaned close to hear better. "Ronald," Louise Jane continued, "knows to keep a close eye on the children, and the gate to the upper levels is always locked when we're open, or who knows what might happen?"

"Louise Jane," I said, "do you have a minute?"

She peered down her nose at me. "I'm kinda busy here, Lucy. Sheila's interested in the . . . other life forms that live in the lighthouse."

Sheila nodded enthusiastically. "Ghost hunting's a passion of mine."

Oh dear. The last thing I wanted was Louise Jane leading a tour group through the upper levels in search of Frances, called the Lady, who, Louise Jane insists, was a young bride locked inside the building by her cruel, much older lighthouse-keeper husband.

To be specific, the Lady—according to Louise Jane—had been locked in *my* room. From which she escaped by throwing herself from the fourth-floor window. That I had not once in the year I've lived here seen the slightest trace of the Lady, or the little son of another lighthouse keeper who supposedly fell to his death when playing on the upper levels, where he'd been forbidden to go, didn't matter to Louise Jane.

"I believe," I said, "you were hired to help us tonight."

"If by hired, you mean paid for my time, I wasn't. And I am helping. I'm entertaining the guests."

"And very well too," Sheila said.

"But if you insist." Louise Jane emitted a martyred sigh.

"Ruth's telling everyone we're going for a walk to the marsh later," Sheila said. "Do you have stories about happenings in the marsh?"

"What an excellent idea," Louise Jane said, "I can tell you some stories on the walk. If you'll excuse me, duty calls."

She followed me into the break room, where the platters of food were waiting. "Is it time to serve?"

"Bertie wanted to wait for Ms. Sanchez, but she hasn't shown up yet, and it's almost eight, so she said go ahead. I hope Ms. Sanchez comes. Bertie's wanting to show her some of the things Charlene and I dug up from the storage rooms at the town hall."

We hefted the platters of canapes and carried them into the main room. The assembled women descended like a pack of wolves.

By eight thirty, the desserts had been decimated, and the canapes thoroughly picked over; only the usual celery stalks, sliced red peppers, and carrot sticks remained. I was clearing dirty glasses, getting no help at all from Louise Jane, who was regaling a group of women with details of her family's history on the Outer Banks.

"A taxi's pulling up outside," Ronald said to me, and I went to get the door as a woman walked up the path with firm, rapid steps. When she stepped into the light thrown by the lamp above the door, I could see that this must be the expected Helena Sanchez, previous director of the Bodie Island Lighthouse Library. She was of average height, but very thin, with small dark eyes and a face that was all sharp angles, deep shadows, and jutting bones. The skin on her face formed deep crevices, and her iron-gray hair was tied in a thick bun at the back of her head. She wore plain brown trousers, a red blouse with a white bow tied tightly at her neck, and no jewelry that I could see. A calf-length brown woolen cloak, far too hot for the warm night, was thrown over her shoulders.

"Good evening," I said. "I'm Lucy Richardson, assistant director here, and you're very welcome."

She studied me, top to toe. Then she nodded and held out her hand. I took it in mine, surprised at its strength. "I'm Helena Sanchez. I believe I'm expected."

"And so you are," Bertie said behind me. "Please come in."

I stepped out of the way, and the new arrival walked into the library.

"It's a pleasure to have you here," Bertie said.

"I'm sure it is," Ms. Sanchez replied.

"You must have missed the Lighthouse Library," I said.

"Not particularly." She glanced around the room. A few of the women smiled at the newcomer, but most of them were occupied with their friends.

Charles leaped onto the bookshelf behind us. Ms. Sanchez stared at him. "A cat," she sniffed, "roaming free in a library.

Wouldn't have been allowed in my day. Standards are slipping, Albertina. You need to guard against that."

"Charles is a valued member of our library family," Bertie said. "The children in particular get a great deal of pleasure out of him, and he's an excellent therapy cat for some of the lonely elderly who come here in search of company."

"Can't abide cats myself. Thoroughly nasty creatures."

Charles hissed.

Ms. Sanchez hissed back.

Charles jumped off the shelf and disappeared in the sea of legs.

Ruth McCray broke out of the pack and approached us, glass of wine in hand. "Helena. It's been a long time."

Ms. Sanchez blinked at her.

"Ruth McCray? We worked in Manteo together before you left to work at the Lighthouse Library."

"Oh yes. I remember you. You've put on weight."

Ruth's eyes widened in surprise. "Well, it has been a few years. I think that's allowed. I hope you're enjoying your retirement. I can't wait until it's my turn."

"I keep myself busy." Ms. Sanchez pointedly didn't ask Ruth anything about what she'd been doing all these years.

"Okay. Well, nice to see you." Ruth wandered away, shaking her head.

Ms. Sanchez glanced around the room. "I recognize some of these women. Is that Lucinda Smith talking to the man in the yellow tie? What on earth has happened to her face?"

"She's Lucinda Lorca again," Bertie said. "After her divorce she went back to her maiden name."

"Looks like she's fishing for a new husband," Ms. Sanchez said as Lucinda laughed at something Ronald said.

I threw Bertie a look. She returned it with a shrug.

One of the other women broke away from the pack and greeted Ms. Sanchez with a smile and outstretched hand. "Nice to see you, Helena."

"Margaret Hurley." Ms. Sanchez did not return the smile.

"You must know some of these women," Margaret said. "Let me take you around."

"I'd rather have a drink." Ms. Sanchez headed for the bar. Margaret hesitated and then followed.

"She's rather . . . blunt," I said when Margaret and Helena Sanchez had melted into the crowd.

"So it would seem," Bertie said. "I didn't know her well. I didn't work here when she was in charge. I was hired from outside. She interviewed me, but that was the extent of our contact. When I arrived to start work, no one said anything, but I got the feeling the staff were not entirely unhappy to see her go. I'm going to show her the display. Excuse me, Lucy."

Bertie stepped away, but before she could reach Helena, another woman came up to her. "Great party, Bertie. I absolutely love your library. It was so nice of you to think of having our opening reception here."

"It's my pleasure," Bertie said.

"I happen to have some pictures of my grandchildren in here somewhere. Would you like to see them? My son Kevin's a pediatrician—did you know that?"

"I don't believe I did." Bertie politely bent over the woman's phone to see the pictures.

I chuckled and looked around for something I should be doing. Three women were at the circulation desk chatting to Ronald, who seemed to be having a great time. Helena Sanchez pushed her way through them and managed to give Lucinda Lorca an elbow in the ribs.

Lucinda stepped out of the way. Whatever she'd been about to say died on her lips. Her eyes widened and her face tightened. She stared at the newcomer.

Ms. Sanchez gave her a glance, dismissed her, and said to Roland, "I'll have a glass of white wine. If you have anything decent that is. I can't stand Chardonnay."

"We have a nice New Zealand Sauvignon Blanc," he said.

"That will do."

Lucinda gripped her glass and melted into the crowd.

Bertie finally finished admiring grandchild photos and caught up with Helena Sanchez. She said something to her predecessor and gestured toward the alcove. They headed for it, followed by a few others, including Sheila, Ruth, and Lucinda.

I spotted a dirty plate and crumpled napkin on a side table close to the alcove and hurried to pick it up. Ronald was pouring drinks and laughing at something a woman said. Charlene stood next to the historical display, ready to show it to Bertie's guests, and Louise Jane hovered at her elbow, prepared to leap in with interpretations of her own. I picked up the plate and had started to head down the hallway to the break room when Mary-Sue Delamont passed me, returning from the ladies room. I heard a sharp intake of breath and glanced at her.

She was frozen in place with a look on her face that I can only describe as one of horror as she stared at the women gathered around the display. No, she wasn't staring at the women. She was focused on Helena Sanchez, who'd pulled a pair of drug-store reading glasses out of her bag and propped them on her nose.

"Are you okay?" I asked Mary-Sue.

She started at the sound of my voice, and the expression faded. She gave me a weak smile. "Perfectly okay, thank you. I saw someone I didn't expect, that's all. That woman wearing the ugly brown cloak wasn't in our class. Why's she here?"

"That's Helena Sanchez, the previous library director. The one before Bertie. She's visiting Nags Head, and Bertie thought she'd enjoy the historical display we put together. Do you know her?"

"No. No, I don't. Never seen her before. Excuse me." She headed for the bar.

Chapter Three

"As well as a few pictures of your class at college," Charlene said, "and old photos we were sent from near and far, Lucy and I—"

"With my advice," Louise Jane interrupted.

"—plus Louise Jane McKaughnan thought you'd get a kick out of these library artifacts. Most of the items were found in the basement of the town hall, where it would seem everything ends up that no one has any use for, but doesn't want to throw out. It's a twentieth-century historian's gold mine down there."

"So that's what happened to Mayor Cardamon," a woman said, to much laughter. I had no idea who Mayor Cardamon was. Which, perhaps, was the point.

"Those things sure bring back memories," another woman said.

"Do you remember," Sheila said to Lucinda, "the time Jackie White knocked over the entire row of card catalogues all by herself?"

"Oh gosh, yes. She fainted. We were worried that she was deathly ill." Lucinda's laugh was loud, her accent as Southern as shrimp and grits and sugar pie.

"Turned out she was so completely hungover, she couldn't see straight," Ruth said. "Old Lady O'Brian threatened to expel her."

"Whatever happened to Jackie White, Bertie?" Sheila asked. "I didn't see her name on the list. I don't remember if she graduated."

"She didn't," Bertie said. "She decided libraries weren't for her. She went to law school and is now a state senator. She sent her regrets—an important vote's being held tonight."

Lucinda let out a bark of laughter. "I could have guessed that. Jackie was perfectly suited to either jail or politics."

"Helena," Bertie said, "are you all right?"

The group stopped talking to peer at the older woman. I put down the plates I'd gathered and took a step toward her. Ms. Sanchez had gone frighteningly pale. She held an old volume in her shaking hand. *The Celestine Prophecy.* The book was open to the flyleaf. A paper pocket had been glued inside the cover to hold the record of withdrawals. With a shaking hand, Ms. Sanchez pulled out the withdrawal slip. Names were written on one side in a variety of hands, and due dates stamped next to them. "Where . . . where did you get this?"

"I'm not sure," Charlene said. "Lucy?"

"I found it in the storage rooms in the basement of town hall in a box of books that have been withdrawn from circulation, but not destroyed. I grabbed a few books at random to show how libraries used to keep track of who had books out, when they were due, and when they were returned. That particular book looks to have had an encounter with a cup of coffee. I guess that's why it was taken out of circulation."

"Is something wrong?" Bertie asked.

Ms. Sanchez's entire body shuddered. She let out a long breath and almost visibly gathered her strength around her. Her shoulders straightened, and she lifted her head to look directly at Bertie. "Wrong? No, not at all. A flood of memories, that's all. How quickly time passes." She glanced once more at the withdrawal slip and then returned it to its pocket. She closed the book and placed it on the table. The other women looked between her face and the book.

"That was most interesting," Ms. Sanchez said. "Thank you, young lady. It's getting warm in here, don't you think?" Beads of sweat had popped out on her forehead. She finished her wine in one swallow. "I could use another." She thrust the empty glass at me.

"What would you like?" I asked.

"A white wine."

"It's going well, I think," Ronald said as he poured the drink for me.

"Seems to be. Something quite odd happened just now."

"What?"

Lucinda flashed her empty glass in Ronald's face.

"Tell you later," I said.

"You're the children's librarian," I heard Lucinda say. "Isn't that lovely? I always said we need more men working in the library system. Does your wife work here also?"

"No," Ronald said, "she's an artist. She works out of a studio in our house."

"Oh." Lucinda tried not to sound too disappointed. Ronald handed her a glass, and she walked away.

By the time I returned with Ms. Sanchez's drink, Charlene was explaining how we'd gathered the old library things and the archive photos. Ms. Sanchez was pretending to listen, but her attention kept returning to *The Celestine Prophecy*.

I'd never read the book, but my mom had. A great many people had. Mom talked for months about how "powerful" and "life changing" it was. It didn't, as far as I could see, change my mom's life one little bit, but I knew other people had been strongly affected by it. More than a few had quit their jobs and abandoned their families to follow the protagonist's supposed spiritual journey. Perhaps it had had a similar effect on Helena Sanchez.

"Here you go," I said.

She started. "Do you have to sneak up on people like that?"

"I'm sorry," I said, although I'd been doing anything but sneaking.

She snatched the glass out of my hand and took a long drink. "I need to sit down for a few minutes. I see that horrid cat is in the best chair. Get rid of it, will you?"

I wasn't about to *get rid of* Charles, but I would lift him out of the chair. I did so and Ms. Sanchez dropped down with another disapproving sniff as Charles ran off to hide behind a potted plant.

"Isn't she a charmer?" Charlene whispered to me when the guests had moved on.

"I wonder what she found so interesting in that book."

"You noticed that too, did you? A blast from the past probably. An unpleasant memory stirred."

Gradually the guests began to disperse. Women called taxis or headed for their cars after thanking us for a lovely evening, exchanging hotel details and phone numbers, and confirming arrangements for tomorrow. Some were going to their hotel bar for another drink, and some were heading back to their beds after a long traveling day. They'd meet again as a group in the morning for a visit to the Wright Brothers Memorial in Kitty Hawk, then spend the afternoon at the beach with a picnic lunch catered by Josie's Cozy Bakery, followed by dinner at Jake's Seafood Bar. More beach time on Sunday and then a farewell lunch at the Ocean Side Hotel, where many of them were staying.

As the evening wound down, Mary-Sue had pointedly ignored Ms. Sanchez and kept herself well away from the older woman. The people she'd been talking to said their good nights, and she was left standing alone. Ms. Sanchez approached her. "Mary-Sue Delamont, I thought I recognized you lurking at the edges of the room."

My ears pricked up. Mary-Sue told me she didn't know Ms. Sanchez.

Mary-Sue's face darkened. "Hardly lurking, Helena. I have a perfect right to be here. I was as much a part of this class as any of the others."

"Your qualifications were never in doubt. It was your behavior that got you sacked."

Mary-Sue glared at the older woman. A vein pulsed in her throat, and she gripped her empty glass so hard I feared it might break. I stepped up to her and held out my tray. "Can I take your glass?"

She turned to me. "Thank you. You and your colleagues have been perfect hosts."

"It's our pleasure having you here," I said.

Ms. Sanchez walked away, not trying to hide her smirk.

Eventually only the three women who'd come with Bertie, Sheila, who was still talking to Louise Jane about ghostly presences, Ms. Sanchez, and the library staff were left.

"It's still early," Ruth said. "Who's up for that walk to the marsh?"

"Is it safe?" Lucinda asked Ronald.

"Perfectly safe. We'll bring flashlights." He glanced at her feet. "If you stay on the boardwalk, you'll be fine in those shoes."

"As long as no one wanders off by themselves," Louise Jane said, "and gets eaten. Or worse."

Lucinda's hands flew to her chest, and she gasped. "What does that mean?"

"She's kidding." Ronald gave Louise Jane a warning look.

"I'm kidding about being eaten," Louise Jane said. "No crocodiles live in these parts, and the mosquitoes aren't bigger—not by much anyway—than anyplace else. Although . . . some say when the wind blows from the north . . ."

"Whatever," I said. "You'll enjoy a walk. It's lovely out there."

"What happens when the wind blows from the north?" Sheila asked.

"I don't think we need to hear that fable right now, Louise Jane," Bertie said. "Don't you have to help with the cleaning up?"

"Charlene and Lucy can manage," Louise Jane said.

I'd been about to decline the walk in order to get started on cleaning up. No way was I going to do it all by myself while Louise Jane entertained guests. "I'll come too. We can do the dishes later, Louise Jane. You remember Charlene has to leave by nine forty-five, don't you?" Charlene's mother was disabled and needed care. Charlene had arranged for a friend to come to their house to have dinner and watch a movie with Mrs. Clayton until ten.

"Sorry," Charlene said. "I can come in early tomorrow."

"Don't worry about it," I said. "Louise Jane, Ronald, and I can manage. Can't we, Louise Jane?"

Louise Jane grumbled but wisely said nothing.

I carried a load of used glasses into the break room and found my keys in a drawer. A tiny flashlight was attached to the chain in case the light over the door was off when I got home one night.

Back in the main room, the handful of remaining guests were gathering to depart. Phones were out, and the flashlight apps being switched on. Ronald carried a solid Maglite we kept in the circulation desk in case of power failure. Bertie explained that the 1000-watt light high above us in the great first-order Fresnel lens flashed in a regular pattern of 2.5 seconds on, 2.5 seconds off, 2.5 seconds on, and 22.5 seconds off. When it was off, it could be very dark outside if the night was cloudy. We were quite a distance from the lights of Nags Head to the north; to the east was the open ocean, and nothing lay to the south but Cape Hatteras National Seashore and a few scattered small communities.

"This is exciting," Mary-Sue said to Sheila.

"I hope we see a ghost," Sheila said.

"I don't," Lucinda said.

"Are you coming, Helena?" Bertie asked. "I've promised you a ride back to town, but you can wait inside if you like."

"A brisk evening walk, I always say, makes for a good night's sleep," Ms. Sanchez replied.

"Off we go then," Bertie said. "We'll only be a few minutes, Lucy, so no need to lock up after us."

"Can Charles come?" Mary-Sue cradled the big cat in her arms.

"He'd love to," I said, "but better not. The birders won't thank us if they hear he's been running through the marsh."

She tapped him on the nose. "Naughty boy." She put him on the floor. He gave me a filthy look and stalked off, tail high, no doubt in search of an overlooked crab cake.

Bertie led the way outside and the women followed. Ronald, Charlene, and I brought up the rear. Charlene called good night and headed for her car. I closed the door behind us. Once we'd stepped out of the light cast by the lamp over the door, we were plunged into near total darkness. The cloud cover was heavy tonight, and not a trace of moon or stars could be seen. Even when the light high above us came on, it didn't throw much illumination down to the ground. It had been designed to be visible thirty miles out to sea, not to show the way to a group of librarians at its feet.

"Is there a word for a collection of librarians?" I whispered to Ronald.

"Not that I know of, but there might be. There is for just about everything else."

"A leaf of librarians?"

"A shelf of librarians?"

"I like that one," I said.

The group began to spread out almost immediately. Some walked faster than others, some stopped to admire their surroundings or take pictures. Lucinda tried to get a selfie with the lighthouse in the background. Louise Jane, who'd taken off her white apron and white lace cap, hung back with Sheila while Bertie walked ahead with Ms. Sanchez, who set a brisk pace. Ronald hurried to catch up with Bertie and shine the Maglite on the ground in front of them to guide their way.

It was a lovely evening, warm and still and quiet. The light from my little keychain barely showed the tips of my toes, but I didn't mind. I enjoyed the peace. Something rustled in the marsh grasses, and one of the women squealed.

"It's only a rabbit," Ruth said. "It's more afraid of you than you are of it."

"I doubt that," Lucinda mumbled.

"Bertie," Ruth called, "you must get a lot of people coming into the library, wanting information about the marsh wildlife. I hope you have a good collection of natural history books."

"We do." Bertie dropped back to chat with her friend, and Ms. Sanchez charged on ahead alone, into the dark, her brown cloak swirling around her. Ronald hesitated, unsure of which person or group to walk with.

"I'm trying to learn," I said to Ruth, "but the names of birds have never exactly been my forte. I can tell a robin from a duck and that's about it." I wasn't lying about that. We kept a guide to birds of North Carolina at the circulation desk, and if people came in and asked about a specific bird they'd seen, I'd learned not to try their patience by attempting to locate the reference myself. I just handed them the book.

Everyone walked at a different pace. As we crossed the lawn, the group spread out, and voices drifted on the light night wind. Lucinda had dropped into step next to Ronald and tried to take his arm, saying her shoes were unsteady. He'd mumbled something about needing to light the way for Mary-Sue, and Lucinda soon fell back. "I've had enough. I'll wait for y'all in the library," she called after us.

The first of our group reached the boardwalk, and I heard the planks settle under their feet. East of the lighthouse, a wooden boardwalk runs from the parking lot down to the marsh, through tall wet grasses and patches of swamp, ending at a pier jutting into the green water. During the day, it's a popular spot for birders. Beyond the marsh, Highway 12 winds along the edge of the open Atlantic Ocean. The calmer waters of Roanoke Sound are behind us, to the west.

Points of light from Ronald's powerful Maglite, my little beam, and the light from iPhones, spread out along the board-walk as we reached it.

"Turn off your flashlights, everyone"—Louise Jane's voice came from somewhere ahead of me—"so we can get the best effect." One by one the lights went out.

A dim yellow glow lit up the sky to the north. Otherwise, all was completely dark. If not for the clouds, the display of stars would be magnificent.

"Imagine," Louise Jane's voice settled into storyteller mode, "it's the year 1611, and you've arrived on this coast after three horrible months at sea. There's no lighthouse. No town. Over there, perhaps, burns a small cooking fire. Maybe a kerosene lamp or a single candle is lit behind the paper window of one of the small houses, but not for long, as fuel is not for wasting."

It was a warm night, and I was surrounded by friends, but I felt the hairs on my arms rise and a shudder run down my spine. Most of us were dressed in some manner of dark clothes, including Louise Jane, Ronald, and I, who were all in black, and the figures blended seamlessly into the darkness of the night.

In the modern world we're rarely, if ever, enveloped by complete darkness. Even I, living so far out of town, have the benefit of the lighthouse light shining through the night and all the electricity I need at a flick of my fingers.

"You're part of one of the first groups of Europeans to arrive on these shores," Louise Jane continued, "but not the first people. Is someone watching?"

I wrapped my arms around myself and reminded myself I was surrounded by friends.

"It's 1715. Caribbean pirates have been known to sail up the coast in search of plunder. Blackbeard himself has a base in Ocracoke. With no lighthouse to warn of the treacherous currents in the Graveyard of the Atlantic, sailing is dangerous. Is that a light from a ship, a single flash as it feels its way in the dark? No ship would be out at sea, this close to shore in the dead of night, if it wasn't up to no good."

Someone sucked in a breath. I couldn't tell who it was. I couldn't see anyone. I could hear nothing but soft breathing, the creak of the boards as people shifted their weight, the rustle of the breeze in the long grasses, the gentle movement of water lapping the pier at the end of the boardwalk, and Louise Jane's steady voice.

"It's 1861, and armies are on the move. A few lamps burn in tents or from the front of supply wagons, but we're a long way from the nearest town, and the night is treacherous. Where you have armies, you have camp followers and deserters and very nervous soldiers."

A loud splash came from ahead and to my right in the vicinity of the pier at the end of the boardwalk.

A light broke the night and shattered the spell of Louise Jane's words. "Wasn't that interesting? Thank you, Louise Jane." Bertie shone her flashlight across the ground. "Shall we carry on?"

"That's enough for me," Mary-Sue said. "Almost scared the living daylights out of me."

"Are there records of Civil War–era soldiers haunting this area?" Sheila asked.

"Oh yes," Louise Jane said. "Sergeant O'Leary lives in the lighthouse."

"He does not," I said.

She ignored me as she usually does. "He died before the lighthouse was built, but he was hastily buried in an unmarked grave, and the building was put up over him. Building the lighthouse itself was a highly dangerous job. Several workmen are believed to still be hanging around outside."

"They are not," I said. As usual, no one paid any attention to my feeble protests. Why bother with the truth, when Louise Jane's stories were so much more interesting? I led the way down the boardwalk to the water.

I was first to reach the small pier marking the end of the trail. Here people can tie up their boats and get out to have a look around. Bertie and Ronald walked behind me. I turned to see a couple of lights bobbing along the boardwalk, followed by dark indistinguishable shapes. At least one person had ventured into the edges of the marsh itself, but I couldn't tell who it was.

"We seem to have lost a few people," I said to Bertie.

"Louise Jane and her tall tales," Bertie said.

"I thought she was pretty good," Ronald said.

"If I didn't know her and her stories as well as I do," I said, "it would have scared the life out of me too."

"Everyone," Bertie called, "it's time to turn back. We don't want to lose anyone."

"I can't see a blasted thing," Mary-Sue called out.

"Don't you have a light?" Ronald asked.

"No. I was with Sheila, but I've lost her."

"Over here," Louise Jane called.

"Come toward my light." Ronald held the Maglite up and waved it over his head. "And we can all walk back together."

No one could get lost, no matter how dark it was, with the lighthouse looming overhead, but we didn't want any twisted ankles or anyone stumbling into the dark waters.

"Lucinda went back by herself," I said.

"Where's Helena?" Bertie said. "Helena!"

No answer.

Louise Jane stepped onto the pier. "Sheila was with me, and then she wasn't."

"I'm here," Sheila said. "Gosh, that was interesting. You should do ghost tours. You'd make a fortune."

Louise Jane preened.

"Ow!" Mary-Sue's voice came out of the dark.

"Are you okay?" Bertie called.

"I stubbed my toe." Mary-Sue hobbled into the circle of light. "No harm done. I think."

We were all here except for Lucinda and Helena. Helena had said nothing about turning around, but she didn't seem the type to worry about other people worrying about her.

"Helena!" Bertie yelled. "Are you out there?"

Silence.

"She probably gave up on the walk and is waiting for us at the library," Ronald said. "Is everyone ready to go back?"

"I need to come out here tomorrow," Ruth said, "and have a proper look around in the daylight. It should be at its best as the sun's rising. Anyone want to join me?"

"Not me," Sheila said. "I'm looking forward to a huge pot of coffee and a long luxurious breakfast in the hotel restaurant."

"Must be nice," Mary-Sue said. "My husband will be wanting a full cooked breakfast as he does every Saturday and Sunday morning." I'd overheard snatches of conversation earlier and knew that Mary-Sue lived in Nags Head. She was no longer a librarian, but worked as a realtor.

"You must get an incredible number of birds out here in the morning," Ruth said.

"It's a popular spot for birders," I said. "Particularly in the fall, when migrating birds stop here for a rest on their way south."

Ruth leaned over the railing and peered into the dark water. "I thought you said there aren't any crocs around here?"

Mary-Sue squealed, leapt back, and crashed into Louise Jane. Louise Jane grabbed her arm to keep them both from falling, and Mary-Sue mumbled apologies.

"There aren't," Bertie said. "You must be looking at a log."

"I don't think that's any log."

I leaned over the railing next to Ruth and peered into the darkness. Something was floating in the water, bumping gently against the pylons holding up the wooden dock, and it was a lot bigger than a duck or a Canada goose.

"Ronald," I said, "shine that light down there, would you?"

He did so. The Maglite caught a flash of white skin and brown cloth and tendrils of gray hair caressing the surface of the water.

"Oh my gosh!" Ruth yelled. "Someone's in there."

Ronald clambered over the railing and jumped into the water. I was right behind him. The rest of the women rushed to the edge. Mary-Sue screamed and kept on screaming. I'd jumped without thinking, but thankfully the water only came up to my waist. Ronald still had a firm grip on the Maglite, and he held it high so we could see. I fought my way the few feet to whatever lay in the water as weeds and long grasses tugged at my legs and thick mud filled my shoes, trying to pull me down. I reached it first, and Ronald helped me turn it over.

The dark, vacant eyes of Helena Sanchez stared up at us.

Chapter Four

R onald began mouth-to-mouth resuscitation while Bertie called 911. Still standing in the warm gentle waters of the marsh, I cradled Ms. Sanchez's head. I felt something warmer and thicker than water on my fingers and lifted my hand. Blood glistened in the light from the women's phones and flashlights. Five sets of wide, frightened eyes peered over the railing down at me.

"They're coming," Bertie called, "but they'll be a few minutes. Is she . . .?"

Ronald glanced at me and gave his head a quick shake. "Bertie," I called, "why don't you take the other women to the library. We'll wait here for the medics."

"Excellent idea," Bertie said. "Come along, ladies. Let's get out of these people's way."

"What's happened?" Mary-Sue said. "Is she okay? Why isn't she moving?"

"How did she get in the water?" Sheila asked. "Did she fall down the ladder?"

"I'll stay here," Louise Jane said. "And help."

"I need you," Bertie said in a voice that tolerated no argument. "Someone has to meet the ambulance and lead them here."

"Bertie!" I yelled.

Her face popped over the railing. "Yes?"

"You might want to tell them to send . . . Sam Watson and his crew." I deliberately avoided use of the word "police."

"You think . . .?"

"I do."

"Understood. Come along, everyone. Keep together. I don't want anyone wandering off." She spoke as if to a kindergarten class on an excursion to the zoo.

"Is she going to be okay?" Sheila asked.

No one answered.

Gradually the babble of voices died away, and the glow of their lights faded. My phone was still lying on the pier, where I'd dropped it before I jumped, the beam of light shining into the sky. Ronald's curly gray hair was soaked, and his no-longer-cheerful bowtie askew. "Am I wasting my time, Lucy?" he said between breaths.

"I think so."

"You think this is a police matter?"

"I do. There's a cut on the back of the neck. Hard to tell in the water, but the bleeding seems to be slowing. I don't think she tripped over a loose board and fell in. I suppose that might have happened and she hit her head on the way over, but that seems unlikely."

"Yeah," he said, "it does."

"I wish I didn't know things like that. But I do." Something crawled across my foot, and I screamed. Then it was gone, and I began to breathe again. "Just a clump of weeds," I said as much to myself as to a started Ronald.

Sirens sounded in the distance, getting closer. Powerful lights appeared on the boardwalk and voices called out. "We're coming!" Louise Jane yelled.

And then people were in the water next to us and hands took the floating body of Helena Sanchez from us.

*   *   *

"I'm coming to no conclusions yet," Detective Sam Watson said, "but I'm also not ruling anything out."

"The wound in the back of the neck does look suspicious, though, don't you think?" I said.

"Lucy, please allow me to be the judge of what looks suspicious and what doesn't."

"Sorry," I mumbled. But I wasn't sorry in the least. Why shouldn't I speculate? I'd been there. I'd seen Helena Sanchez's long gray hair released from its bun and floating among the weeds. Sam Watson hadn't arrived until the medics had lifted her out of the water, laid her on the pier, checked her over, and then covered her with a blanket.

After that, Ronald and I, along with Louise Jane, returned to the library to give the others the news. We'd passed Watson running down the boardwalk. He told us to make sure no one left the area before he could talk to them.

I was in the break room, making hot tea and coffee, when Watson came in. I'd run upstairs, torn off my wet clothes, and thrown on yoga pants and a loose T-shirt. Ronald didn't have anything dry to change into, but Bertie had tucked the wrap she keeps in her office around his shoulders. She and the others were in the main room. Our guests were huddled into themselves, in shock. When we walked into the library, they jumped to their feet, their faces full of questions. I gave Bertie a quick shake of my head, and she told her friends Helena Sanchez had died. I added that the police wanted to speak to them before they left, and after changing out of my wet clothes, I went into the break room to put the kettle and coffeepot on. Watson found me arranging mugs and jugs of cream and sugar on a tray.

"Coffee, Detective?" I asked.

"No thanks. I spoke briefly to Bertie, and she told me the woman's name, but she suggested I talk to you while she stayed with her friends. What was going on here tonight? Who are those women? I don't recognize them. Was the dead woman part of their group?"

"They're here for a reunion of Bertie's college class. Tonight was the first night of a planned weekend."

He waved his hand at the pile of used dishes, cutlery, and glassware on the countertops and stacked in the sink. "Judging by all this, you had more guests than just them. How many people were here tonight in total do you think?"

"Nineteen students from the class, plus Bertie, which makes twenty. Plus Helena Sanchez, the"—I swallowed— "dead woman. The three of us who work here and Louise Jane."

"Always Louise Jane," he said.

"Where else would I be?" Louise Jane marched into the break room. "I'll be happy to give you the benefit of my observations, Detective. I was paying close attention all evening to the conversation and the body language of those present. What do you need to know? Ask me anything." She faced him, feet apart, hands on hips, eyes intense.

"When did the others leave?" Watson asked.

"I'm not entirely sure," she admitted. "I didn't have my eye on the clock the entire time. Lucy?"

"Most of the guests left between nine thirty and quarter to ten. I remember the time because Charlene had to get home to her mom by ten, and she walked out of the library with us, on our way to the boardwalk."

"Why did you go there?" he asked.

"I suggested it," Louise Jane said. "The women are interested in the history of this area. They are librarians after all."

"That's not right," I said. "It was Ruth's idea. She seems to be a nature lover, and she mentioned going for a walk as soon as she arrived."

"I meant," Louise Jane said quickly, "that they begged me for stories, so I agreed a walk would give us the proper atmosphere."

"Which one's Ruth?" Watson asked.

"The short one with frizzy red hair." I poured coffee into a carafe and added hot water to the teapot. A handful of canapés and desserts were left, so I took them out of the fridge and arranged them on a platter.

"The dead woman—this Helena Sanchez—she went with you?"

"Yes," I said.

Louise Jane helped herself to a pecan square.

"Did you stay together?"

I scrunched up my face. "I'm afraid not. We spread out almost immediately. Some walked faster than others. Some lingered. Lucinda—that's the tall one—"

"The one who's had plastic surgery done," Louise Jane interrupted. "You might want to watch out for her, Sam. Apparently she's in search of her next husband."

"I'll bear that in mind," he said dryly. "Other than that, what about her?"

"She didn't come all the way to the end of the boardwalk with the rest of us. She turned back. Her shoes weren't suitable."

"Did you see her go back? Into the library?"

"No," I said.

Louise Jane shook her head.

"Other than this Lucinda . . . last name?"

"Lorca. Lucinda Lorca."

"Other than her, did you lose track of any of them for a period of time?"

"All of them," I admitted. "I lost track of every one of them. I can't say for sure where anyone was between leaving the library and arriving at the pier."

"Does that include Bertie and Ronald, and each other?"

"'Fraid so," I said.

"I was talking to Sheila," Louise Jane said. "She's particularly interested in the paranormal history of—"

"Were you with her all the time?" he asked.

"Uh . . . no . . . I guess not." Louise Jane popped the last bit of the square into her mouth. "Sorry."

"I don't think we can help you, Detective," I said. "I'd never met any of those women, including Ms. Sanchez, before seven o'clock tonight." I thought about Mary-Sue's obvious antagonism toward the dead woman but said nothing. There was a history there, but it was up to Mary-Sue to tell the detective.

"Me neither," Louise Jane said.

"Even Bertie hasn't seen most of them for years."

"I'll talk to them now." Watson left the kitchen. I picked up the tray, loaded with mugs, teapot, coffee carafe, containers of cream and sugar, and napkins.

Louise Jane grabbed a crab cake and followed Watson. I sighed, put down the tray, balanced the plate of food on the edge, and staggered out under the load.

Mary-Sue rose to her feet to help me when I came into the main room. She took the coffee jug and teapot, and I put the tray on the circulation desk. "Please," I said, "help yourselves."

Ruth and Lucinda gave me weak smiles. Sheila kept her head down, twisted her hands in her lap, and said nothing. Mary-Sue stared out the window, although all she'd be able to see was darkness. Bertie and Ronald stood together in the alcove, Ronald dripping dirty water on the floor. Charles had resumed his place in the wingback chair.

Officer Holly Rankin stood against the door, watching and listening, saying nothing. My friend Butch Greenblatt had been the first officer to arrive, and he was down at the water, overseeing the forensic examination of the pier and adjacent area.

I studied each of the women, their feet in particular, trying not to be too obvious about it. Whoever had killed Helena—and it still had to be determined if someone had and, if so, whether it was one of the women gathered here—had reached the pier before the rest of us. That scream, abruptly broken off, I'd heard as Louise Jane spun her tale must have been Helena. It had come from the direction of the pier.

Most of the women's shoes were damp, and some had long grasses or a bit of mud stuck to the soles, but none of them looked as though they'd been in the water.

Meaning the killer, if it was one of these women, hadn't climbed over the railing of the boardwalk and run off. She'd either slipped around us on the boardwalk, unnoticed in the dark, or remained where she was and fell in with the rest of the group as we reached the pier.

She must have nerves of steel.

Watson allowed Bertie and her friends to serve themselves refreshments, and then he cleared his throat and said, "If I can please have your names, where you live, and what brings you here tonight."

Bertie's guests glanced at each other.

"I might as well go first," Sheila said. "I'm Sheila Jameson, and I live in Virginia Beach, where I'm a librarian at the public library. I'm here for the college reunion and staying at the Ocean Side Hotel."

"Mary-Sue Delamont. I'm a real estate agent in Nags Head. I'm part of the reunion. Because I live locally, I'm not staying at a hotel, but at my own house." She gave the police the address, and Holly Rankin wrote it down.

"My name is Lucinda Lorca. I live in Los Angeles, California. Like Mary-Sue, I don't work as a librarian anymore, but I wanted to catch up with my old friends. I'm also staying at the Ocean Side Hotel. Most of the out-of-towners are."

"Ruth McCray. Baltimore. I'm a librarian at Johns Hopkins University. Like the others, I'm staying at the Ocean Side."

"Thank you," Watson said. "Can you tell—"

"Louise Jane McKaughnan. Nags Head. I—"

"Thank you, Louise Jane. I know who you are."

"Just stating it for the record."

"Noted. Bertie, you go first. What can you tell me about Helena Sanchez?"

"She was the director here immediately before me. She moved to Mount Dora, Florida, I believe, when she retired. That was ten years ago, and until tonight I haven't seen her since. I'd heard she was visiting the area, and I thought she'd enjoy seeing the display Lucy and Charlene put together. So I invited her to join us tonight."

"You say she was visiting. Visiting who?"

"Whom." I said.

"Pardon me, Lucy?"

"Visiting whom. Not who." I ducked my head. "Sorry."

Bertie gave me a fond smile. Then she turned back to Sam Watson. "I don't know, except that it was somewhere in Nags Head. I don't know anything about her private life. I've had no contact with her since she left the library ten years ago, and I didn't know her before that."

"How'd you know she was in Nags Head?"

"She ran into Ellen O'Malley in town, and they exchanged phone numbers. Ellen told me. I thought . . . I guess I thought Helena would enjoy seeing the library again. I was wrong about that."

"What do you mean?"

"She didn't seem to be having a good time. That's all. Maybe she had something on her mind. I can't say what that might have been, if anything."

Lucinda and Sheila glanced at each other and said nothing. Mary-Sue fiddled with her coffee mug, and Ruth studied her fingernails.

"How did she get here?" Watson asked.

"She came in a cab. I said I'd give her a lift after the party, which is why she came on the marsh walk with us. She was waiting for her ride."

"Did any of you know her prior to this party?" Watson asked.

Ruth tore her attention away from her nails. "I worked with her in Manteo for about a year. That would have been twenty or so years ago, before I moved to Baltimore. Helena moved between libraries quite a lot in her early years. She was never . . . much of a people person."

"You can say that again," Mary-Sue said. "Although she did stay here, at the Lighthouse Library for the last fifteen years of her career."

Watson looked at her. She flushed and cleared her throat. "I don't mean to speak ill of the dead, but Helena Sanchez was a horrid person. I worked here when she was director."

"I didn't know that," Bertie said.

"Not for long, and it wasn't a pleasant time in my life. Because of that experience I gave up being a librarian and got my realtor's license. I was surprised to see her here tonight, but other than that, I didn't really care. It happened a long time ago, and I haven't given Helena Sanchez a single thought since." She gave Sam Watson a big smile.

I studied Mary-Sue's face. The smile disappeared when she caught me looking, and she flushed and dipped her head. She was lying; she'd been very upset to see Helena. Upset enough to initially tell me she didn't know the other woman.

"I didn't find her difficult," Ruth said. "She was perfectly fine to work with. A bit of a perfectionist sometimes, but I've known people to be worse. She was never what I'd call friendly, and we didn't socialize outside of work, but she wasn't nasty to anyone either."

"I guess you were just lucky then," Mary-Sue snapped.

"I never worked with her," Lucinda said, "but the librarian world's a small one, and I met her at conferences and training days and such. I moved to California a long time ago and haven't seen her since."

"I'd never met her before tonight," Sheila said.

"I'll need the names of everyone who was here tonight," Watson said, addressing Bertie.

"I'll e-mail you a copy of the guest list. It has everyone's e-mail addresses also."

"You don't seriously think someone killed Helena, do you?" Ruth said. "She fell into the water. She obviously got to the pier before the rest of us. It was dark and she didn't have a light of her own. She must have tripped. Tragic, but an accident."

"I haven't come to any conclusions," he said.

"It's routine," Lucinda said, "for the police to investigate any unexpected death. Isn't that right, Detective?"

"Right," he said. "I'd like to speak to each of you privately, one at a time. Bertie, can I use your office?"

"You know the way," she said.

Which, much to our regret, he did.

"I'll start with you," Watson said to Ronald, whose lips were turning blue as he shivered under the wrap. "Then you can go home and get yourself warmed up."

"Th–th–thank you. Just this once, I won't be a gentleman and say 'Ladies first.'" Ronald got to his feet and headed for the hallway, followed by Watson. Officer Rankin stayed in the main room with us, probably to keep us from talking and "getting our stories straight."

Not that we had a story to get straight.

"Once more," Louise Jane said, "strange happenings are afoot at the Lighthouse Library. I'm available to offer any help you need, Lucy."

"Why would I need your help?"

She jerked her head toward the listening officer.

"This has nothing to do with me," I said. "I'm not getting involved."

"Are you a private detective?" Sheila asked. "That's exciting. I thought you worked here."

"I do work here. And I am not a private detective."

"Lucy has sometimes helped the police with their inquiries," Louise Jane said.

Four sets of eyebrows rose.

"I don't think that expression means what you think it means, Louise Jane," I said.

"What does it mean?"

"Helping the police with their inquiries doesn't mean you are 'helping the police with their inquiries.' It means you're being questioned prior to being arrested."

"It does?"

"Yes, it does. Don't you read British police procedurals?"

"Why would I do that? In my limited free time, I prefer to read North Carolina history or historical fiction."

"I hope this doesn't spoil our weekend," Lucinda said.

"It shouldn't," Mary-Sue said. "Most of us didn't know the woman, and if we did, we didn't like her."

"That's rather unkind, isn't it?" Ruth said.

"I'm being honest. That's all." Mary-Sue checked her watch. "I hope this doesn't take too long. I'm tired."

Ronald was soon back. He said good night and left. Watson asked Mary-Sue to join him in Bertie's office.

"While we're waiting our turn to talk to Detective Watson," I said to Louise Jane, "we can finish the cleaning up."

"You go ahead," she said.

Bertie started to stand. "I'll give you a hand, Lucy."

"I meant *we* as in Louise Jane and me. Not you. This is your party."

"I need to be doing something productive."

"So do I," Ruth said. "Come on, everyone. Many hands make light work."

And they did. Before long we had the library spic and span and ready to open tomorrow.

If we did open tomorrow.

"Do you think Watson's going to order us to keep the library closed until further notice?" I asked Bertie as I rinsed out the coffee maker.

"I see no reason. The death happened outside."

"They were stringing police tape around the boardwalk when we left."

"That should be enough then. I hope."

Watson finished questioning Mary-Sue, Ruth, Lucinda, and Sheila, and called for a police car to take them back to their homes or the hotel.

"Can I ride in the back?" Ruth said as they prepared to leave. "I've always wanted to ride in the back of a cruiser."

"See you tomorrow, Bertie," Mary-Sue called. "Are you coming to the Wright Brothers with us?"

"I was planning to, but I'll have to see what happens here."

"I hope they get the boardwalk open before I have to leave," Ruth said. "I asked Detective Watson about that, but he wouldn't say."

"Is Detective Watson married?" Lucinda asked me.

"'Fraid so," I said. "I know his wife well. They're very happy together."

"Too bad," she said.

I glanced across the room to where Watson was talking to Officer Rankin. The tips of his ears might have turned pink.

"We can talk in here," he said when the women had left. "Tell me what happened tonight, after you started on this walk."

"First," I said, "there's something you should know. Mary-Sue wasn't at all blasé about seeing Helena. She was, in fact, extremely upset. I might even say horrified. At first she lied to me, told me she didn't know her. Then, obviously, it came out that she did, and not at all fondly."

"Lucy's right," Bertie said. "She cornered me and demanded to know why Helena was here. I explained my reasoning, and she said I should have sent out a full guest list. If she'd known she'd bump into Helena, she wouldn't have come. She was furious. I apologized and said if she wanted to leave early, I'd call her a cab. She said she was here now and wouldn't be driven away as though she were the one who'd done something wrong."

"Which implies," Watson said, "that she believes Helena Sanchez did something wrong. I thought she was hiding something. I'll have another chat with her tomorrow. Thank you. You don't know what might have caused this animosity between them?"

"No," Bertie said.

"I can take a guess," I said. "I've heard that Helena wasn't very popular with the Friends of the Library when she was director here. Aunt Ellen was on the verge of quitting when Helena retired. Mary-Sue worked under her and then left the profession all together."

"I'll ask around," Bertie said.

"I'll get the full story from Aunt Ellen," I said.

"The ever-reliable Nags Head grapevine," Watson said with a chuckle.

"And the even better librarian grapevine," Bertie said.

"I can't help you there, Detective," Louise Jane said. "Activities a mere twenty years ago are not something I concern myself with."

Watson then asked us to take him step by step through what happened on the boardwalk. I struggled to remember, but I had to admit I couldn't account for the whereabouts of anyone all the time. Bertie and Louise Jane said the same.

"Lucinda turned back," Bertie said, "but no one went with her. She would have been alone for several minutes until we came back here after finding Helena. She was in the library when we came in."

"It was very dark," I said. "And many of us were wearing black clothes, so we were hard to see." I indicated Louise Jane and myself. "We, and Ronald, were the waitstaff for tonight and we tried to dress accordingly." Bertie's attire wasn't much lighter. She wore a calf-length navy-blue dress with long sleeves. "Points of light were moving through the marsh, but they weren't bright enough to show who was carrying them, except for Ronald, who had the big Maglite. And the lights were out entirely for several minutes."

"You turned your flashlights off? Why?"

I glanced at Louise Jane. "Uh . . ."

"I was creating a mood, Detective," she said, "to illustrate what it must have been like for our ancestors when they first arrived on these shores. Although that's not entirely possible, is it? Not with airplanes flying overhead, and the lights from town bouncing off the clouds, and—"

"You're saying when the lights were out, you couldn't see anyone at all?"

"Not even Louise Jane," I said, "who was talking. Hey, I've just cleared you of suspicion, Louise Jane. Your voice stayed in one place."

"I'm quite sure I was never under suspicion, Lucy."

"No one," Watson said, "who was here tonight is entirely above suspicion."

Louise Jane harrumphed.

"Other than Mary-Sue, who reacted badly to seeing Helena, did you notice anything else about her relations with the guests?"

Bertie, Louise Jane, and I exchanged glances. "Nothing stands out," Bertie said.

"She could be extremely blunt," I said. "She told Ruth she'd put on weight. Ruth didn't like that, but she pretended to laugh it off."

"If every woman killed a person who commented on her weight," Bertie said, "there wouldn't be many people left. In jail or out of it."

"I wouldn't know about that," scrawny Louise Jane said smugly.

"I have to say," I continued, "Helena Sanchez didn't exactly try to be friendly. She was blunt, as Bertie said, and rude, and didn't much care who she offended." I remembered her shoving people out of her way to get to the bar.

"Thank you for this," Watson said. "You can go home now. We won't need to close the library, Bertie, but we will keep the boardwalk sectioned off for a while yet. I have people trying to track down where Helena Sanchez was staying so we can notify her next of kin, and I'll have officers calling the guests who were here tonight, the ones who left before you went for this walk."

"Have you considered that maybe this didn't have anything to do with Helena coming here tonight?" I asked. "Perhaps someone was following her, saw their chance, and took it. Anyone could have been out in the marsh tonight, beyond the beam of our lights. Silently following us. Watching us." I shivered at the thought.

"Lucy," Louise Jane said, "for once you've come up with an excellent idea."

"I wouldn't say that's all that rare," I said.

"I said I couldn't help you, Detective," Louise Jane said, "but perhaps I can after all. As we all know, the marsh can be a hive of supernatural activity on the darkest of nights."

"We all know that, do we?" Watson said.

"Those of us who've gone to the trouble to expand the scope of our thought beyond worldly thinking, at any rate. We've suggested that Helena might have fallen into the water, tripped in the dark perhaps, but what if she was frightened into jumping? What if she saw something that terrified her so much she jumped off the pier, thinking that was her only escape?" Louise Jane sprang to her feet. "I'll try to contact the spirits tonight. Perhaps they can tell me something."

"The entire boardwalk and area is off-limits, Louise Jane," Watson said.

"Surely not for me."

"Particularly for you," he said. "We'll have no séances being conducted in the middle of my investigation, thank you."

She sat down with a thud and a pout.

That, I knew, wasn't the end of that. The minute the tape was taken down and the cops left, Louise Jane would be creeping around out there, trying to get someone—anyone—to talk to her. I could only hope I'd be able to avoid being roped in.

At that, I usually failed.

Watson stood up. "Thanks for your help. I know where I can find y'all if I need anything more."

"I hope it'll turn out to be an accident after all," Bertie said. "Poor Helena. Will you let me know, Sam, when you locate her next of kin? I'd like to offer my condolences and help with arrangements in any way I can."

"Of course," he said.

Bertie and Louise Jane left, but not until Louise Jane reminded Detective Watson that "there are more things on heaven and earth—"

"I know the saying, Louise Jane," he said. "Hamlet, Act One, Scene Five. When the Nags Head PD takes instruction from Shakespeare, I'll give you a call."

"I'll be waiting," she said. "In the meantime, Bertie, have you thought about offering guided tours in the marsh at night? We could find some way of incorporating my stories into library programs. My fee will be entirely reasonable and . . ." Her voice faded away.

Louise Jane never did take offense when people didn't take her stories of the supernatural seriously. She just drove straight over them in a bulldozer.

I walked Watson to the door. "I wasn't aware you're a Shakespearian scholar, Detective. Many people would get that reference, but not many know the exact scene from which it comes."

"Can I tell you something in the strictest of confidence, Lucy?"

"My lips are sealed!"

"In school I wanted to major in theater. I planned to be a classical stage actor."

"Goodness. I never would have thought."

"Nor did anyone else. Including, eventually, me. I soon discovered that my talent didn't match my ambition, and I switched courses."

I could see Sam Watson, tall and lean, square of face and lantern of jaw, piercing gray eyes, nose like a hawk's beak, bestriding the stage, delivering the bard's immortal lines in his deep North Carolina accent.

Watson and I stood together, looking out into the marsh. The scene had completely changed from a few short hours ago. The peace and quiet vanished as bright lights were brought into the marsh and onto the pier, and men and women ran back and forth calling to each other. Cars filled the parking area next to the boardwalk, engines running, blue and red lights flashing.

If, I thought, there really is something out there, it would not be happy at the disturbance.

"Good night, Lucy," Watson said to me. "You have my number if you think of anything."

"I do," I said.

A figure broke out of the dark and jogged toward us. Butch Greenblatt, imposing in his dark uniform, jangling utility belt, and sheer size, appeared in the circle of light. "Hey, Lucy. Can't say I'm surprised to see you here."

"Just another fun night at the Lighthouse Library," I said.

"What's up?" Watson asked.

"Found something." Butch glanced at me.

"Might as well tell Lucy too," Watson said. "She'll find out anyway."

"Coroner's been and the body's been taken away. He had a quick look at it and found what looks like a puncture wound at the base of the neck."

"Is that so?" Watson said.

"Small, neat, round hole. They'll know more after the autopsy but it's unlikely, he said, to have been caused by any sort of fall. Meaning . . ."

"Meaning," I said, "Helena Sanchez was murdered."

Chapter Five

"What on earth has happened now?" Charlene asked the moment she set foot in the library the following day. "There's a police car parked by the boardwalk and crime scene tape around that part of the marsh."

I told her about last night's ill-fated expedition.

"That's terrible. Bertie was so looking forward to hosting her college reunion here. The police think it's murder?"

"That's the assumption they're going with. At least it was when Watson left last night. I haven't heard anything new since."

"We're opening as usual today?"

"Again, I haven't heard anything to the contrary. You're early this morning."

It was eight thirty. The library opened at nine. I'd slept surprisingly well, untroubled by dreams of long gray hair trapped in weeds or ghostly figures lingering just beyond reach of my light, but I'd woken early and had not been able to get back to sleep. Rather than lie in bed, thinking about Helena Sanchez and what had happened to her, I got up. Charles and I came down early to get the coffee on and our day started.

Charles had begun his day by settling down for a nap in the wingback chair.

Charlene fiddled with her iPhone and settled her earbuds around her neck, where they'd remain for most of the day unless she actually had to talk to someone. She did a great deal of her job online as she helped high school and college students and historical authors from all over the world research events from Outer Banks history. "In case you didn't get fully cleaned up after the party, I thought you might need a hand." She glanced around the room. "But everything looks good."

"Some of Bertie's guests helped out. They didn't have anything else to do while waiting to be questioned by Sam Watson."

"What do you think happened, Lucy?"

"Me? I have no idea and I'm not going to speculate. This has nothing to do with the Lighthouse Library community, so it's no business of mine."

"You could say Helena Sanchez, as a former library director, was a member of our community."

"No," I said firmly. "I'm staying well out of it."

"To change the subject, I'd say our little exhibit was a big hit with the visitors."

"The women loved it," I said. "It's amazing to think how fast everything has changed in our world."

"And how well we've adapted. Some people think libraries are a thing of the past, but nothing could be further from the truth. We're needed now more than ever to help people sift through the mountains of information, and misinformation, constantly falling on their heads."

"And help those who don't have access to any of that information on their own or the ability to get it."

As we chatted, we wandered to the display. We hadn't asked people not to touch—these weren't rare or valuable artifacts, just things that appealed to Charlene and me. Some of the books on the table had been picked up and put back in the wrong place.

Charles roused himself from his nap and came to join us. He stood on top of *The Celestine Prophecy*. Charlene put him on the floor. "Silly cat. He's been playing with this stuff."

"I wouldn't have thought he could do much damage to a bunch of old books."

"Where's the letter opener?"

"The letter opener?"

Charlene bent over and peered under the table. "I don't see it."

Something closed over my heart. I stopped breathing. "The letter opener."

"It's not here. It's pretty heavy, but Charles might have been batting it around."

I tried to calm my breathing as I helped Charlene search. "We have to find it," I said. We crawled across the floor, and checked under chairs, bookshelves, the magazine rack, the circulation desk, the returns cart. Charles thought this was great fun and roused himself to help us. "Ruth swept the floor before we rolled the bookshelves into place. If she'd found something as big as that letter opener, she'd have picked it up." I opened the desk drawers and frantically shuffled through the usual office rubbish stuffed into everyone's drawer. Colorful post-it pads, pens, a stapler, paper clips, elastic bands. A tattered paperback copy of *The Moonstone* by Wilkie Collins, this month's book club selection. The book was one of my favorites, and although I've read it many times, I'd put it aside to leaf through and refresh my memory before the meeting of the club.

"It's not here," I said at last.

Charlene pushed herself off the floor. "Do you think someone took it? It's not at all valuable, even sentimentally. Hundreds of those things must still be around."

"Valuable? No. There's something I didn't tell you about Helena's death. First, I have to call Sam Watson."

*   *   *

Bertie, Charlene, and I watched the detective. He stood in the alcove, studying the display of library artifacts. Butch Greenblatt was next to him.

"You're sure it was here, Lucy?" Watson asked.

"Positive."

"As am I," Charlene said.

"When did you last see it?"

"I can't say for certain," I said. "We checked the display one last time around six forty-five, just before Bertie and her friends arrived. I didn't notice it in particular, but if it hadn't been there, I probably would have realized that." I sighed. "Although, I have to admit, I didn't even know it was missing until this morning when Charlene pointed it out."

"I saw it," Bertie said, "at some point during the course of the evening. But I can't remember exactly when."

"Charlene?" Watson asked.

"I'm thinking. It was there—I'm sure of it—when Helena Sanchez arrived. I showed her the exhibit, and she genuinely seemed interested. She told me a few stories about how they'd done things back in the old days."

"I hate having most of my career referred to as 'the old days,'" Bertie said.

"Try being in law enforcement," Watson said as Butch chuckled. The detective turned to face us. "If you do find it, let me know right away. The autopsy's scheduled for noon, so I'll know more about the cause of death then."

"You could try asking someone at town hall to find you one of those," I suggested. "To compare with the missing one. Some might still be around."

"I'll do that," he said.

"You don't have to go far," Butch said. "Ed Jones has one in his pencil holder. I've seen it myself, and not long ago."

I mentally slapped myself. "I can't believe I forgot!"

"What did you forget?" Bertie asked me.

"When Charlene was showing Helena the display, she was interested. But something happened that seemed to genuinely bother her, and she walked away abruptly. Do you remember, Charlene?"

"Now that you mention it, I do. I thought one of the women must have said something to upset her."

"That wasn't it. She picked up that book." I pointed to *The Celestine Prophecy*, lying on top of a stack of books.

As one we leaned over and studied it.

"It's prophesizing something," Butch said. "Do you think that means something?"

"It's fiction," Charlene said, "but a lot of people thought it was real. It was an enormous bestseller in the mid-1990s."

"Can I open it, Detective?" I asked.

"Yes, but put something on your hands first. I know your prints will be all over it, but if this book is significant, I don't want to mess it up any more than it already is."

"Be right back." Charlene ran for the stairs.

We studied the book. The jacket was black with gold and white print. The title of the book filled the center of the book, with the author's name in smaller print below. The cover design was plain and stark: no picture, just a marketing blurb about the book across the top and an endorsement at the bottom. A small tear marked one corner of the jacket, and the worn paper indicated that the book had been well used over the years. The remains of spilled coffee discolored and warped some of the pages.

"As you can see," I said, "the book was damaged. Probably a coffee spill. Which is why it would have been removed from circulation. How or why it ended up in the basement of Town Hall is anyone's guess."

"I'm convinced," Watson said, "that one day we're going to find an intact skeleton down there."

Charlene was soon back with a pair of white gloves, ones she used for handling rare and fragile papers. She handed them to me, and I slipped them on. I opened the book. Everyone leaned closer.

It was a common edition, nothing special that I could see. It hadn't been signed by the author.

I flipped carefully through the book. Pages were dog-eared, paper yellowing, passages underlined. "This book's seen a lot of use," I said.

"By people who used a pen or pencil to highlight passages," Bertie growled. "I'd like to get my hands on them. That was done deliberately; we can assume the coffee spill was accidental."

"Is there anything noteworthy, do you think, about the parts that are marked?" Butch asked.

"That would need a close study," I said, "but offhand, doesn't look so."

"Might this book have any particular value?" Watson asked. "Monetary, I mean."

"I suppose it could be a special edition, although it doesn't look like it. I can ask Theodore to check," I said.

"Thanks."

"We pulled it out of the basement for no reason other than it came quickly to hand. We displayed it open to the flyleaf so we could see the withdrawal record with its signatures and date stamps."

As one, they all stared at the book. Even Charles, perched on top of a high shelf, moved closer for a better look.

Charlene sucked in a breath. "That's it! Helena wasn't interested in the book itself. She pulled out the withdrawal record and looked . . . the only word I can think of is horrified."

"You're right," I said. "Now I remember." I slowly turned to the cover.

We all leaned in. I'm sure I was holding my breath.

The little paper envelope glued to the inside of the cover was empty.

I breathed. "It's gone."

"What's gone?" Butch said.

"The card," Charlene said. "In the days before computers, libraries used paper to keep a record of who'd taken out books and when they were due."

"I remember. I think," Watson said.

"Can I show you another?" Charlene said.

"If you can without leaving prints."

"My prints are all over everything," Charlene said. "So are Lucy's, Bertie's—probably everyone who was in the library yesterday. This isn't a hands-off display. We made it for people to enjoy."

"Nevertheless, let Lucy and her gloves do it."

I opened the next book on the stack, a history of the Civil War in North Carolina, and pulled out the card. It was almost full, dates stamped on the right column and handwritten signatures in various colors of ink on the left. The final date was November 15, 1996, and it had been signed out by one Jane Jones.

"When someone took out a book, they wrote their name here, or the librarian did it for them," Bertie explained, "and the librarian stamped the date the book was due back. This card was then filed away as a record until the book was returned. A slip was put into the book with the due date on it as a reminder to the borrower."

"Why would someone take the card out of that first one?" Butch asked.

"That's the question, isn't it?" I said.

"You're sure there was a withdrawal slip in this book?" Watson said.

"Absolutely," Charlene said. "That was the only reason it was part of our display."

"Ms. Sanchez had a strong visceral reaction to seeing it," I said. "No, wait, that's not right. She reacted to seeing what was written on it. The card itself was exactly the same as any other."

"Where's this card now?" Butch asked.

Charlene, Bertie, and I glanced at one another. We shook our heads.

"The letter opener's missing as well as the withdrawal record card from that particular book," Watson said. "Anything else?"

I scrunched up my forehead and studied the display. I couldn't exactly remember everything that had been in it. A few items had come from other library systems, but mainly Charlene and I had simply helped ourselves to books and other abandoned things in the town hall basement. We hadn't had to sign anything out: nothing was of any value. It would all have been thrown out long ago, if anyone had bothered to get around to it.

"I don't think so," Charlene said at last.

"Me neither," I said.

"Butch," Watson said, "take that book into evidence. I'm not waiting for the result of the autopsy. I'm going to get divers into the marsh to look for that letter opener."

"Good morning!"

I was so startled I squealed and jumped into the air.

"Goodness," Bertie said, "you scared me there, Ellen."

"Sorry. Is everything okay?" My aunt Ellen stood in the doorway, holding her loaded book bag, looking from one of us to the other. "Are you open? It's after nine."

"Are we open?" Bertie asked Watson.

"You'll be late today," he said. "I want all this stuff taken into town. Butch, call for a forensic van."

Bertie groaned.

"You might as well come in, Ellen," Watson said. "As long as you're here. Everyone else, can you stand back, please."

"I don't know what you're going to find," Charlene said. "Everyone at the party last night had a chance to handle those things. Fingerprints will be useless."

"I won't know what I hope to find until I find it, now will I?" he replied.

"I stopped in to return my books and to ask how your reunion went, Bertie." Aunt Ellen glanced at Watson. "Not all that well, at a guess."

"Helena Sanchez died," Bertie said.

"Oh," Aunt Ellen said, "I'm sorry to hear that."

Butch stepped outside to use his radio to call for someone to come out and take away our things.

"You can open the library once the forensic team has removed the historical display," Watson said. "I see no need for us to go through anything else here. I have to get back to town. If you think of anything . . ."

"We'll let you know," Bertie said.

He smiled at her. "I'm sorry this happened to you again."

"It didn't happen to us," she said. "It happened to Helena Sanchez."

"Aunt Ellen," I said, "you knew Helena when she was the director here. You might want to tell Detective Watson about her."

"I'm all ears," Watson said.

"I'll help if I can, but I can't say I knew her well," Aunt Ellen said. "I've been a member of the Friends of the Library for a long time, under various library directors. But to be honest, Helena Sanchez was by far the worst."

"In what way?" Watson asked.

"Dictatorial. Opinionated. Rude. Completely dismissive of anyone else's opinion. The Friends of the Library are, as you know, all volunteers. We help out here when we can because we believe in the importance of libraries in general and this library in particular. Helena Sanchez treated us as though we were serving staff. I'd been a library volunteer when my children were little, and enjoyed it, but I didn't have a lot of time when they got older and I started helping out at Amos's law office. I came back a few years later, and it seemed as though everything here had changed. I was on the verge of quitting the group, when Helena announced she was leaving. I don't really remember why—it wasn't anything in particular, a straw that broke the camel's back sort of thing—but I decided I couldn't work with her anymore." My aunt shrugged. "She left. I stayed. When Bertie took over, we all breathed a sigh of relief."

"Was her leaving sudden?" Watson asked.

"It was announced suddenly to us. I don't know how long she'd been planning to go."

"When was this?" Watson asked.

"I started in the summer of 2010," Bertie said. "Helena's leaving was sudden. I was hired with much haste, and she didn't hang around to help me get into the job, but she was of retirement age, and there was never any indication she'd been asked to leave."

"Here one day, gone the next," Aunt Ellen said.

"Not quite that fast," Bertie said, "but close. She not only left the library but left town as well, almost the day after her job ended."

"I've been told it was you who told her about the party here last night," Watson said to Aunt Ellen. "How did that come about?"

"I was surprised to see her in town," Aunt Ellen said. "If I could have, I would've avoided her, and she probably wasn't all that keen to talk to me, but we recognized each other at the same time, so we stopped to chat. The only thing we have in common is the library, so I mentioned Bertie was doing an excellent job as director. She told me she'd enjoy talking to Bertie and gave me her phone number so I could give it to Bertie. We then went our separate ways. I didn't tell her about the party."

"That, unfortunately, was me," Bertie said. "Ellen gave me the number, and I called her to invite her."

"Give me a minute," Watson said, "I want to check my phone."

Cell phone coverage inside the thick stone walls of the library is, to say the least, unreliable. I walked the detective to the door, and the minute he stepped into the open air, his phone beeped. He answered it with a gruff "Watson," listened for a brief moment, and then said, "I'll handle it," and hung up.

"A woman called the hospital just now, looking for her sister, who didn't come home last night."

"You think . . .?"

"The description sounds very much like Helena Sanchez. I'm heading there now. Butch, I need you to stay here and guard the historical display until our people arrive. A guard is probably not necessary, and far too late, but I have to do what

I can to preserve the chain of evidence. That means I need a ride. Lucy, you're with me."

"I am?"

"You are. Let's go. There's a chance the woman who's looking for her sister might be elderly, and the news I have for her isn't good. Your presence might calm her."

"I'll get my purse." I ran back inside. "I have to go," I called to Bertie. "I'm needed to . . . assist the police with their inquiries."

"Doesn't that mean—?" Charlene began.

Just this once," I said, "it means what it says."

Chapter Six

Tina Ledbetter lived on a quiet street of small houses on sandy lots set back from the bustling tourist thoroughfare that is the Croatan Highway. The garden consisted of nothing but sand, scruffy bushes, struggling grasses, and determined weeds. The house was small, a single-story above an open space that was intended to be a parking area but was stuffed full of assorted junk, some of which didn't seem to ever be used, judging by the amount of rust and dust I saw when I peeked into it on our way to the rickety wooden steps leading from the driveway to the front door.

A dented and battered old red Honda Civic, held together as much by rust as metal, was parked in the weed-choked driveway. I left my teal Yaris on the street, and Watson and I walked up the crumbling path together and climbed the steps. He knocked firmly on the door, and it was opened almost immediately by a woman.

My jaw fell and I stared at her. *Helena Sanchez?*

Watson flashed his badge. "Good morning. I'm Detective Sam Watson of the Nags Head Police. Are you Mrs. Tina Ledbetter?"

"I am." The woman's dark eyes studied me. I closed my mouth and gave her a feeble smile. Not Ms. Sanchez, but a darn good imitation. The skin was less lined, the lips not quite so thin, the hair slightly darker, but the face was so very much like her, and she was almost the exact size as the dead woman. A sister for sure. Probably a twin. Even the eyeglasses were the same as Helena Sanchez had worn.

"May we come in?" Watson said.

She stepped back. "You're here about Helena?"

I followed Watson into the house. The front door opened onto a small foyer containing nothing but a pair of sneakers, standing side by side on a rubber mat, and a yellow raincoat hanging on a hook. I could see into the living room beyond. The furniture was cheap, faded, and dated, but the place was spotlessly clean.

"Perhaps you should take a seat," Watson said.

Mrs. Ledbetter didn't move. "No need. You've come to tell me my sister is dead. I'm aware of that." The woman's face showed no emotion.

"Do you mind my asking how you know?"

"I don't mind at all. I dreamt last night of dark water and tangled gray hair drifting in the weeds."

I sucked in a breath, and the woman looked at me for the first time. "You were there," she said. It was not a question.

"I . . . I . . ."

"What's your relationship with Helena Sanchez?" Watson asked.

"She's my identical twin sister. She's here for a short visit. I don't know why. We haven't seen each other for years and I was surprised when I got her e-mail asking me . . . telling me . . .

she planned to stay with me while she was in town. How'd she die?"

"She was found in the marsh near the lighthouse."

Mrs. Ledbetter nodded.

"You seem to have some knowledge of that fact."

"As I said, I saw it. I dreamt it. Do you have a twin, Detective?"

"No. I don't."

"Then you can't understand. There was a bond between my sister and me that nothing could break. Even though we might have wanted it to. When she departed this life, I knew it. If I had gone first, she would have seen it and known. Thank you for coming to give me the news." She opened the door.

"You called the hospital looking for her?" I asked. Watson had told me not to say anything, to let him do the talking, but I couldn't help myself. The words burst out all on their own.

Although he probably wouldn't see it that way.

He said nothing.

"I didn't know if she'd been found," Mrs. Ledbetter said.

"What do you mean when you say you might not have wanted these bonds between you?" Watson asked.

"I assume you want the truth, so I'll give it to you. We couldn't stand each other, Detective. Over the course of her entire life, I don't think Helena ever gave a thought to anyone else. What Helena wanted is what Helena wanted. And what Helena wanted is what Helena usually got. For some reason she convinced our parents that she was the golden twin, and I was the devil incarnate."

"Yet you invited her to stay with you on this visit. Or didn't refuse her at any rate."

Mrs. Ledbetter stared at Sam Watson over the top of her glasses with such intensity he actually looked away. "She was my sister," she said at last. "Of course she stayed with me."

"Why did she come back to Nags Head? Was she hoping to repair her relationship with you?"

"Repair it?" Mrs. Ledbetter snorted. "Our father died when we were in high school, and our mother moved to Raleigh about twenty years ago. Mother died last month."

"My condolences," Watson said. I muttered something sympathetic.

"On Father's death, Mother had her will written by a Nags Head lawyer. Helena was in town this week to make sure she got her share in case there's any dispute over the contents of that will."

"Is there likely to be?" Watson asked.

"Dispute? Not a dispute, no. Helena's share, in her eyes, would be nothing less than the entire amount. Our mother was a weak and foolish woman. She did whatever Helena told her to do. We were never close."

"When did you last see your mother?" Watson said.

"Twenty years ago. The day she left for Raleigh. I was in town doing my shopping and saw her drive past. I don't know if she saw me or not, but she did not acknowledge me."

Not close was an understatement.

"Did you . . . uh . . . have a warning of your mother's death?" I asked.

She shook her head. "Why would I? I found out about it from the lawyer. I did my duty and went to the funeral. It was a sad affair. Rained steadily all day. Her church put on a dreary lunch of overly sweet tea and dried-up sandwiches."

"Was Helena there?"

"Oh yes. Standing under an umbrella. She wasn't aging well, I thought." Mrs. Ledbetter let out a bark of laughter. "She's stopped aging now, hasn't she? We exchanged air kisses and lied about how we'd missed each other. We also lied when we told the church ladies the tea was excellent."

"You had no plans to dispute your mother's will?"

Mrs. Ledbetter grinned at Detective Watson. Her teeth were small and closely crowded together. "No. Looks like now I'll get it all, won't I? Serves them right."

"What were you doing yesterday evening?" he asked.

"Not out killing my sister—or anyone else, if that's what you're asking. But if my word's not enough for you and you insist on the details . . . I'd been at a movie and got home around seven o'clock. Helena was here. She was going, she said, to a party, of all things. I didn't know she had any friends. She called a taxi and it came for her around quarter after eight. I watched television until midnight and went to bed. She had not come home, nor had she called to say where she was."

"Were you concerned that she hadn't come home by then?"

"Of course not. What do I care what she got herself up to? I slept soundly and woke shortly before seven. I remembered my dream vividly and knew my sister was dead."

Chapter Seven

"There's a family Christmas dinner I don't ever want to be invited to," Watson said.

I drove us back to the police station. Watson wanted to check in with the forensic team and make a few phone calls. He also wanted to pick up a car so he wouldn't need me to drive him around anymore.

Drat!

"What do you think, Sam?" I dared to ask. I used his first name, hoping he'd think we were friends or something and he could talk freely to me.

"I scarcely know what to think, Lucy. At least she didn't try to pretend she and her sister got on well. I'll call the mother's lawyer and ask to see the will. Although I can't imagine why she'd lie to me about that. I'll find out if Helena had a will of her own. Tina Ledbetter might not be in line to inherit everything—not if Helena, who got her mother's inheritance first, had other ideas."

"Do you suppose there's much of value to inherit?"

"I've no idea. Sometimes it doesn't matter. People can kill over who gets Grandma's favorite teapot. If one sibling was favored over the others, the principal of the thing can be all that matters. As for her knowing her twin had died because she dreamt it . . ." He shook his head. "She heard the news somewhere. It may be that someone at the hospital or in the coroner's office has loose lips."

"Tina wasn't at the library last night," I said. "She didn't come inside anyway. That means she didn't take the withdrawal slip or the letter opener."

"We don't know the letter opener was used in the killing, Lucy, so don't speculate. We also don't know if the withdrawal slip is of any importance. It might have fallen on the floor and someone tossed it in the trash."

"No librarian," I said firmly, "would ever throw away a piece of library property. No matter how old." I pulled to a stop at the front of the police station and Watson got out.

He shut the car door and then hesitated. He turned back and tapped on the window. I lowered it.

"Do something for me, Lucy," he said. "Ask Louise Jane what she knows about the sisters. Tina Ledbetter in particular. I want to know if Tina was messing with me because it amused her to do so, or if she genuinely believes she has some psychic abilities. If she moves in that sort of circles, Louise Jane is likely to know."

"Happy to be of help," I said.

Watson ran up the steps of the police station. Before driving away, I eyed the front of Town Hall, on the other side of the laneway. I thought of dropping in to see Connor. Maybe I could convince him to take a break and join me for a cup of coffee at Josie's Cozy Bakery. I gave him a call, but it went to voicemail. Perhaps he was in a meeting.

I waved in the general direction of the mayor's office and drove away. I might be helping the police solve a murder, but merely thinking of Connor McNeil took me to a happy place.

I hoped thoughts of me did the same for him.

* * *

By the time I arrived at the library, more police cars were in the parking lot, and more yellow tape cordoned off the path to the water's edge. A police boat was anchored off the pier, and I could see signs of divers in the water.

A handful of people milled about at the top of the boardwalk, trying to get a look at what was going on, while Officer Rankin, the very picture of boredom, told them to keep back.

Inside the library, the police had removed the display of historical artifacts (as well as our trash) and allowed us to open.

Saturdays are normally the busiest day of the week, and today was no exception. Parents were arriving with their primary school children for today's North Carolina history story time; locals were loading up on books to enjoy at the beach; and tourists were checking out the lighthouse as well as the library itself.

Unfortunately, we didn't have a display of library artifacts to show them. The police had taken everything away, and the alcove was empty.

On the second floor, Ronald was getting ready to receive his little patrons, along with Charles, who loved nothing more than story time; above him, Charlene was in her office, surrounded by reference books; on the ground floor, my aunt

Ellen, in the role of library volunteer, staffed the circulation desk while Bertie shelved books off the returns cart. Bertie didn't normally work on Saturdays, but in light of what happened here last night, she'd come in in case of any new developments.

"Learn anything?" she asked me.

I glanced at the patrons, pretending not to be listening.

Bertie jerked her head and led the way down the hall to her office. I trotted along behind.

"Did you know Helena has a twin sister living in Nags Head?" I asked her when we were behind closed doors.

"No, I didn't. I don't know anything about her private life."

I told her quickly what Tina Ledbetter had had to say.

"Quite the family situation," Bertie said.

"Let's hope Helena's death was a family affair, Watson clears this up quickly, and you and your friends can get on with your reunion. Is the group expedition to the Wright Brothers still on?"

"It is. I'll be leaving shortly to join them. I don't know that the trip's entirely appropriate in light of Helena's death, but to be fair, Helena wasn't part of our reunion. I heard from Ruth earlier. The police sent a couple of officers around to the Ocean Side this morning to take statements from the party guests who'd left last night before our walk. They—the women, that is, were quite excited about being questioned. Most of them said they hadn't even spoken to Helena, but they had noticed her."

"The police are searching the water under the pier. Looks like they've brought in divers."

"They're looking for the letter opener, I assume. Ronald will have his hands full trying to keep the children interested in his story when they could be watching police divers at work."

"I assume there's been no sign of the missing withdrawal slip?"

"No," Bertie said.

"I think that's more important than Detective Watson seems to realize. Why would someone steal an old library card?"

"Assuming it was stolen, and didn't get thrown in the trash or someone used it to wipe their fingers and then put it into their bag."

"Did you search the party trash?"

My boss grinned at me. "Charlene did that as soon as you left, under the careful supervision of Butch. It's been taken away for further inspection."

"If we'd had a pack of pre-teenage boys here last night, I'd agree it might be possible they threw it out or used it as a napkin. But librarians?"

"That's pretty much unthinkable." Bertie rummaged in the bottom drawer of her desk and got her purse. "I'm off. Call me if there are any developments, please, Lucy."

I accompanied her to the main room and waved her out the door.

"I remember Helena Sanchez," a patron was saying to Aunt Ellen. "Meanest woman on God's green earth." She dropped a stack of books on the desk, and I caught a glimpse of swords, leather jerkins, horses, and dragons. She came in every Saturday morning to return one bulging bag of books for another. I wondered where she found the time to read them all.

"I wouldn't go that far," a second woman said. "She was never what you'd call friendly, but she did her job efficiently and was always polite to me." She carried one book, the Michelle Obama memoir, for which we still had a long wait list.

"Did you know her well?" I asked.

"Only from the library," the second woman said. "We never socialized."

"I don't think she socialized with anyone," her friend said. "She kept to herself. Which was just as well. No one liked her."

"You're being unfair, Joanie. I've been visiting the library longer than you have, so I knew her better. They say she had some health problems that caused her pain, so in her years here she wasn't always in the best of moods."

"I'm sorry she died," Joanie said, "but I believe in being honest. Whatever Helena's problem was, she didn't make any attempt to be nice to anyone, and I didn't see any need to be nice to her in return. Bye. See you next week."

I watched them go, thinking that a lot of people hadn't liked Helena Sanchez. I hadn't liked her much in the short exposure to her I'd had. But did people dislike her enough to kill her? She'd been gone from Nags Head for ten years. Wasn't that long enough for old resentments to die? Unless someone feared her presence here would stir up trouble long forgotten.

"Do you mind watching the desk for a few more minutes?" I asked Aunt Ellen. "I've a couple of phone calls to make."

"I never mind," she said with a laugh. "This desk is Nags Head Gossip Central."

"That's what Bertie calls it." I went outside to make my calls. To give myself some privacy, I wandered away from the front steps of the library. I enjoyed the feel of the hot sun on my bare arms, although as always I worried about what the sea air was doing to my hair. At the end of a particularly humid day, my mop resembles a circus clown's wig. Connor always says he loves my out-of-control curls. I was thinking about Connor a lot this morning, I realized.

Then again, lately I was thinking about Connor a lot all the time. I pushed that thought aside and made my first phone call.

"TK Rare Books. How may I be of assistance?" The voice was that of a distinguished Englishman in his fifties or sixties, tempered by years of cigars enjoyed in gentlemen's clubs and good whiskey served in crystal tumblers, with just a splash of water, by hovering waiters.

"Hi, Theodore. It's Lucy here."

"Hey, Lucy. What's up?" This voice belonged to the same man, but it was that of a Nags Head native in his thirties who'd never smoked a cigar or enjoyed a glass of good single malt in his life. Theodore Kowalski thought the accent, plus the Harris Tweed jackets and spectacles of plain glass, gave him gravitas in the world of rare books.

"I'm wondering if you know anything about *The Celestine Prophecy*. Apart from what everyone knows, that is."

"I saw a copy of it in your historical display. Is that the one you're asking about?"

"It is. It was published in 1993 by Warner Books, and ours appears to be a first edition, but a later printing. If that means anything."

"Warner Books is now Grand Central Publishing. Hundreds of thousands of copies of *The Celestine Prophecy* were produced, and it's still in print. Unless the copy you have is signed by the author or contains some sort of error that caused that particular print run to be pulled, I can't imagine it's of any value. Do you think it's of some significance?"

"That's the question. Did you hear about the death at the library last night?"

"I did. I was on Twitter this morning and saw news of it there. Most unfortunate. I didn't see mention of the deceased's name or anything about a missing book."

"The book's not missing. The police have it. We don't know if it means anything at all. It might not, but the dead woman saw it shortly before she died, and she had a strong reaction, that's all. So we're curious."

"I can check into it," he said. "But that won't necessarily mean anything. Perhaps the book was of some personal importance to this lady?"

"Perhaps. When we're talking books, potentially rare and valuable books, you're my go-to person, Theodore."

"I appreciate the thought, Lucy. Let me see what I can find out for you." I smiled at the pleasure in his voice. Some people thought Teddy, with his false English airs and his moldy old books that barely provided him a living, a fool. But I knew him to be a loyal friend of the library, a true lover of literature, and a kind man.

We hung up and my next call was to Louise Jane.

"More police activity," she said. "I was hoping they'd be gone by now so I could get in there and solve this murder for them, but instead they've brought in more people."

"How do you know what's going on here?"

"Because I can see them. I can see you. You're wearing a yellow dress."

I whirred around. I couldn't see Louise Jane anywhere. I threw my head back and looked up, way up, to the walkway that runs outside at the top of the lighthouse tower. The gate to the upper levels is always closed and locked when the library's open, particularly when children's programs are in progress, but we open it for visitors who want to go up and see the view, which is truly spectacular.

Whether she had keys or not, Louise Jane always seems to be able to get herself wherever she wants to be.

"No," she said into the phone. "I'm not up there. I'm on the side of the highway, currently standing on the roof of my car."

"You must have good binoculars."

"Did you doubt it?"

"I guess not. I hope you have a good roof on your car as well."

"Why are you calling?" she asked, blunt as always.

"Do you know a woman named Tina Ledbetter?"

"Why are you asking about her?" Suspicion filled Louise Jane's voice.

"So you do know her?"

"I know of her. Again, why are you asking?"

"Her name came up in relation to the death of Helena Sanchez."

A long pause came down the line. Pulling teeth came to mind. "Louise Jane? This is important."

"Tina Ledbetter thinks of herself as some sort of psychic powerhouse. As if. The old fraud. Her family's originally from

Raleigh." Spoken as though having family from Raleigh was equivalent to being an old fraud.

"How long has she lived in Nags Head?"

"I can't say for sure. Since she was a child, I think, which isn't long enough to be a true Banker, as you know, Lucy."

I ignored that comment.

"She approached my grandmother a number of years ago with some crazy idea about setting up some sort of group to combine energies to contact the spirts. My grandmother saw through her right away and sent her packing. Again, why are you asking?"

"She was Helena Sanchez's identical twin sister."

"Was she now? Interesting. Even more interesting that they both lived in Nags Head at one time and I didn't know that."

"I gather they didn't exactly get on."

"She told you she foretold Helena's death, I suppose."

"Not foretold exactly."

"What exactly, Lucy? Sometimes talking to you is like pulling teeth."

I didn't have to explain myself to Louise Jane. Somehow, despite that, I always found myself doing precisely that. "She says her sister's death came to her in a dream."

"I thought so. The old fraud. Check Twitter, that'll be where she heard it. Oh, something's happening. The divers are waving. Gotta go. Bye."

I put my phone away and trotted over to the police tape. "Good morning," I said to Officer Rankin.

"You can't go past," she said.

"I know that. I'm out for a walk. Getting some fresh air. Something seems to be happening down there."

She turned and looked. Louise Jane was right. The divers had surfaced, and the men in the boat were leaning over the gunwales, talking to them. A wetsuit-clad arm reached up and passed something over. From here, I couldn't tell what it was. If I didn't have a few remaining scraps of pride, I'd call Louise Jane and ask if she could pick it up with her binoculars.

Instead, I walked back to the library. I'd have to wait to hear from Sam Watson. If he wanted to tell me what they'd found. Might have been nothing more exciting than an old boot.

Before going inside I called up Twitter and searched for Nags Head and the Lighthouse Library. @MSyourOBXrealtor had put up a series of posts about the reunion last night. Pictures of groups of laughing women posing outside the library and circulating inside. I saw myself in the background of one, offering the guests a platter of crab cakes. If my mom saw me acting as a cocktail waitress, she'd have a fit. My mother's very sensitive about the proper placement of our family on the social ladder.

The last post said: *Fun day ends in tragedy. Unknown woman found dead in the water. RIP.*

I thought it tasteless in the extreme to post about a sudden tragic death. I checked the profile of @MSyourOBXrealtor. The picture was of Mary-Sue Delamont, and the link provided led to Antonio Francesco Realty.

Mary-Sue's final post had gone up at 1:15 AM. Had Tina seen it? When her sister didn't come home that night, and when the police knocked on her door the next morning, it would be easy enough to guess they were here to tell her Helena was the one who'd died.

If it had been just a guess, why would Tina pretend to have "foreseen" the death? Sam Watson wouldn't care if Tina had a reputation as a psychic, but pretending to know the circumstances of someone's mysterious death would pretty much be guaranteed to ensure police attention.

Games people play.

I thought of Louise Jane, standing on the roof of her van with her binoculars, and went inside.

Chapter Eight

"*The Moonstone* is generally considered to be the first detective novel."

"I thought that was Edgar Allen Poe?"

"Poe wrote short stories, not novels, and he didn't write about professional detectives. *The Moonstone* was genuinely groundbreaking. It contains almost all the tropes we know today as common in a mystery novel. The family with secrets, the incompetent local police, the big-city detective, the limited circle of suspects." I handed a copy of the book to Aunt Ellen. "You don't have much time to read it. Book club meets on Monday."

"I guess we know what I'll be doing all day tomorrow, then," my aunt said.

I smiled at her. Aunt Ellen and I were close. She and my mom had grown up together on the Outer Banks, in the same house, in the same family, but their life paths had diverged widely. Mom met my dad when she was in high school and he was a law student on vacation, and she never looked back. My father's family is not only one of the most socially prominent in Boston, with roots reaching back to prerevolutionary days, but my grandfather founded one of the city's most illustrious corporate law firms. Dad joined Richardson Lewiston the day he finished law school, and Mom threw herself wholeheartedly into the life of a Boston society matron, whereas Aunt Ellen persuaded her Louisianan fiancé to move to Nags Head to set up his own law practice. When we were young, my brothers and I spent much of our summers in the Outer Banks, never with Dad and often not even with Mom, who preferred the social whirl of the big city. My brothers stopped coming as soon as they were old enough, but I cherished my carefree summers in the big comfortable home of Aunt Ellen and Uncle Amos and my three cousins. A year ago, I quit my job at Harvard, fled my life in Boston and my mother's expectations, and came to my favorite place on earth and the loving arms of Aunt Ellen. Fortune had been kind enough to smile on me, and at that time the Lighthouse Library was searching for an assistant director. So here I am. And so very happy to be so.

The summer I was fourteen, I met Connor McNeil. He'd been fifteen, and we'd had the sweetest, most innocent of holiday romances. Summer had ended, and I'd gone back to life and school in Boston. I hadn't seen Connor again until I began work at the library, and we found that the feelings we'd had for each other so long ago still existed.

"If you're okay to take over here, Lucy," Aunt Ellen said, pulling me out of my memories, "I'll be off. I need to get a start on my reading." She studied the thick volume I'd placed in her hands. "I hope this book isn't too dry. Some of the classics can be."

"It's wordy, yes, and not what I'd call fast paced, but it's a good read. The Moonstone of the title is a fabulous yet infamous jewel all sorts of mysterious people are hunting. You'll enjoy it."

"See you on Monday, then." She gave me a peck on the cheek and left the library. I settled behind the circulation desk.

With the children's program going on upstairs, the main library was full of parents waiting for their kids, chatting between the shelves, or searching for books for themselves.

"Terrible about Helena Sanchez," Glenda Covington said to me. "Although it's fitting in some way, I think, that she died near here, where she'd spent so much time. She truly loved the Lighthouse Library."

"Did she?" I asked. That wasn't the impression I had of her. I thought she'd come last night out of some sense of obligation, not a desire to have a stroll down memory lane. And according to her sister, she was only in town to make sure she got her hands on her inheritance.

"Oh yes. I know some people didn't get on with her, but I always had a soft spot for Helena. We all have disappointments in our lives, don't we? Some of us handle it better than others." Glenda waved goodbye.

The children's story time ended and excited kids clattered down the twisting iron stairs. Parents gathered them up, helped them check out their books, said goodbye to their friends, and left. I heard several children ask if they could go to the pier to see the police boat. Only a scattering of patrons remained, but we'd be full again in another hour, when it was time for the preteens book club.

* * *

Louise Jane came in as we were going through the end-of-day routine. She was dressed in multi-pocketed nylon pants, a beige jacket, and sturdy hiking boots. A pair of powerful binoculars hung around her neck.

"What have you been up to?" Charlene asked. "You look like you're heading off on an expedition in search of the source of the Nile."

"Someone has to keep an eye on things out there while y'all are so busy in here," Louise Jane replied. "Sitting on the top of a metal car in the hot sun all day isn't fun you know. Never mind the filthy exhaust some cars spit out." She coughed. "They oughta be taken off the road."

"What's happening out there?" I asked. We'd been so busy for the rest of the day, I hadn't had time to take a peek out the window.

"They've gone after having dredged up a bunch of junk from the bottom of the marsh. I couldn't tell if anything important was among it. They also carried off the contents of the trash containers that line the boardwalk. Searching through that muck is a job I would not want. Have you heard anything more from Sam Watson, Lucy?"

"Me? Why would you expect him to contact me?"

"You've been of help to him on past cases. You and I have been of help, I should say."

"Oh, right," Charlene said. "Like the time he thought you'd broken into the library at night, engaged in a fight to the death with a man, and then ran off with the treasure map and code page."

"That was never a serious consideration," Louise Jane sniffed.

Charlene winked at me. "I'm off home now. Do you have any plans for tomorrow, Lucy?"

"Connor and I are going to the beach. It's supposed to be a hot day. Would you and your mom like to join us?"

"Sounds good," Louise Jane said. "Are you planning a picnic?"

"Thank you, but Mom and I will not join you," Charlene said, "and neither will Louise Jane."

"Why not?" Louise Jane asked. "I've no better plans for the day."

"Because Lucy only asked out of politeness. She doesn't want us tagging along on a date."

"Oh," Louise Jane said.

I said nothing. Charlene was right: I had only invited them to be polite.

Ronald clattered down the stairs, briefcase in hand. "'Night all. See you on Monday."

He and Charlene left together. I looked at Louise Jane. Louise Jane looked at me.

"Good night," I said. "I'm locking up now."

"So," she said, "things with Conner are progressing well, are they?"

"Whatever 'well' means," I said as heat rushed into my cheeks. "We enjoy spending time in each other's company."

"If you're thinking of spending any more time in each other's company, remember I'm only renting my place from Uncle Gordon. I can move out at any time."

"What? Oh, you want to move into my apartment. Sorry, I'm not leaving."

"Whatever you say, Lucy, honey." She gave me her patented smile. The one that put me in mind of a shark circling a particularly oblivious minnow. Then she said, "I have to be off. I'm going to the Ocean Side for drinks."

"You're going to the Ocean Side Hotel for drinks?"

"Didn't I just say that, Lucy?"

She wouldn't have dangled that bit of information in front of me if she didn't want me to beg for more details. I shouldn't have asked. Somehow, as usual, I found myself giving her what she wanted. "Well, yes. You did. I mean, who are you having drinks with?"

"Sheila called me earlier and mentioned that some of the reunion group will be gathering in the hotel bar before dinner. She thought they'd be interested in hearing things I know about the history of the hotel—the stories the hotel management doesn't want the guests to hear."

"Oh, right. Those stories." I knew all about the maid who supposedly haunted the second floor of the hotel after killing herself because her lover had convinced her to steal from the guest rooms to raise money for his mother's desperately needed medical care, and then he'd abandoned her. The maid, not the mother. Who'd never existed. As well as that one, Louise Jane had plenty of other stories about supposed hauntings at the hotel. Staff had been told to keep an eye out for her and put a stop to her scaring the life out of their guests.

I had no interest in hearing those stories again.

But I was interested, very interested, in chatting to the women who'd been here last night. Maybe one of them had noticed something she hadn't thought to tell the police. The death of Helena Sanchez didn't have anything to do with the library community, and this time, thank heavens, there was no reason for me to become involved.

Nevertheless, it wouldn't hurt for me to listen to what they had to say. Sometimes, I've found, I can learn more from casual conversation among friends than the police can in an interview room.

"Sounds good," I said to Louise Jane. "I've no plans for tonight. I'll join you."

She eyed me suspiciously. As well she might. Louise Jane knew I didn't believe her tales of ghostly happenings and restless, wandering spirits. Which is why, I suspect, she continues to tell them to me.

I smiled at her. "You can give me a lift. That way I can enjoy a drink and take a cab back."

* * *

They'd taken a big table in the lobby bar of the Ocean Side Hotel and pulled additional chairs from all over the room. Bertie was there, along with Shelia, Lucinda, Ruth, Mary-Sue and several others whose names I hadn't caught. Sheila saw us first and sprang to her feet to wave us over. Bertie glanced between Louise Jane and me, clearly surprised to see us together. Louise Jane pulled up a chair, but before I sat down, I leaned close to Bertie and whispered in her ear. "Okay if we join you? Sheila invited Louise Jane to tell stories, and I thought I might check things out. I've heard nothing more from the police today."

"Happy to have you," she said.

The table was piled high with drinks and bar snacks, and the women chatted and laughed.

The Ocean Side Hotel is one of the nicest, and most expensive, in this part of the Outer Banks. My mom always stays here when she comes to visit. She says she doesn't want to impose on her sister; what Mom really means is that she knows my aunt Ellen won't wait on her.

After a few years of slipping standards, the hotel owners had recently spent a lot of money to get everything back into shape. One wall of the bar was all glass, giving a view over the well-maintained gardens, the umbrellas and lounge chairs surrounding the swimming pool, and the dunes and beach grasses lining the oceanfront. Inside, it was all bright shades of blue and yellow, with colorful whimsical art, comfortable furniture, giant-leafed plants in large pots, a gleaming mahogany bar, and rows and rows of bottles against a mirrored background. The room was full of the laughter and conversation of vacationing couples or families and locals relaxing after their workweek.

I took a seat and a waiter immediately appeared at my side, asking what I wanted to drink. I ordered a glass of white wine. The woman next to me nodded politely and shoved a platter of deep-fried calamari toward me. I thanked her, helped myself to a piece, and dipped it into the spicy sauce provided. I popped it into my mouth and chewed happily.

"I could tell you stories about this place that would have your hair standing on end. Stories *they* don't want me to be telling. If you know what I mean." Louise Jane looked around her as though suspecting the hotel manager was standing behind a potted palm, ready to leap out and eject her from the premises if she said a word out of turn.

"Oh, do tell!" Shelia clapped her hands. "I always say the untold stories are the most fascinating, don't you agree?"

A couple of women concurred, in tones ranging from eager to reluctant. Others turned to their neighbor and began private conversations.

"If you insist," Louise Jane said. "This hotel is quite old, although it's been renovated recently. Even the best renovations only serve to throw a thin veneer over the surface. To those who've been . . . shall we say, living here for a long time . . . all remains as it had been. The staircase by the car park, for example, is where . . ."

"I've no time for ghost stories," the woman beside me said. "You're Lucy, aren't you? From the library. Bertie speaks very highly of you. I'm Margaret Hurley. Retired librarian." She looked the part, I thought, with her pale lipstick, neatly cut gray hair, thick glasses hanging from a chain around her neck, pink silk blouse tied in a bow at her throat.

"Pleased to meet you," I said.

"I enjoyed myself very much last night. I left before . . . before what happened."

"Did you know Ms. Sanchez?"

"I knew her vaguely from when she worked at the Lighthouse Library. I said no more than a few words to her at the party, but I can still be sorry for her death." She turned to the woman on her other side. "You knew Helena better, didn't you, Lucinda?"

"Briefly, but not well," Lucinda Lorca said. She, on the other hand, didn't look at all like the stereotypical image of a librarian with her long, sleek blond hair curling around her chin, diamond earrings and matching tennis bracelet, high-collared shirt with the top three buttons undone, and tight white capris. The skin around her mouth and eyes was fractionally too tight, and I suspected she'd had some plastic surgery done. "I was a librarian in the Outer Banks, and I might have run into her at conferences and the like now and again, but we never worked together. We certainly weren't friends. Until last night, I hadn't seen Helena for a long time. Not long after my marriage to Ed Smith ended, I quit and moved to California."

"When was that?" I asked.

"Nineteen ninety-three." She laughed lightly. "So long ago. Best thing I ever did, move to California." She patted her hair. "I'm in television now."

"That must be exciting," Margaret said.

"It is. I love every minute of my job. I'm not an actor, although I think I would have made a good one. I work strictly behind the scenes. I'm an assistant to one of Hollywood's most successful showrunners." She went on to mention the TV programs her boss was responsible for, including my mom's favorite legal drama.

The waiter arrived with my glass of wine and a beer for Louise Jane. Several of the women ordered another drink.

"If you want to talk to someone who knew Helena much better than me," Lucinda said, "you should try Mary-Sue. Mary-Sue!"

Mary-Sue had been studying the contents of her glass and not taking part in any of the conversations swirling around her. Her head jerked at the sound of her name. "Yes?"

"You knew Helena," Lucinda said. "Didn't you work together at the Lighthouse Library?"

Mary-Sue's face tightened. "As you well know. We talked about that last night. I don't need to be reminded again."

"But I do, dear." Lucinda smiled at her. I'd seen that expression before, when I'd been roped into watching TV with Mom: when the really nasty woman got her supposed enemy in a corner at a cocktail party. "I don't think I ever heard the full story of why you gave up your career."

Mary-Sue drained her glass. She said nothing.

"You're in real estate, I believe," Lucinda said. "That must be *so* interesting."

"It's a living," Mary-Sue muttered.

Margaret glanced between Lucinda and Mary-Sue. "You must see some wonderful homes around here," she said.

"Sometimes," Mary-Sue said.

"I loved every minute of my library career," Margaret said. "I can't imagine having done anything else. I wasn't ready to retire, but George—that's my husband; he's a few years older than me—when he retired, he wanted to travel. I have to admit, we've been to some marvelous places. Last year we were in Vietnam, and this year we're planning a Mediterranean cruise, and—"

"She forced me out," Mary-Sue snapped. "She fired me because I needed to take time off when Roger took sick. It was the absolute lowest time of my life. I had one child still in college, a husband without a job, and then him getting so sick and not nearly enough health insurance to take care of him. And Helena Sanchez fired me because she said I wasn't able to do my job anymore. Not only that but she blackballed me all over eastern North Carolina. No other libraries would hire me. You think I want to spend my time showing shoddily made, overpriced beach houses to stuck-up rich people from New York City? What other options did I have after

Helena Sanchez ripped my dreams as well as my livelihood away from me?"

All conversation at the big table died. Even Louise Jane was left with her mouth hanging open. Everyone stared at Mary-Sue. Tears filled her eyes. She rubbed at them and twisted in her chair. "Where is that waiter!" She snapped her fingers together, and he hurried across the room to our table.

"Can I get you ladies anything else?"

Mary-Sue tapped the rim of her glass. Louise Jane asked for another beer, and Sheila ordered a plate of bruschetta and more calamari.

"Aren't we going out for dinner?" Bertie asked.

"Eventually," Sheila said. "You say you've seen the maid yourself, Louise Jane? Do you get a sense of how she's feeling?"

"If it was me," Ruth said, "I'd be feeling trapped. Twenty years wandering around a hotel corridor? No thank you."

"It's interesting how small the library world is, isn't it?" Lucinda said. "Did you ever work with Helena, Ruth?"

"I did. We were at Manteo Library together, but not for long. She left there when she got the director job at the Lighthouse. After that we continued to run into each other at conferences and the like. She had a good reputation at one time, although in her later years people didn't speak as favorably of her. Bertie?"

"She was an excellent librarian," Bertie said. "When I took over at the Lighthouse Library, I found everything in admirable shape." Notably, Bertie didn't say anything about Aunt Ellen and the volunteers being on the verge of quitting because of Helena's leadership.

"I remember now," Lucinda said. "Gossip had it that she was bitterly estranged from her sister and her parents. Does anyone know what that was about?"

"Her sister," Louise Jane said, "is a nut case. I wouldn't put stock in anything she has to say."

"You told me you don't know her," I said.

"I hear things, Lucy. I listen and I pay attention. Unlike some people, I don't take things at face value."

"Please," Bertie said, "we're not here to gossip about Helena." Bertie might as well have tried to turn back the tide now lapping against the sand outside the windows as stop this conversation once it had started.

"The police paid a call on me this morning," Margaret said. "Such a handsome young man."

"When," Ruth said, "did they get to be so young?"

"Around the time my doctor did," a woman said.

"Have any of you ladies seen the mayor of this town?" Lucinda said. "My goodness, but they didn't make politicians that handsome in my day."

I felt myself blushing and blushed even more when I caught Bertie smiling at me.

"It was exciting being questioned by the police," Margaret said. "Unfortunately I had to tell him I couldn't be of help. I spoke to Helena last night, but not for long, and we said not much more than hello. When I left the party, she was still alive. What are the police saying happened to her, Bertie?"

"Nothing they're sharing with me," Bertie said. "Tell me about this cruise you mentioned, Margaret. Where are you going? I'd love to do a Mediterranean cruise someday. It's top of my list for when I retire."

"You should ask Lucy to show you her apartment," Louise Jane said. "Frances, known as the Lady, lives there. Her story is a fascinating one. Such a tragedy."

"That would be great," Shelia said. "How about tonight, Lucy?"

"What?" I said.

"Can I visit tonight? I'd love to try to contact one of the lighthouse spirits."

"There are no lighthouse spirits," I said, "and definitely none who are living in my apartment. I have a cat. He wouldn't allow them in."

"Shelia," Lucinda said, "do you have any memories to share of Helena?"

"Me? Didn't know her. Never heard of her before yesterday."

"Will you stop talking about Helena Sanchez," Mary-Sue snapped. Her glass was already empty. "She ruined my life. I'll never forgive her. I'm glad she's dead, and I'm not afraid to say so."

"Isn't this fun?" Ruth said in an attempt to change the subject. "So nice we could all get together."

"What are your plans for tomorrow?" I asked.

"Some beach and pool time after breakfast," Bertie said. "A group lunch here and then everyone's on their way."

"I'll have to miss the lunch," Lucinda said. "I have an early flight."

"I'm staying on for a few days," another woman said. "My parents live in Duck, so I'm going up to visit them."

"We have a reservation at Jake's Seafood Bar at seven," Bertie said. "We should finish our drinks and settle up the bill."

A Death Long Overdue

"If I can't see your apartment tonight," Sheila said to me, "how about tomorrow?"

I didn't answer her. Something, or rather someone, had caught my eye. Tina Ledbetter had slipped into the room when I wasn't looking and had taken a stool at the end of the bar. Despite the low lights, she wore enormous sunglasses, and her hair was hidden under a big straw hat. An untouched glass of beer rested on the counter in front of her, and she was staring at our table. She caught me watching and didn't look away.

Chapter Nine

Connor picked me up at eleven on Sunday. I was already wearing my bathing suit under a loose beach wrap and had flip-flops on my feet. My beach bag was packed with a book, a big towel, sunscreen, and a refillable bottle of water. Connor had promised to provide our picnic.

I was waiting downstairs when he drove up. It was going to be a perfect beach day. The sun was a bright yellow ball in a sky of the deepest blue, and the temperature was scheduled to hit the high eighties, with little wind. The top was down on Connor's BMW, and I got eagerly into the passenger seat. I leaned over for a kiss, and he kindly provided me with one.

A very long, very delicious one.

I'd been afraid that, despite Charlene warning her off, Louise Jane would show up, bathing suit on, beach bag in hand, ready to go with us. But I saw no sign of her.

Not yet anyway.

"Let's go," I said when Connor and I separated.

"You sound like you're in a hurry."

"I am in a hurry. A hurry to get sand between my toes and salty water on my bathing suit. As well as in a hurry to get out of here before someone shows up wanting my help with something."

He threw the car into gear. "Any news about the police investigation?"

"Not a peep. I'm going to assume that's a good thing. The autopsy was scheduled for yesterday afternoon. Maybe they concluded it wasn't murder after all, but an accident. That would be nice."

"Is Bertie enjoying her reunion?"

"I think she is. Aside from the death, of course. Louise Jane and I had drinks with some of the women last night at their hotel. It's nice to talk to older librarians. They have some great stories."

"You had drinks with Louise Jane?"

"Believe it or not, yes. We're getting on better these days. I think."

The waiter had brought the bill for my glass of wine, and I'd fumbled through my bag searching for my credit card. When I finally found it, paid for my drink, and looked again, Tina Ledbetter's stool had been empty. None of Bertie's group had noticed her. They weren't paying attention to their surroundings, of course, but the sunglasses and the big hat had gone a long way toward hiding Tina's resemblance to Helena.

I wondered what had brought her to the hotel and what her interest was in that group of librarians. Maybe nothing. Perhaps she regularly came to the Ocean Side for a drink. It wasn't far from her house.

The women paid their bills, gathered purses and wraps, and got to their feet. I managed to get out of the hotel without having to invite Sheila to my apartment to meet the Lady.

Who, of course, doesn't exist.

Traffic was heavy on the highway this morning. The perfect weather had Sunday crowds streaming out of Nags Head to explore the beaches further south and the small, charming towns of Rodanthe and Buxton; see the Cape Hatteras Lighthouse; or hop on the ferry to Ocracoke. Plenty of cars were in the parking lot at Coquina Beach, but the beach is long enough for everyone to enjoy without feeling at all crowded.

Connor got the picnic basket out of the trunk, and I carried the blanket and umbrella over the dunes. We found a perfect spot and set ourselves up. He put up the umbrella and I laid out my towel. I took off my beach wrap and handed him the sunscreen. He rubbed it over my back and shoulders with deep, penetrating strokes that went on long after the heavy cream had been absorbed. I then did the same for him.

Well protected from the sun, shivering with pleasure, happy in each other's company, we gripped hands and ran laughing and splashing into the surf.

We swam and played in the water, and then we collapsed onto our towels in the shade of the umbrella and read in companionable silence. Connor is in my book club, and he was also reading *The Moonstone*.

"The local cops aren't all that efficient in this book, are they?" he said at one point.

"One of the standard tropes of traditional mystery fiction," I said.

"Don't let Sam Watson hear you say that."

I chuckled. "Which is why they had to call in Sergeant Cuff, the hotshot from Scotland Yard."

"You about ready for lunch?"

I closed my book and sat up. "I am."

Together we unpacked the basket. He'd stopped at Josie's Cozy Bakery for sandwiches, cold drinks, and desserts. "You have your choice of roast beef, ham and cheese, hummus and roasted red peppers, or tuna salad," Connor said.

"You bought four of those enormous sandwiches for two people?"

"You make it sound as though there's something wrong with that. I'll have leftovers for dinner."

"Tuna, please."

He handed me my sandwich, and I unwrapped it and dug in. As we ate, we watched the activity on the beach. Waves along this stretch of the coast can be high and the riptide dangerous, but today the sea was calm, so some people swam close to shore while others played in the surf. Small children filled plastic pails with sand and dumped them out again while older ones kicked balls around. Families enjoyed picnics, and further down the beach fishermen sat in folding chairs next to their long arching poles, beverage of choice in hand. Colorful kites bobbed and swooped in the distance.

"A perfect day." I peeked into the picnic basket, hoping he'd bought one of Josie's famous coconut cupcakes. My favorite. Other than her pecan squares, which are also my favorite. Of course, I also love the dream cake she makes from an old family recipe.

Connor cleared his throat. "Lucy."

The tone in his voice had me stop thinking about baked treats. I looked up. His face was flushed and his eyes bright. I wondered if he was suddenly coming down with a fever. "What? Are you okay?"

He cleared his throat again. "It is a perfect day. Lucy. There can be many more prefect days."

"Yes," I agreed. "The weather's supposed to stay good all week."

"I mean . . . I mean . . . beyond this week. Lucy, what I'm saying is—"

From the depths of my beach bag, my phone rang. Instinctively, I reached for it.

"Leave it," Connor said. "Let them leave a message."

"I'll just take a peek and see who it is. Oh. It's Detective Watson." I looked at Connor. "I should get this. It might be important."

He sighed. "Yes, I guess you should."

"Good afternoon, Detective," I said.

"Sorry to bother you, Lucy, but we've found something I need you to have a look at, and Bertie's not answering her phone."

"She's having a farewell lunch with her college crowd. What is it?"

"You'll see when you get here. How long will it take?"

"I'm at Coquina Beach with Connor. Ten minutes."

"See you then." He hung up.

"He needs me to come to the police station right now," I said. "They've found something important."

Connor began gathering up the picnic debris. "Did he say what it was?"

"No."

"I guess we should go then."

"What were you talking about when he called? Did you want to make some sort of plans?"

"Some sort," he said. "It'll keep."

*　*　*

I felt somewhat odd walking into the Nags Head police station in my bathing suit, beach wrap, big straw hat, and flip-flops. Connor didn't look all that mayoral in shorts with a rip in the right pocket, sandals, T-shirt, and Boston Red Sox cap (my Christmas present to him). But it was the Outer Banks on a hot Sunday in July, so no one had a right to expect anything more formal.

Sam Watson was waiting for us by the front doors when we arrived.

"You didn't invite me to see this, Sam," Connor said. "Whatever it is. Do you want me to wait out here?"

"No need. It won't take long." Watson led the way through the station to an interview room. The office was quiet on a Sunday afternoon. Butch Greenblatt was the only other person at work, pounding at a computer keyboard, his fingers almost too big for the keys, and he lifted a hand in a wave as we passed. The air-conditioning was turned up far too high, reminding me I was seriously underdressed.

The interview room was sparsely furnished, but not intimidating and not too dreadfully uncomfortable apart from the temperature. Sam nodded toward a chair and I sat, trying not to shiver too obviously. Connor stood behind me. A plain beige paper folder lay on the table. It wasn't thick, so it couldn't contain much more than a few sheets of paper. Watson opened it, took out a sheet of plastic that he laid in front of me, and then he closed the folder.

I leaned in for a closer look, and I felt Connor do the same over my shoulder. "It's a library withdrawal slip," I said.

115

"We found this in a trash can near the boardwalk at the lighthouse. Does this look like the slip you told me was missing from the library?"

I studied it carefully. The card was about four inches square, yellowing with age. The title of the book and name of the author were typewritten across the top. A line of names in different hands and inks ran down the left hand column, and dates were stamped on the right. "It does. I'm pretty sure it's the same one. *The Celestine Prophecy*. I suppose it could be a slip from another book with the same title, but that stretches coincidence to the breaking point, don't you think?"

"I do," Watson said. Connor muttered his agreement.

The paper had been torn into many pieces. Some of them were smudged with traces of I didn't want to know what. Someone had carefully reassembled the card as though it were a jigsaw puzzle.

"We put it back together as best we were able, and checked it for fingerprints," Watson said. "We came up with a lot of prints. Some older than others. One partial's a match to Helena Sanchez."

I thought back to Bertie's party Friday night. The women gathered in the alcove exclaiming over the historical display. "I'm almost certain Helena touched it. She started to take it out of the pocket, and seemed to see something that upset her."

"Find any other identifiable prints, Sam?" Connor asked.

"Charlene Clayton's."

"Natural enough," I said. "Charlene and I put the exhibit together. I don't think I touched this particular item, though."

"Some smudges, some partials that will be too small to identify without a good match. Lucy, you said no librarian would throw something like this in the garbage. Do you still maintain that?"

"Absolutely. No one is more protective of a written legacy than librarians. Not even the police. You'll destroy this if you don't need it anymore. We would need a very good reason to do that."

"Not all the women in Bertie's class are still working librarians," Watson said.

"No, but they were trained to be. I'm not saying none of the women at the party threw this away; all I'm saying is no one did it mindlessly. Someone didn't want it found."

"Yet you have found it," Connor said. "What does it mean?"

"Lucy?" Watson asked.

And that was a very good question. *Why would someone think they needed to get rid of this common withdrawal slip?* I studied it carefully. The title of the book was typed in capital letters, the signatures handwritten in various types of ink, the dates stamped. I didn't recognize any of the names, and the dates themselves, ranging over six months from the beginning of 1995, were of no significance I could see. "I've absolutely no idea. Sorry, Sam."

"That's okay. I'm going to show you one more thing. This is a photograph of something our divers found in the water under the pier." He took another page out of the folder.

I recognized it immediately. "That's the souvenir letter opener that was part of the exhibit."

"Or one of the same," Connor said. "Those things were handed out by the bucketful in 1986 to celebrate the twenty-fifth anniversary of the incorporation of the town of Nags Head. There are plenty of them floating around. Pardon the pun."

"This one hasn't been in the water long," Watson said. "No more than a couple days at a guess. Probably less. There are no prints on it, not even any partials, meaning it was probably wiped down before being thrown in the marsh."

"Is there any . . . uh . . . trace of it being used?" I asked.

"It's in the lab now and they're checking it over. The blade, as you can see, is completely smooth. No serrations to trap residue in. But we might be able to pull something off. The town's seal is stamped in the handle."

"You said Helena's prints were on the withdrawal slip. Do identical twins have identical prints?"

He grinned at me. "We'll make an investigator out of you yet, Lucy."

"Perish the thought," I said with a shudder that wasn't entirely because I was half-dressed and the air-conditioning was blowing directly on me.

"The answer to your question is no," Watson said. "There may be similarities between them, more than between two random people, but one twin's prints are not identical to the other's. In this case, however, we only have partials. Which may be important. Or it may not."

"Why did you ask that, Lucy?" Connor said.

"Helena Sanchez has an identical twin sister," Watson said.

"Interesting," Connor said.

"Isn't it?" Watson picked up the folder and slipped the pages inside. He crossed the room and opened the door. "Thanks for coming down so promptly, Lucy, Connor. I hope I haven't spoiled your day."

Connor shifted from one foot to the other.

"No problem," I said. "We were about to leave the beach anyway. What happens now?"

"I'm concentrating on the women who went on the walk on the boardwalk after the party on Friday. Present company excepted, of course. Unless you knew Helena Sanchez and haven't told me?"

"I never met her before Friday evening," I said firmly. I didn't know the woman and I had no reason to kill her, but being involved in a police investigation, no matter how innocent one might be, is always stressful. Watson hadn't included Bertie in his statement, and I wasn't pleased about that. Surely he couldn't be thinking Bertie might have been responsible for the death of Helena Sanchez?

"My officers spoke to the women who didn't go on the walk, and every one of them can be accounted for. They shared cabs or lifts into town; a few went for a drink in the bar once they got back to the hotel; some are sharing rooms. It would have been difficult, although nothing is impossible, for one of them to return to the library unnoticed in time to kill Ms. Sanchez. The four women who went on the walk with you have been asked to remain in Nags Head for the time being."

"How did they react to being told that?" I asked.

"Not always well," he said dryly. "I sent an officer to the Ocean Side Hotel first thing this morning, to inform that group they are not to leave Nags Head until further notice. The autopsy results conclude that Helena Sanchez was killed by a sharp thin object driven into the back of her neck. An object much like a letter opener. She was dead by the time she hit the water."

"Meaning she was murdered by someone who was in our library that evening," I said.

"So it would appear," he replied.

Chapter Ten

Sam Watson's phone rang. He pulled it out of his jacket pocket and checked the display. He held up one finger, telling us to wait a minute. "Watson. Whatcha got?" He listened for a moment and said, "On my way." He put the phone away and spoke to Connor and me.

"As for what happens now, that call was to tell me Bertie and her friends have finished their lunch and are waiting for me. I'm taking a copy of this withdrawal slip to the hotel to show it to them. It means nothing to you. It must mean something to whoever stole it and then threw it away, hoping we wouldn't search the trash."

"I wonder why that person didn't take it with them," Connor said.

Watson shrugged. "Who knows why anyone does anything? Maybe they were uncomfortable having it on their person. I need to know what this piece of paper means. If it means anything. Despite what you keep telling me, Lucy, it's possible someone wiped their fingers on it and tossed it in the garbage at the first opportunity."

"You're going to the hotel now," I said. "How about I come with you? I was there, remember. Seeing them with the withdrawal slip might remind me of something."

"Bertie was there also," Watson reminded me.

"Yes, but she was enjoying catching up with old friends. I was working. There's a difference."

Watson glanced at Connor. Connor held out his hands. "She's got a point, Sam."

"You're not exactly dressed for participating in a police inquiry," Watson said.

I tugged my beach wrap tighter around me, grateful that it was large and loose and all-covering. "It's an Outer Banks resort hotel in July. I'll be dressed like half the people in the place. Besides, I'm not pretending to be a police officer." I didn't add *this time.*

"Okay," Watson said. "You might as well come. I see no need at this point to question the women privately or individually about the withdrawal slip. Discussing what happened among themselves might help jog memories."

"Thanks," I said.

"Connor," Watson said, "you up to joining us?"

"I think not. I wasn't there that night; I don't know any of the people involved. Lucy'll be with you, not prowling around in the dark by herself. Besides, I have reading to do for tomorrow night."

I waved to Butch as we walked through the police station, and he gave me a big grin and a thumbs-up. "How's CeeCee liking this month's book?" I asked Watson, referring to his wife, who was part of my classic novel book club.

"She likes it a lot. She wants me to read it after she's done. There's nothing, she says, like a stolen jewel with a mysterious deadly past to make a story intriguing."

We parted at the bottom of the steps. Connor gave me a light kiss and headed for the BMW. I got into Watson's car with him, and we drove the short distance to the Ocean Side.

We found fourteen of the women, plus Bertie, waiting for us in a meeting room under the stern eye of Officer Holly Rankin. Three of the reunion attendees, we were told, had left late Saturday night, after dinner, and two early this morning. Watson confirmed he had their contact information and said he'd give them a call later.

Most of the women had taken seats around the table; a couple stood against the wall; Lucinda paced back and forth; Sheila stared out the window. The hotel had provided a pot of coffee and pitchers of juice and ice water, but no one had served themselves.

Bertie raised one eyebrow when she caught sight of me following Watson into the room, but she didn't say anything. Again, I felt ridiculously underdressed. Watson was in ironed gray slacks and a blue buttoned shirt under a brown leather jacket, and Rankin wore her dark, heavy uniform. The women attending the reunion were nicely dressed for lunch with friends and then traveling in brightly colored dresses or white capris with patterned T-shirts. They all wore proper shoes, and most had earrings in ears and necklaces around necks.

I slapped my way across the room in my flip-flops to stand behind Bertie. I jerked at the belt of my beach wrap to tie it tighter around my waist. At least the air-conditioning in this room was at a level above bone-chilling.

The detective put the folder on the table in the center of the room. "Thank you all for agreeing to speak with me."

"I wasn't aware we had a choice," Sheila said.

"You don't," he replied. "Not if you want me to find the person who killed your friend."

"So it was a murder, then." Sheila turned away from the window.

Watson didn't reply. The word had been put out there, and that was enough. The women shifted uncomfortably in their seats and murmured to their neighbors.

"I know nothing about that," Lucinda said. "I keep telling you, over and over, I hadn't seen Helena for years. I don't know why I can't go home. I have work tomorrow morning."

"I'm sure your employers will understand," Watson said.

"I for one am more than happy to help," said a woman I didn't know.

"Which might be because you're not under suspicion," Mary-Sue said. "And you're free to leave."

The woman smirked at her.

"At least you can sleep in your own bed, Mary-Sue," Lucinda snapped. "I'm being kept here against my will."

"There are worse places," Ruth said. "Like a cell in the police station."

Lucinda glared at her.

"I expect to be fully reimbursed by the Nags Head PD for the cost of changing my flight and any extra nights in the hotel," Ruth said.

"That goes for me too," Lucinda said.

Watson did not reply. "If you wouldn't mind taking your seats, we can get this over with quickly."

"And then *some of us* can be on our way," a woman said.

"I'm going to hand around photocopies of a piece of paper. You'll notice that the original of the page has been torn and reassembled. Y'all will recognize it for what it is. What I want to know is if this one in particular has any meaning to you. No matter how small." He took photocopied pages out of the folder and passed them around.

"It's an old-time withdrawal slip," Sheila said. "Before computers, we used these to keep track of who had books out and when they were due to be returned."

The women murmured their agreement.

"*The Celestine Prophecy*," Margaret Hurley said. "I never read it, but it was a huge bestseller. Some people said it changed their lives. We couldn't keep it on the shelf."

"What about the people's names?" Watson asked. "Do any of your recognize any of them?"

The women studied the slip.

I watched their faces. I realized Bertie was doing the same.

"This was in one of the books at the library on Friday night," Sheila said. "Helena looked at it. I'm sure she did."

"Yes, she did," Ruth said.

"Jeff Applewhite," Lucinda said in a low voice that was barely a whisper.

Mary-Sue narrowed her eyes and held the page closer to her face. She sucked in a breath. "Oh my gosh. Lucinda's right. I didn't see it at first."

I leaned over Margaret's shoulder. She stabbed her finger onto the name on the page. Jeff Applewhite had taken out the book, and it was due to be returned on May 25, 1995. Some of the women looked complexly blank, but a few exchanged glances and muttered to themselves. Clearly, the name had sig-nificance to some of them.

"Who's Jeff Applewhite?" Watson asked.

"Were you working here in 1995, Detective?" Margaret asked.

"No. I was with the NYPD."

"Do a record search at your station," she said. "You'll be sure to find it. I remember the case well."

"As do I," Mary-Sue said. "It was a nine-day wonder around the time I . . . left the library."

I threw a questioning look to Bertie. She shrugged, indicating that she knew no more than me.

"What are you talking about?" Watson asked.

Several women began speaking at once, their voices rising in excitement.

"One at a time, please," Watson said.

"Jeff Applewhite disappeared in spring of 1995," Margaret said. "I don't remember the exact date, but I remember the story very well indeed. He himself was no one of any particular importance, and people come and go all the time around here. The only reason any of us remember the circumstances is that he was last seen in the vicinity of an extremely expensive dia-mond necklace. Neither the necklace nor Mr. Applewhite were ever seen again."

Chapter Eleven

At that, the women began to talk all over each other. Some nodded sagely and repeated the story. Some asked breathless questions.

"He disappeared from my library?" Bertie asked.

"Not from the library, no," Margaret said, "but it looks like he might have checked out a book before he left."

"Why would anyone who stole valuable jewels be interested in a fiction book?" someone asked.

"Are you sure the necklace was stolen?" Ruth said. "I heard the owner wouldn't cooperate with the police."

"Because she was embarrassed most likely," Sheila said. "What was her name again?"

Sam Watson, I thought, looked stunned. But he recovered quickly and lifted one hand. Gradually the excited chatter died down. Watson ran his penetrating gray eyes over the watching faces. "Were any of you personally acquainted with this Jeff Applewhite?"

The women shook their heads.

"Were any of you personally involved in events surrounding the disappearance of this necklace?"

More head shaking.

"Not exactly the circles in which I mixed," sniffed Mary-Sue.

"In that case," he said, "I'd prefer to read up on the case myself rather than be influenced by fading memories and secondhand gossip. In the meantime, I'll remind you we're here about the death of Helena Sanchez. I have another picture to show you. Please tell me if you recognize this."

He took the photograph of the letter opener out of the folder and passed it around. Almost everyone said they'd seen it on Friday night as part of our historical exhibit.

"Is that the murder weapon?" a woman asked with what I thought an unseemly delighted shudder.

"He's not going to tell us that," Ruth said. "But we're free to speculate."

"I thought you said she drowned," another woman said. "Didn't she?"

"She had to get into the water somehow," Mary-Sue said. "She wasn't enjoying a moonlight swim."

"I can't believe no one saw anything," a woman said. "How could you have lost track of her? We're hardly in the middle of nowhere."

"It was as dark out there that night as though we were in the middle of nowhere," Lucinda replied. "And I resent your implication."

"Not implying anything. Just making a comment."

"As for this letter opener," Watson said. "Did anyone see it *not* on the display table in the alcove?"

Women glanced at each other. Heads shook again.

"Hard to prove a negative, Detective," Margaret said.

He rephrased the question. "Did anyone who'd seen it earlier, happen to notice when it was no longer on the display table?"

More shaking of heads.

A small, gray-haired woman slowly raised her hand.

"Yes, ma'am," Watson said. "Do you have something to add?"

"I have to be leaving for the airport soon. I don't want to miss my flight."

"It's a long drive to Raleigh," said another. "I don't like to be on the roads after dark."

"I think we're finished here." Watson gathered up the papers and put them back in the folder. "Thank you for your time. If anyone remembers anything, anything at all, about events of Friday night or Helena Sanchez, please get in touch with me. I have your contact details if I need further information. Those of you who need to be on your way are free to leave now. If you've been asked to remain in Nags Head pending further developments, I trust you'll do so."

Some women bounded out of their chairs and bolted for the door. Some lingered, unsure. A few hugged and exchanged kisses and promises to keep in touch.

"I want it on record that I object to being treated like a common criminal," Lucinda Lorca said. "Television is a highly competitive business. If I have to stay here much longer, I might not have a job to go back to."

"Duly noted," Watson said.

"Mary-Sue, do you have room for me at your house?" Lucinda asked.

"What?" Mary-Sue said.

"I don't want to stay in this hotel a moment longer. It'll be much nicer to move into a friend's home. I'm sure it'll only be for a day or two."

"I don't—"

"Great! That's arranged then. I'll get my stuff packed and meet you in the lobby in a jiffy." Lucinda ran past Holly Rankin and out the door.

Mary-Sue looked at Bertie.

"You can say no," Bertie said.

"Too late now," Mary-Sue said.

"I don't suppose you have room for me too, do you?" Sheila asked. "This is an expensive hotel."

"No. Sorry. Our house isn't very big and my son . . ." Mary-Sue's voice trailed off.

"Why don't you and I get a room together, Sheila?" Ruth said. "If we share, it'll help with the cost a bit."

"I'd like that," Sheila replied. "Thanks."

"Mrs. Hurley," Watson said. "I have one question about this Jeff Applewhite and the stolen jewels. What was the name of the owner?"

"Rachel Blackstone," Margaret said.

Bertie's jaw dropped.

"Rachel Blackstone," I said. "You don't mean—"

"She does," Mary-Sue said. "The same Rachel Blackstone who still lives in Nags Head and chairs all those fundraising committees for the hospital and other charities."

"Do you know this woman?" Watson asked Bertie and me.

"We do. Very well," Bertie said.

"She's a regular at the library," I said. "She's a close friend to my aunt Ellen."

"Did either of you know about this theft?"

"No," I said.

"Me neither," Bertie said. "It happened before my time here. I find it interesting that no one talks about it anymore."

"Out of respect for Rachel most likely," Margaret said. "It was a long time ago."

"I'm going back to the station, and I'm going to read up on the records of the case. The fact that the name of a man who disappeared after allegedly stealing a valuable piece of jewelry is on the withdrawal slip that appears to have some nebulous connection to a current case is probably meaningless. Plenty of other people took out that book and wrote their names on the slip. But stranger things have happened. Officer Rankin, let's go."

Rankin moved herself away from the wall.

I picked one of the photocopies off the table. "May I keep this, Detective?"

"Sure," he said.

Mary-Sue followed Watson to the door. "How long are you going to keep them here? I don't want that woman in my house any longer than necessary."

"I can't say, Mrs. Delamont. But I'll remind you that you also are not to leave town without my permission."

"I haven't done anything!" she protested.

"Glad to hear it." Watson paused in the doorway and then turned around. "Sorry, Lucy. I forgot. You came with me. Do you need Officer Rankin to drive you back to the lighthouse?"

"I'll take her," Bertie said.

He gave us a nod and left. Rankin followed him out.

"We'd better get that room arranged, Ruth," Sheila said. "I hope the hotel's not fully booked. Otherwise, we'll be at your place, Mary-Sue, son or not."

Mary-Sue tried not to groan.

"It would be just like our college days," Ruth said. "We can watch scary movies and stuff ourselves with potato chips and pizza, and throw sleeping bags on the floor."

"I doubt my sixty-year-old bones would care for that," Sheila said as they left the meeting room.

"I haven't thought about that business of Rachel's necklace for a long time," Margaret said. "Imagine it popping up now. I wonder if it did have something to do with Helena. I don't suppose we'll ever know. It was nice seeing you, Bertie. It's been too long. I'd like to keep in touch."

"As would I," Bertie said with a smile.

Soon only Bertie and I remained in the meeting room. A housekeeper slipped in and began clearing away the untouched drinks.

"Are you thinking what I'm thinking?" Bertie said to me.

"Oh yeah." I dropped into the chair next to her and took out my phone. "It might well be a coincidence that this Jeff Applewhite took out that book from what's now our library around the time he disappeared with a purloined necklace. But I saw the look on Helena's face when she saw that withdrawal slip. She read something there that meant something extremely important to her. And that something was not a happy memory."

We began tapping on our phones.

In 1995, the internet was in its infancy. There wasn't a lot of detail available about the case, but Bertie and I were able to find some information, mainly because the necklace that apparently had been stolen was of considerable significance and people who care about rare gems had followed the case closely at the time and speculated ever since.

The night of April 30, 1995, Rachel Blackstone threw a party at her family's beach house in Nags Head. The party had gotten out of control, and neighbors called the police. It was not, apparently, the first time that happened. Rachel was known to be what was euphemistically described as a "wealthy, fun-loving young woman."

"Doesn't sound like the Rachel I know," Bertie said.

"No, it doesn't. It might not be the same person."

"It has to be her. Same name, right age, home in Nags Head. Rachel's a woman of considerable means. Family money."

We read on. The police had left after asking a few partygoers to move their cars, and the party continued. Much to the annoyance of the neighbors.

"This is interesting," I said. "Rachel didn't report the theft. Her mother did, and then not until several days had passed."

"Perhaps Rachel didn't realize it was missing. Police searched for a man by the name of Jeffrey Applewhite, who'd attended the party. He's described as having recently moved to Nags Head. And there the story seems to end. Applewhite was never found, and the necklace is still missing. To the dismay of gemologists everywhere."

"Do you really think this has something to do with the death of Helena?"

"I can't see how, Lucy. I didn't know Helena at all well, but she stayed in Nags Head for a long time after this happened.

She didn't abscond with a lover and a diamond necklace and live off the proceeds of its sale."

"I'm wondering about her sister," I said. "Her twin sister. Maybe Tina Ledbetter had something to do with it. Although I've been to her house. Not exactly the mansion of a master criminal."

Bertie put her phone away. "You must be freezing in that outfit. I'll take you home. Why are you dressed like that anyway?"

"Connor and I were at the beach when Watson called saying he needed me to come down to the station and look at the withdrawal slip." Grains of sand were trapped in the seat of my bathing suit, and my body felt sticky from the drying salt. I didn't dare think about what my hair must look like.

Bertie frowned. "Really. Sam Watson needs to stop working all the time and expecting us to be at his beck and call."

"I don't mind. It's important."

"Personal time is also important," my boss said.

We left the meeting room and walked into the hotel lobby. Some of the reunion guests were checking out, and others stood at the front doors next to their suitcases, waiting for taxis. It took a long time for us to leave. Bertie stopped to talk to everyone, and they all exchanged hugs and promises to keep in touch.

"Did you enjoy the weekend?" I asked when we'd finally been able to make our escape and get into Bertie's car.

"Very much. Aside from what happened with Helena, of course. I can't believe how much I laughed last night at dinner as we repeated the old stories. I was very close to some of those women at an important time in my life. Some of them I couldn't stand back then, and one or two I found I still can't stand."

"I don't believe that," I said. "You like everyone, Bertie."

She turned to me with a smile. "I pretend to like everyone, Lucy. There's a difference. Although, I've found over the years that if you try to get along, almost everyone turns out to be good at heart."

"Mary-Sue wasn't happy at Lucinda's coming to stay with her."

"No. Mary-Sue's very bitter. She doesn't hide it at all well. I don't think she even tries."

We drove through Whalebone Junction, and Bertie sped up as the traffic thinned as we sped out of town. I looked out the window at the narrow line of houses lining the seafront on my left. The houses soon faded away, and we drove past miles of sand dunes and scruffy beach grass. The Bodie Island Lighthouse appeared in the distance to our right, its black and white bands serving as a landmark to ships at sea, the paint as individual as the pattern of the light at night.

Something about a lighthouse—any lighthouse—always brings a lump to my throat. On one of my first dates with Connor, he recited the words written on the walls of the Currituck light: *To illuminate the dark space.* He'd told me how people built lighthouses to protect people they might never meet. A flash of light in the preelectric world would guide ships on their way and keep them safe from the perils of the sea.

I think, now that I look back on it, it might have been that night, at that dinner, that I fell in love with Connor McNeil.

"I suspect Lucinda," Bertie said, pulling me out of my pleasant thoughts and back to the unpleasant matter at hand, "has some deep insecurities, which make her inclined to brag and show off. Not a good situation in the company of an angry woman like Mary-Sue."

"Do you think Rachel would mind talking about what happened all those years ago?" I asked as Bertie turned into the long lane and passed between the lines of tall red pines.

"I don't know. I'd never heard that story before today, so it's obviously not a point of conversation for her. Doesn't mean it's a sore point. Maybe she thinks it's old news and no one cares."

"Could we pay her a visit? I can get changed quickly."

"I'm having dinner with Eddie tonight. He'll have left Elizabeth City already, so I can hardly call and tell him it's off." Eddie was Edward McClanahan, a professor of ancient languages at Blacklock College. He and Bertie had been an item in their grad student years. They'd reconnected a few months ago when Bertie and I went to the college in search of the dirt—I mean, important information—on two of his colleagues. "Why don't you speak to Ellen first? She might know if it's a sensitive subject for Rachel."

"Good idea." The car pulled up in front of the lighthouse, and I grabbed my beach bag and got out.

"I forgot to ask," Bertie said, "did you and Connor have a nice afternoon? Before you were so rudely interrupted."

"We did. Thanks for the lift. See you tomorrow." I shut the car door and ran up the path.

Chapter Twelve

Charles greeted me in his normally effusive manner. I always hope it's me he's happy to see, and not just that he's hoping to soon hear the pop of the tab being released on the cat food can. He ran ahead of me, balancing nimbly on the staircase railing. I ran after him, not nearly so nimbly, and let us into the Lighthouse Aerie. I threw my bag on the bed, and before doing anything else, I called Aunt Ellen from the landline in my apartment. Charles paced across the kitchen and wound himself around my legs, reminding me that I had more important tasks to attend to. I wagged my finger at him. It was still too early for dinner.

Although, for Charles, it was never too early for dinner.

"Good afternoon, Lucy," Aunt Ellen said.

"Hi. I know this might sound strange, but I do have a reason for asking."

"Go ahead."

"Rachel Blackstone. Her name came up today in connection with a missing necklace."

"Oh yes. That."

"So it was hers? I heard that a valuable piece of jewelry had been stolen from her many years ago."

"That's true. And 'valuable' is the word. It was a family heirloom containing a legendary diamond and worth a considerable amount of money. It was never recovered, and Rachel feels guilty to this day about it."

"You mean she had something to do with its disappearing?"

"No, not at all. Guilty that she didn't take better care, I mean."

"Do you think she'd be willing to talk to me about it?"

"I don't see why not. She feels guilty, as I said, but it's not a sensitive subject for her."

In the background, I heard my uncle Amos yelling at Aunt Ellen.

"Amos says it's been too long and you're to come to dinner tonight. He's grilling fish, and there's always room for one more. Josie will be here."

"Sounds mighty tempting," I said, meaning it. No one on planet Earth does grilled fish better than Uncle Amos. I grew up eating it in those long, lazy summers I spent on the Outer Banks.

"I have an idea," Aunt Ellen said. "I'll invite Rachel too. I know she's in town. We have a meeting of the museum board tomorrow."

"That would be great. If she's not comfortable talking about what happened, I'll drop the subject."

"Josie's expected around six. Come when you're ready. If Rachel's not free, I'll tell her you want to pay a call on her another time."

We hung up and I checked the time. It was five o'clock now. I fed Charles (who was attempting to make me believe he was about to expire from sheer starvation any minute now) and then jumped into the shower. I stood under the hot water for a long time, grateful to be washing all that sand and salt out of my hair and off my skin.

I pulled on a light summer dress of red cotton splashed with yellow and blue. Expecting that we'd sit outside to eat, knowing the evening breeze off the ocean can be cool, I added a light black sweater to the outfit.

Charles waved me out the door, and I was on my way by quarter to six.

* * *

When Aunt Ellen and Uncle Amos's three children grew up and moved away, they sold the big, rambling home I'd visited so often and bought their dream place on the beach, not far from Jeanette's Pier in Nags Head. It's a beautiful house, painted a cheerful yellow, made up of several stories in the standard Outer Banks beach style, perched on the edge of the dunes, with a view of the open ocean. It's smaller than the house they used to have, but more than adequate for their needs now and for visitors they continue to get regularly.

Like most beach houses, theirs stands on stilts, with the garage and storage rooms on the ground level and the living areas on the upper floors. I climbed the steps, and Aunt Ellen opened the door to me with a smile. She wrapped me in an enthusiastic hug.

"Sorry, I didn't bring anything," I said, "but you did give me rather short notice."

"You never need to bring anything except yourself, honey, and you know that."

"I do," I said.

"I spoke to Rachel and she accepted my invitation to dinner with enthusiasm. She was pleased to hear you and Josie will be joining us."

Aunt Ellen led the way upstairs. The main living area is open plan, the walls painted white and the rooms full of cheerful, comfortable blue and yellow furniture. Paintings of Outer Banks scenes by local artists add to the riot of color.

Josie and Uncle Amos were waiting for us on the deck that runs off the thoroughly modern steel and glass kitchen. Josie jumped to her feet to greet me with a hug, and Uncle Amos said, "Get you a drink?"

"A tea would be nice. I'm driving, so I'll have a small glass of wine with dinner."

The table was set with five places. "Did you tell Rachel why I want to talk to her?" I asked.

"No," Aunt Ellen said. "I'm happy to have her as a guest in my home. You can ask, but if she doesn't want to talk about it, I trust you'll respect that."

"I will." I accepted a frosty, ice-filled glass from Uncle Amos and sat down.

"Why do you want to talk to her?" Josie asked.

"There's the door now," Uncle Amos said, and Aunt Ellen excused herself.

I sipped my tea, delicious and sweet without being cloying, in the true Southern manner, and gazed over the baloney railing to the beach below and the sea beyond. It was still daylight but the shadows thrown by the houses lining the dunes were long. No one was swimming, but people strolled through the surf, sending sandpipers scurrying on their long, thin legs. Gulls swooped overhead, and out to sea the fishing charters returned to harbor after a day on the water.

I sighed happily.

I turned to see Josie grinning at me. "What?" I said.

"You were in your happy place. I could see it on your face."

"Guilty as charged," I said. "How's things at work?"

"Good. All good." If the bakery were falling down around her, my cousin would say everything was falling perfectly.

"I'm sorry I haven't been in for a while. We've been busy at the library. It's that time of year."

"That time of year for us all," Uncle Amos said. "Even for me, although Steph's taking on more of the workload these days." Stephanie Stanton was one of my closest friends, girl-friend of Butch Greenblatt, and Uncle Amos's law partner. As my uncle edged slowly, perhaps more slowly than Aunt Ellen would like, toward retirement, Steph began shouldering more of their cases.

Uncle Amos rose to his feet as Aunt Ellen and Rachel Blackstone came onto the deck. My aunt carried an enormous bouquet of fresh, short-stemmed red roses, accented by white daisies and leaves of green Hosta. "Look what Rachel brought me," she said with delight. "And at such short notice too."

"They're gorgeous," Josie said, giving Rachel a hug.

"Grown by my own hand," Rachel said.

"You know Lucy, don't you?" Aunt Ellen said. "From the library?"

"Of course," Rachel said with a light laugh. "Everyone knows Lucy."

"Everyone loves Lucy," Josie said. "Hmm, that might make a good name for a TV show."

"Never heard that one before," I said, and we all laughed. Oh yes, I'd been reminded of the old Lucille Ball TV show *I Love Lucy* many times, particularly when I'd been dating a man named Ricky. *Thank heavens,* I always thought, *I don't have red hair.*

Uncle Amos offered drinks, Rachel accepted, and she and I sat down. Aunt Ellen took her flowers into the kitchen, and Josie went to give her a hand. Rachel accepted a glass of wine and complimented Uncle Amos on the view. She was a striking-looking woman, but without the veneer of being over-pampered (my own mom came to mind) some wealthy women have. She was probably in her mid-fifties, taller than even Josie, and whippet thin, with sleek black-and-gray hair that curled under her chin, and wide hazel eyes brimming with good humor. She'd dressed for a casual dinner with friends, in white jeans, a navy-blue T-shirt, and a white linen jacket. Her only jewelry was discreet gold hoop earrings.

Josie and Aunt Ellen were soon back, carrying platters of cheese, a sliced baguette, and a bowl of mixed nuts. Uncle Amos fired up the grill.

"I haven't seen you since your wedding, Josie," Rachel said. "My congratulations."

"Thank you."

"I'd ask how married life is working out, but I don't have to. You still have that glow. Happiness simply pours from you."

Josie smiled and blushed. She'd been married over the winter to Jake Greenblatt, Butch's brother. Jake owned Jake's Seafood Bar, one of the most popular restaurants in Nags Head, where he was also the head chef. With his work hours, he didn't often get to family dinners.

Aunt Ellen sat down and accepted a glass of wine from Uncle Amos. My uncle went into the kitchen and was soon back carrying a tray on which lay an enormous red snapper, which he'd earlier prepped and stuffed.

I picked up my glass of tea and twisted it in my hands. I spoke hesitantly, unsure of the reception my question would get. "I hope you don't mind, Rachel. I have something I'd like to ask you. If you don't want to talk about it, that's okay."

"That sounds serious," she said. "Go ahead."

"Did you hear about the woman who died outside the library on Friday night?"

"I did. It was on the news."

"Her name was Helena Sanchez. She was the library director until about ten years ago. Did you know her?"

"I don't believe I did. She would have been there before my time. It's only since Bertie took over that I got involved in the library. I knew of her, when she lived in Nags Head, but I don't recall having any contact. I knew her sister, though. Tina."

"You did?"

"Tina and I were friends at one time. In our wild youth. Tina Sanchez she was then. She has since married and divorced, I've heard. I haven't seen Tina in ages; I don't know if she's still living in this area."

"She is."

Rachel put down her glass. She studied my face intently. Perhaps she saw something there she could trust, because she gave the slightest of nods and began to speak. "When I say 'wild youth,' Lucy, I mean it. That was not a good time in my life. Why are you asking about Helena?"

"The police are calling her death a murder."

Rachel nodded. "So I've heard."

"Something strange happened a short while before she died, and your name came up."

She looked surprised. "It did? How odd. In what context, may I ask?"

I glanced at Aunt Ellen. She gave me a slight nod, telling me to continue. Uncle Amos stood next to the gas grill, beer in one hand, metal tongs in the other, supervising the cooking of his fish but still listening closely to our conversation.

"Jeffrey Applewhite."

"Goodness. That is a blast from the past." Rachel glanced at my uncle. "Is there news about the necklace?"

"Not that I know of," he said.

She picked up her glass, took a sip, and said, "Go on, Lucy." I couldn't help but notice that her hand shook ever so slightly.

"We thought it would amuse Bertie's guests to be reminded of the way things used to work in a library. Charlene and I dragged a lot of old library equipment and artifacts out of storage. Among them was a book titled *The Celestine Prophecy*. Does that mean anything to you?"

"I remember it. I don't believe I ever read it, but many of the people in my . . . circle of acquaintances had. They raved constantly about it, about the meaning and the quest for enlightenment. More than a few talked about heading off to South America in the footsteps of the author. What was his name again?"

"James Redfield."

"That's right. As far as I know, not one of them ever did end up either in Peru or enlightened. Enlightenment was something a certain type of person sought, Lucy. In the circles in which I mixed in those days, 'sought' meant talk about and have another drink. Not actually doing anything to achieve it." She scrunched up her face in thought. "If you're asking if there's something specific I know about that book, I can't think of anything."

"Attached to the flyleaf of the book was a withdrawal record. The sort libraries everywhere used before computers. I was with Helena when she saw that slip. She reacted strongly to it. Very strongly. I didn't know why then, and I haven't been able to find out why since. When the police later showed a copy of the slip to Bertie's class, several of them recognized a name on it." I took my copy of the slip out of my bag. "Would you mind having a look?"

Rachel held out her hand. "Not at all."

I gave it to her, and she studied it for a long time. She passed it to Aunt Ellen, who then gave it to Josie. "I don't recognize any of those names except for Jeff Applewhite," Rachel said. "I most definitely remember Jeff Applewhite. It's dated May 25, 1995. Do you know the significance of that date, Lucy?"

"It was mentioned that something happened around that time."

Rachel leaned back in her chair. She cradled her glass in her hands. Her nails were freshly painted a soft pink. "I appreciate you realizing this might be sensitive to me, Lucy, but don't worry about it. I'm happy to talk about it. Jeff Applewhite, and what subsequently happened, was a turning point in my life. The major turning point, I might say. Some people need therapy, some need intervention, some need time in rehab. Some even get jail time. I was lucky none of those things were needed in my case. They might have been, without Jeff and what he did."

Uncle Amos flipped the fish. Josie sipped her drink, and Aunt Ellen smiled encouragingly at her friend.

"I was a wild one in my youth," Rachel said. "I dropped out of school. I drank to excess. I drank beyond excess. I did drugs. Plenty of drugs. I was on a very bad path. My family has money—lots of money—which was made by my grandfather who'd started his life as the son of a shoemaker and a seamstress. My own father, unfortunately for us all, didn't inherit the work ethic of his father and grandparents. My father pretended to work in the family firm, and my mother pretended to be a pillar of East Coast society, but what they mostly wanted out of life was to spend money. I'm their only child. The only thing I can say in my defense is that they pretty much left me to raise myself, watched over by a series of nannies and housekeepers, some of whom were kind. Some of whom were not.

"My parents are still alive, by the way. These days they spend most of their summers on Long Island and winters in Arizona. My father's no longer involved in the day-to-day running of the family business, which is the main reason it continues to do well. I'm not telling you I'm a poor little rich girl, Lucy. I'm well aware all my life choices were my own. Anyway, to continue the story . . . in the spring of 1995, my parents were in New York. Dad was still pretending to manage the company and Mom was playing socialite. I was in Nags Head at the house I still live in today. The housekeeper was a woman by the name of Juliette Ramirez."

Aunt Ellen nodded.

"Juliette no longer works for me, but we're still close. It was her, most of all, who made me see the dangers of the path I was on. Anyway, to continue the story, my grandfather bought his wife, my grandmother, a necklace. It featured a large white diamond in the center, which was surrounded by smaller diamonds, sapphires, and rubies. The main diamond was one hundred carats."

"That's a lot," Josie said with considerable understatement.

"It is. The necklace was, truth be told, a truly hideous piece. Suitable perhaps for the Queen of England to wear at her coronation, but not anyone else. My grandfather, whom I loved very much by the way, was a plain, practical, down-to-earth, level-headed man, who made a fortune by the time he was thirty. He loved his wife, my grandmother, with a passion. Or so people tell me. Sadly, I never knew her. He gave her the necklace as a grand, extravagant gesture on the birth of their first child. My father. My father turned out to be their only child, as she died a few months later in a car accident. They'd been invited to a state dinner at the White House, which took place the month after she died. She'd planned to wear the necklace to that for the first time. Grandfather was completely devastated at her death and threw himself totally into his businesses, thus making even more money. My father was raised by servants, so I guess I can't blame him too much for abandoning me in my childhood. It was all he knew."

Uncle Amos held the wine bottle over Rachel's glass.

"Thank you," she said, and he poured.

"Grandfather died when I was in high school. I went off the rails not long after that, and my life entered a downward spiral. Anyway, in the spring of ninety-five I was at the beach house. The necklace was usually kept in a safe in the Manhattan apartment, but my parents had been to some big fancy charity affair in Raleigh, and Mom had worn it. The necklace, by the way, originated in India, and the diamond itself was famous enough to have a name: the Rajipani Diamond. It had been the property of some minor princeling who'd fallen on hard times and had to sell all his wife's jewelry. My parents stopped off in Nags Head for a couple of days after the Raleigh event, and for some reason they left the necklace in the house when they returned to New York.

"I had a party once they were gone. I had a lot of parties in those days. I had a lot of friends, many of whose names I couldn't have told you the next day. People realized I had a lot of money and not much sense, and they moved into the house for weeks at a time, or asked me for loans they had no intention of ever repaying. I provided the booze and the drugs. They flattered me and made me think I was popular."

Rachel sipped her drink and stared into space. "What a fool."

Aunt Ellen reached across the table and touched her hand. Rachel gave her a big smile. "Of all the things in life I'm grateful for, the fact that I've learned what friendship truly is, is perhaps the most important. Jeff Applewhite was one of those so-called friends that spring. He came, he partied, he left. He was not a boyfriend of mine or even anyone special; he hung with the crowd who hung around me. I learned later he was from Iowa, had arrived in Nags Head the previous summer, and got a job with a construction firm. The night of April thirtieth, the usual crowd of hangers-on were at my house. Someone lit a bonfire on the beach, it got out of control, and the neighbors complained. I remember that. They were always complaining. I never paid any attention—my parents' lawyers would smooth it all over when it got too serious to ignore. At some point in the night, I thought it would be amusing to wear the necklace. I put it on and pranced around the house in it. So funny." She shook her head.

"Was Tina Sanchez at the party?" I asked.

"She might have been, Lucy. I don't remember her being there, but I honestly don't know. The point is, people wandered in and out all the time. They drank my booze, ate my food, borrowed my things and never returned them. I woke up the following morning on the floor of my bedroom, which wasn't an uncommon occurrence. I didn't realize I didn't have the necklace on anymore. I didn't know it was missing until my parents came back a few days later and wanted it. I couldn't find it. They called the police."

"It was never seen again," Aunt Ellen said.

"Not by me, at any rate. The police talked to everyone they could locate who'd been in my house that night. People told them I'd been wearing it early in the evening, but no one had seen me take it off. A necklace of that value, with stones of that quality, isn't something you sell on the street corner. The police were confident it would turn up. It never did."

"And Jeff Applewhite?" I asked.

"He went to work the morning following the theft, and on the day after, but by the time the time the police got involved and went to his workplace, he was gone. They said he simply hadn't shown up the morning of May third and hadn't been heard from since. He hadn't even come in to collect wages owed. He was working for a company called Reynolds Renovations, which isn't around anymore."

"Roy Reynolds died a few years later," Uncle Amos said, "and his children didn't want the business."

"I remember them," Aunt Ellen said. "Didn't they do the family room extension we put on the old house? They were sorely missed when they closed, because their work was excellent and their prices good. I think they did some work on the interior of the library years ago, modernizing it and such. Sorry, Rachel. Please go on."

Rachel sipped her drink. "Most of Jeff's stuff was still in his apartment, but no one was able to say if anything was missing or when they'd seen him last. The police searched for him. They never found him. They eventually located his truck, or at least the truck registered to him, parked near the bus station in Elizabeth City. They concluded that Jeff stole the necklace and left town with it. What happened then"—she held out her hands—"no one knows."

"And you?" I asked. "What did you do?"

She smiled at me. "My parents yelled and screamed and called me irresponsible. I yelled and screamed and blamed it all on them. But I was smart enough—and still not totally lost—to realize what I'd done. Juliette, who'd known my beloved grandfather and out of loyalty to him patiently stayed with me over my difficult years, helped me realize I'd lost his most important possession because of nothing but sheer stupidity. He would have been devastated. And so dreadfully disappointed in me. I'd like to say I immediately devoted myself to doing good works, but that took a while. I can say I never threw another wild party again. I never again saw most of the people who'd been there that night. I stopped taking drugs completely, although . . ."—she lifted her glass of wine—"I do like a drink now and again."

"And fish," Uncle Amos said, "I hope you like fish, because dinner's ready."

Josie sprang to her feet. "You sit, Mom. I'll bring everything out."

"My father fought the insurance company for a long time," Rachel said. "The company refused to pay on the grounds that I'd been negligent in handling the necklace. Which I had. My parents found themselves out of a heck of a lot of money. They've never forgiven me for that. A few years later, I hired a private investigator to search for Jeff Applewhite. He had no more luck than the police. He located Jeff's family back in Iowa, but they said he didn't keep in touch much once he moved to North Carolina, and they never heard from him again after April 1995. Remember, this was before the days of texts, cheap phone calls, and everyone having e-mail. People had to make an effort to keep in touch."

Josie laughed as she put a giant wooden bowl of salad on the table. "Sounds like the Dark Ages."

"Also known as our youth, right, Ellen?" Rachel smiled at my aunt, and I thought how very lucky Rachel had been. She could so easily have continued down that dark path.

"Jeff's family and friends in Iowa said they had no idea what could have happened to him. My investigator believed them. His mother in particular was upset just talking about her missing son. She insisted Jeff would not have cut off contact completely, but my investigator said that didn't mean much. If he was on the run he'd have known not to call his family. Nags Head people told him they thought Jeff had a girlfriend, but no one knew her name or anything about her. His friendships, it seemed, were as nebulous as mine."

"Could it have been Helena Sanchez? Or her sister, Tina?" I asked.

"It could have been anyone," Rachel said. "No woman reported him as missing to the police or came looking for him. Not officially anyway. The police believed she left town with him. No one reported a woman missing around the time, so she was probably just a drifter too. It's likely the necklace was broken up, the smaller jewels pried out of it and sold separately, the big diamond cut up into smaller ones. It really was an ugly thing. The story got a lot of press, nationally as well as locally. If a woman had suddenly started sporting rare and precious jewels, people would have talked."

Josie came back, carrying a tray loaded with plates and cutlery, a bowl of potato salad, and a pineapple and mango salsa to accompany the fish. Uncle Amos carefully lifted the fish off the grill and laid it on a platter. It smelled marvelous.

"Thank you for telling me your story," I said as I held out my plate to be filled.

"Not a problem, Lucy," Rachel said. "I'm ashamed and embarrassed at losing my grandmother's necklace, but I've come to believe my grandfather might have considered it a price worth paying to get me off that track of self-destruction."

"One more quick question," I said, "What would you esti-
mate is the value of the necklace today?"

"Twenty-five million dollars," Rachel said. "This fish smells
and looks delicious, Amos. Thank you. Now, Ellen, I want to
hear this idea of yours for a fundraiser for the museum."

Chapter Thirteen

I climbed into bed with my iPad and Charles, full of fish and salads and some of Josie's marvelous pastries that she'd brought for our dessert. I searched for more information about the Rajipani Diamond and the Blackstone family treasure. I found a picture of the necklace and studied it. I agreed with Rachel: it was incredibly ugly, designed to show off excessive wealth rather than good taste. I chastised myself for the unkind thought. Rachel said her grandfather had loved her grandmother very much. Perhaps, he gave her this necklace, thinking it matched the strength of the feelings he had for her.

The main feature was a ginormous white diamond, about the size of a golf ball, which the article confirmed was a hefty one hundred and one carats, set in gold and surrounded by sapphires. The pendant hung from a chain covered with smaller diamonds, more sapphires, and rubies. A smaller circle of equally precious gems lay inside the first.

Not something that'd drop between the floorboards and be forgotten, or would easily slip into the Nags Head criminal underworld. If Nags Head had a criminal underworld. That was something I didn't know and didn't want to know.

Articles on the necklace told me the main feature, the big diamond, was named the Rajipani Diamond after the Indian prince who'd had it cut into its current form. It had been found in South Africa in 1903 and had passed through several hands, eventually ending up with Prince Rajipani, who had it cut and inset into the necklace. Around the time India got its independence, the newest Rajipani prince had fallen onto hard times and was forced to sell almost all his family's assets at fire-sale prices. Apparently his son had later gone into the movie business and made a new fortune as the producer of Bollywood flicks. The articles I read said nothing about him trying to get back the diamond, and there was no indication he'd ever come under suspicion for the theft.

From what I read, if he wanted it, he had the funds to simply offer to buy it. No need to pretend to be an American drifter working construction and hanging around beach house parties waiting for a chance to grab it.

I couldn't help but think about our book club's current selection, *The Moonstone*, which concerns the search for an Indian jewel known as the Moonstone. In the book, members of a religious cult come to England in pursuit of their sacred jewel, stolen by one Colonel Herncastle, who gave it to his niece for her eighteenth birthday. And there the story begins.

As far as I could tell from my search of the internet, the Rajipani Diamond had no supernatural or religious significance. It was simply worth a heck of a lot of money.

I expanded my search and found a picture of Jeff Applewhite taken about a year before his disappearance. He seemed to me like an average-looking guy. Late twenties, scruffy dark hair in need of a wash, messy beard, big eyes in a thin face with prominent cheekbones.

What importance did Jeff Applewhite, with or without the Blackstone necklace, have to Helena Sanchez? Her reaction indicated that the name meant something to her.

If not Helena herself, maybe she knew it meant something to her sister, Tina?

That was only one question.

The big one was: *Did Helena die because of it?* And if so, why?

I crawled across the bed, upsetting Charles, and reached for my bag. I pulled out the photocopy of the withdrawal slip.

Jeff Applewhite had withdrawn *The Celestine Prophecy* from the Lighthouse Library. It was due to be returned on May 25, 1995. If at that time the library's withdrawal period was the same as it is now, three weeks, he would have taken the book out on May 4.

The party at Rachel's had been on April 30.

What had Jeff done in the four days following the fateful party? Other than visit the library to check out a book?

What day had he disappeared? Rachel said he hadn't shown up to work the morning of May 3.

Was it possible Jeff Applewhite had stolen an incredibly valuable diamond and planned to skip town with it, with or without an unknown girlfriend, but he stayed long enough to drop into the library and sign out a book? Charlene and I had found the volume in the library's box of damaged books in the town basement, so he must have returned it.

That made absolutely no sense.

I had to call Detective Watson. He might not be aware that the date on the withdrawal slip was the day the book was due back, not the day it had been taken out.

I climbed out of bed with a sigh and walked across the room to the phone. It rang as I put my hand on it, and I jumped.

"Hello?"

"Lucy. I hope I'm not calling you too late," Watson said.

"No. I'm still up."

"I have a library question, and CeeCee's not home yet."

"Shoot," I said before thinking maybe that was a poor choice of words.

"In 1995, how long could you take a book out of the library?"

I laughed. "Good question. Such a good question, I was about to phone you with the answer. Three weeks. Meaning Jeff Applewhite took out *The Celestine Prophecy* on May fourth."

"Four days after the disappearance of the Blackstone necklace and two days after the disappearance of Jeff Applewhite himself."

"Right."

"I have to wonder," Watson said, "if a man who's in illegal possession of a multimillion-dollar necklace has the concentration to be thinking about reading."

"I was thinking much the same thing."

"Good night, Lucy."

"Good night, Detective."

* * *

The following morning, I told Bertie what I'd learned about Jeff Applewhite and the Blackstone necklace and the Rajipani Diamond.

She let out a sharp puff of air, leaned back in her chair so far the springs squeaked, and said, "My goodness."

As I always did when I came in this room, I studied the painting hanging on the wall behind Bertie's desk, showing a woman doing a downward dog on the beach as the sun rose behind her.

"Twenty-five million dollars," she said at last. "For a necklace."

"Hard to believe, I know. Not just a necklace, but one that originated with some minor Indian prince. Have you read *The Moonstone*?"

"Long ago. The Moonstone of the title is a jewel, right?"

"Right. An extremely valuable jewel people from India have come to England in search of, with the intention of returning it to their idol from which it was stolen."

"You're thinking international criminals took the Blackstone necklace?"

"Not at all. I'm pointing out the coincidence, that's all. It's quite likely Jeff Applewhite stole it that night, probably with no idea of what he was going to do with it, maybe even as a prank. Very funny. Ha-ha. Sounds like the type of thing the people who hung around Rachel in those days might have done. Then people of the sort who do know what to do with something like that found out about it and took it off him, either before or after he left Nags Head. He's probably at the bottom of the ocean. But that's nothing but conjecture on my part. Perhaps I've read too many mystery novels."

"One can never read too many mystery novels," Bertie said.

"What's of interest to us—to the police, I mean—is what Helena Sanchez knew about Jeff and why that information might have gotten her killed. I asked Rachel if Helena had been at her party, and she said no, she didn't associate with Helena, but it was possible Tina was there. Tina and Rachel were friends when Rachel was in her wild period."

"You want to talk to Tina?"

"If you don't mind?"

"It's Monday and we're usually slow here on Mondays. Ronald's off today, but I can watch the desk for a while."

"Thanks, Bertie. I'll try not to be too long."

"Are you going to phone and let her know you're coming?"

"I never like to do that. Always better to catch people off guard, I've found. I'll try her house first. If she's at work or out, I'll have to call and arrange a time."

"I don't like how experienced you're getting at things like this."

"Believe me, Bertie, I don't like it either."

* * *

I didn't call ahead, and I did find Tina Ledbetter at home. She opened the door a crack and peered out at me. "Yes?"

"Hi! I was here the other day with the police. Do you remember me?"

"Yes."

"Great! I was hoping you had a few minutes to talk to me?"

"What about?"

That was the question, wasn't it? I could hardly come straight out and accuse the woman of stealing a necklace twenty-five years ago. "Does the name Jeffrey Applewhite mean anything to you?"

She stared at me. I studied her face intently. Not a flicker of emotion crossed it. "Never heard of him," she said at last.

"Never? Are you sure? He lived in Nags Head in the mid-nineties."

"I'm sure."

"It's rather uncomfortable standing here on the porch. It's so hot today. Do you mind if I come in?" I gave her what I hoped was my biggest, friendliest smile.

She didn't smile in return. But she did open the door a crack and take a step out of my way.

I slipped past her into the house. The foyer was small and dark, and the first thing I noticed was that it was crowded with large cardboard boxes. I took a discreet peek into one of them: empty. "Are you moving?"

"Is that any of your business?"

"Uh, I guess not. Just asking."

"If you must know . . . yes, I'm moving. I'm leaving this dump at last and going to Mount Dora. That's in Florida."

"I know." Someone had mentioned Mount Dora recently. I struggled to remember.

"Do you know when the police will be releasing Helena's body?" she asked. "I'd like to get the funeral over and done with."

"No, sorry, I don't know." I didn't mention that I am not with the police, and I wouldn't be someone they'd tell about something like that. I'd first met Tina in the company of Detective Watson, and if she wanted to believe the police involved me in their investigations, maybe I wouldn't look quite so much like a nosy librarian.

"It'll be up to me to make the arrangements, I suppose," she said. "We didn't get on, but Helena was my sister. My twin sister. I feel as though part of my soul has been ripped out of me. It's not a nice feeling."

That was where I'd heard mention of Mount Dora. Helena had lived there. "You're going to Helena's place?"

Tina nodded. "She left it to me in her will. She owns her house free and clear. One thing I'll say for Helena, once she settled down and got rid of ridiculous notions about finding her Prince Charming, she became careful with her money. She didn't make a lot as a librarian, but she carefully invested what she did make and had a nice sum to take her into her retirement."

I was about to offer my condolences once again, when Tina let out a burst of laughter and punched the air with her fist. "And now it's all mine! She nagged me constantly, criticizing me as a wastrel. I guess she thought I'd go first so she could make the gesture and mention me in her will." Tina held out her arms, indicating the small house, the empty foyer. "I did the same for her, but that didn't mean much. The mortgage on this dump is pretty large. Helena's house and savings, plus what our mother left her, will set me up nicely. I've never been to Florida, but I've been reading up on it. The paranormal history of Mount Dora is nothing like here in Nags Head, but it does have some interesting points. I'm sure I can get up to speed quickly, with the *proper* influences."

"Uh, yeah."

"Unlike that Louise Jane McKaughnan and her flake of a grandmother. Bunch of frauds in that family, every last one of them, but they think they're so high and mighty with their airs about being a longtime Outer Banks family. She's a friend of yours, isn't she?"

"A friend? I wouldn't say we're friends exactly. We know her at the library."

"Which is why I've never been there. Look, I'm sorry if I don't have time to offer you a glass of tea, but I'm busy here. What do you want?"

For a moment I couldn't remember what I wanted. All I could think was that Tina had clearly benefited from the death of her twin sister. What do they say in the classic mystery novels? *Cue bono.* Who benefits.

Tina Ledbetter benefited.

"Oh, right. I was wondering about Jeff. Jeff Applewhite. Did Helena know him?"

"Considering I told you I've never heard of the guy, it's unlikely I'd know if Helena did."

Rachel told me Tina moved in the same circles that she had in her wild days. Even if Tina had never met Jeff, she had to have heard of him. His name was linked to the disappearance of the necklace, and that had been a big story at the time. "Jeff Applewhite was in the news in May of 1995, in connection with a theft from Rachel Blackstone's home."

Tina shrugged. She tried to look nonchalant, but something moved in her eyes. "Oh yeah. That. I'd forgotten about that. It happened a long time ago. Nothing to do with me."

"Did you know Rachel?"

"Everyone in Nags Head knows Rachel Blackstone."

"Back then, I mean. Were you friends?"

She gestured toward the open door. "Like I said, I'm busy."

"Were you at a party at Rachel's house on the night of April 30, 1995?"

"You expect me to remember what I was doing on one day twenty-five years ago?"

"Not in normal circumstances, no, but a valuable necklace was stolen that night, and the police would have been asking everyone who'd been there about it. It got a lot of press. Things like that make events stand out in people's minds."

"Whether I was at this party or not, I don't see that it's any of your business."

"Just curious. Was Helena there? Did you and Helena go together? Was Helena friends with Jeff?"

She stepped toward me and loomed over me, invading my private space. I don't like these questions, and I don't think I like you. If you don't leave, right now, I'm calling the cops."

"No need to get aggressive," I said.

"Isn't there?"

I took a step backward. Then another. "Thanks for your time." The door slammed shut, barely missing the tip of my nose.

Chapter Fourteen

Monday evening, The Bodie Island Lighthouse Library Classic Novel Reading Club met to discuss *The Moonstone* by Wilkie Collins, written in 1868. As I'd told Aunt Ellen, *The Moonstone* is considered to be an important novel in the evolution of crime and mystery fiction, and I was looking forward to discussing that with the group.

The club has a core component who come to most meetings and decide which books to read, but anyone's welcome to attend. The full club rarely meets in the summer months, as people have other things on their mind in the long, warm, lazy evenings, so I was surprised at the number of people who made their way down the long driveway between the tall red pines tonight.

As I usually did, I stood at the front door, greeting people as they arrived and directing them to the meeting room on the third floor. Josie was one of the first to get here, and she brought, as she usually did, bakery boxes full of delicious treats to get the meeting started. Earlier, I'd arranged jugs of tea and lemonade and glasses and napkins on the table in the meeting room. Josie went up to lay out her offerings and then joined me downstairs.

"I don't think I've brought enough," Josie said as we watched cars jostle for position in the parking lot.

"I wonder what's brought all these people out tonight? I would have thought a stroll on the beach or dinner on the patio at Jake's would be a better option."

"Word's gotten around that Jeff Applewhite's name has been linked to the death of Helena Sanchez," Josie said. "I overheard several groups talking about it in the bakery today. Nothing like a long-ago mystery to get everyone interested in it again. And as Jeff's name was also linked to the disappearance of the Blackstone necklace, and—"

"*The Moonstone* is about the theft of a rare jewel." I sighed. "I bet most of these people haven't even read the book."

Butch Greenblatt and Stephanie Stanton, my uncle Amos's law partner, walked up the path, hand in hand. We exchanged hugs and kisses. "Did you read the book?" I asked.

"Loved it," Steph said.

Butch studied the ground at his feet. Butch meant well, but I suspect he rarely managed to get through the club selection. Butch came for the food. And, I hoped, the company. He was a good friend.

"If you want a pecan square," Josie said, "you'd better get up there fast. I brought nowhere near enough."

Butch practically dragged Steph to the stairs. That wasn't hard. At six feet five inches of solid muscle, Butch loomed over tiny Steph, who was even shorter than my five foot three and probably didn't tip the scales much past a hundred pounds. The differences didn't stop there either. Butch was a cop, and Steph a defense attorney. They'd hated each other at first sight.

The enmity hadn't lasted long, and I was delighted that my two friends had found each other.

"Bertie doesn't usually come, does she?" Josie pointed to the newest arrivals walking down the path.

"She never has before," I said.

My boss was with two of her college friends, Mary-Sue and Lucinda.

I greeted them and introduced Josie.

"You two go on upstairs and find seats," Bertie said. "I'll be up in a minute."

Once she was sure the women were out of earshot, Bertie turned to me with a shrug. "Hope you don't mind my coming, Lucy—"

"Of course not."

"We were supposed to be meeting for dinner, but Mary-Sue heard about the meeting tonight and wanted to come, although she's never been to your book club before. She told Lucinda, who's staying with her, much to Mary-Sue's displeasure. And Lucinda decided to tag along, so they called me and roped me into it too."

"They're not the only ones of your friends joining us," I said as Louise Jane's van came to a shuddering halt and three women stepped out. "Looks like Louise Jane's brought Sheila and Ruth."

"I left them messages earlier about dinner plans but never heard back."

"Look who I just happened to run into," Louise Jane said when they reached us. I doubted any such happenstance had been involved.

"Louise Jane told us you're discussing *The Moonstone* tonight. I love that book," Ruth said.

"I jumped at the chance to have another look at your library." Sheila shifted her big canvas tote bag from one shoulder to the other. "I didn't get upstairs the last time I was here. Is it possible to go all the way to the top?"

"Yes, but—"

"I'll unlock the gates for you," Louise Jane said. "No clouds are out tonight, so you'll get a great view of the sunset. Come on. Uh, Lucy, where did you last put the keys?"

I glanced at Bertie.

"In the second drawer of the circulation desk, Louise Jane."

"I have the run of the place, you know," Louise Jane said as they went inside. "That's the least they can do for me, considering all the help I give them with research and . . ."

Bertie gave me a "what can you do?" shrug and went inside.

A few more people arrived, including several I didn't know. I welcomed them all warmly.

"Should be an interesting discussion." Theodore Kowalski had come tonight in his Harris tweed jacket, paisley cravat, plain-glass spectacles, and full-on upper-crust English accent.

"I hope so," I said.

He stepped closer to me, and I caught a whiff of tobacco. I know Teddy doesn't smoke. He must spray the stuff on like other men do aftershave. He lowered his voice. "I was planning to come early, to catch a private moment with you, but I was delayed."

"What about?"

He glanced at Josie.

"My lips are sealed," she said.

"Very well. You asked me to look into the providence of that old copy of *The Celestine Prophecy*."

"Oh yeah," I said. "Right. Did you learn anything?"

"I learned nothing, which is itself momentous. The copy you have here, the one I saw on Thursday afternoon, was mass-produced as part of a regular print run. The book is still in print. Your copy is not only not signed, nor distinctive in any other way, but it's water damaged. It is, in fact, of no more value than to assist one in lighting a fire on a frosty winter's night."

I suppressed a shudder. "Please don't ever say that to a librarian, Theodore. We have nightmares about burning books."

"Just making my point."

"Point taken. Thanks. I appreciate your help."

"Any time, Lucy, any time." He adjusted his spectacles, gave us a small bow, and went inside to join the meeting.

The line of cars coming down the driveway had thinned. I checked my watch. Ten minutes after seven. "Might as well get this show on the road," I said to Josie. "If anyone's late, they can ring up." I locked the front door and led the way through the main room to the twisting iron stairs. The metal clattered beneath our feet as we climbed. The gate between the third and fourth floors was open, meaning Louise Jane and Sheila hadn't come down yet.

The meeting room was packed, and all the seats were taken, leaving Butch and Theodore to lean up against the walls. The platters on the refreshments table contained nothing more than crumbs, and not many of those. Charles had taken his usual place for book club: on Mrs. Fitzgerald's lap. Charles loved book club. Josie and I took places next to Butch.

"Before we begin the meeting," Mrs. Fitzgerald sniffed with disapproval as she looked around the crowded room. She stroked Charles steadily, and Charles purred in return. "So nice to see such an enthusiastic turnout to our little book club. But, I have to say, I hope no one here has such incredibly bad taste as to be interested in discussing *The Moonstone* only because of the real-life events that transpired here recently."

One or two people had the grace to flush.

"We're Bertie's old college friends," Mary-Sue said. "We're all either current or former librarians."

"Then you are welcome," Mrs. Fitzgerald said.

"I've always loved Wilkie Collins," said a woman with a mop of unnaturally red hair the approximate texture of a Brillo pad. I'd never her seen before. The woman next to her, with her hair dyed a deep black, nodded enthusiastically.

I considered asking them a skill-testing question but decided to let it go. At the Bodie Island Lighthouse Library, everyone is welcome. If these two hadn't arrived as lovers of classic literature, maybe they'd leave as such.

Louise Jane marched into the room, but Sheila wasn't with her. I glanced at Bertie. She nodded at me to say we could let Sheila get her fill of the view from the top if she wanted.

"Welcome, everyone," I said. "It's nice to see so many people here tonight."

Everyone muttered some sort of greeting.

"I hope you all had time to read the book."

Theodore pulled a tattered paperback out of his ever-present leather satchel and waved it in the air.

"*The Moonstone*," I said. "Is considered a classic novel of—"

"It's about a jewel theft right?" The Brillo-haired woman asked.

"Uh . . . yes," I said.

"Like the one everyone's talking about in town?"

"No, not like—"

"I remember the story. Rachel Blackstone lost her family's heirloom."

"Lost—ha!" said the black-haired woman. "I always figured she was in on it with that Jeff Whatshisname." She turned to her friend. "What was his name, Annalisa?"

"Applehouse."

"Right, Jeff Applehouse. Strange name."

It was Applewhite, but no one corrected them.

"It looks like he's come back," she continued. "They say he checked a book out of this very library just the other day. Is that right?"

Sheila slipped into the room. Seeing no free seats, she leaned against the wall next to Theodore. He gave her a vacant smile. She shifted her bag from one shoulder to the other.

"We're not here to talk about local events, either past or present," I said. "What parallels do you see between *The Moonstone* and your favorite movie or—"

"Come back?" Louise Jane said. "Surely, Annalisa, you're not suggesting Jeff's . . . here?"

Several people gasped and cast furtive looks into the corners. Not that the room, being round, had any corners.

"That's not—" I struggled to regain control of the conversation.

Josie attempted to leap to my aid. "Let Lucy—"

"There's a thought." Sheila shifted her bag again. "I've been looking into that. The last time we have any record of his movements was in this library. When he signed out the book. Is it possible that he never left?"

"No, that is not possible," I said.

"Louise Jane," Sheila said, "what do you think?"

"I've never known any such presence," Louise Jane admitted, "although it could be a new one and so far unfamiliar to me."

"It could not be anything of the sort," Bertie said. "Louise Jane, I've warned you about making up stories about the lighthouse."

"So you have. Except in this case not only did I not *make up* any story, I specifically said I know nothing about one."

"She's got you there," Theodore said.

"Enough about Jeff Applewhite," Lucinda said. "I'm sick and tired of hearing about him."

"Did you know him?" Mary-Sue asked.

"I did not," Lucinda snapped. "I'd left Nags Head before he did . . . whatever it was he did. Neither, it seems, did anyone else know him, but it's all you people talk about around here. Oh, for heavens' sake, not that dratted cat again." Charles had leaped onto her lap, and she shoved him off.

"He's only trying to be friendly," Mary-Sue said, "although I can't imagine why." She bent over and rubbed her fingers together. Charles went to join her, and she scratched behind his ears. I swear he threw a smirk over his shoulder at Lucinda.

"Has anyone seen a picture of the Blackstone necklace?" Annalisa asked. "Does it look like the Moonstone?"

"It does not look like the Moonstone," I snapped. "And it has nothing whatsoever to do with the book we're here to discuss."

Butch came to my rescue. He stepped away from the wall and crossed his arms over his powerful chest. Even out of uniform, dressed in casual chinos and a short-sleeved blue T-shirt with the logo of the Toronto Blue Jays on it, he looked like nothing but a cop. "The case of Jeffrey Applewhite and the Blackstone necklace is still open at the NHPD. Anyone who has any information about it is welcome to come down to the station during business hours and make a statement. Otherwise, I wouldn't like to see such a sensitive matter being subject to common gossip. I might be forced to assume that a prurient interest indicates that an individual, or individuals, know details they're not willing to discuss with the police." He had everyone's attention, although more than a few people pretended not to be embarrassed.

"Good." Butch resumed his post against the wall. "Lucy, I'm particularly interested in the character of Sergeant Cuff. He doesn't come into the story until it's well underway. How does everyone feel about that? Would you like him to have made an appearance earlier, maybe learn more about him? We don't know anything at all about his personal life, do we?"

"Uh," I said. "Yes. Good question, Butch. You did read the book."

"Of course I did," he said. "I always do."

Annalise and her companion were embarrassed into silence and the meeting continued along the lines I'd hoped for. Bertie and her friends seemed to enjoy the discussion. Ruth in particular had an in-depth knowledge of not only the book itself but the work of Wilkie Collins and his friends and contemporaries. I gratefully gave up leading the conversation and settled back to learn something.

"And then it turns out that Godfrey Ablewhite—" Mrs. Fitzgerald said.

Annalise sat to attention. "There's a character in the book named Jeff Applewhite? Surely not?"

I refrained from pointing out that Annalise had earlier claimed to be a big fan of the book. "Not Applewhite, but Ablewhite. And not Jeffrey, but Godfrey. The similarity is nothing but a minor coincidence."

"Heck of a coincidence," Annalise whispered to her black-haired friend.

Butch cleared his throat, and Annalise said no more. Before much longer, she nudged her companion and said, "Oh my goodness, I forgot a prior appointment. We have to go, so sorry." They jumped up, and I said, "I'll walk down with you and let you out."

"No need," Annalise said. "We can find our way."

I smiled at them. "No trouble."

The meeting broke up shortly before nine. People grabbed their bags and left, chatting excitedly about the book. I heard several say they wanted to try Collins's other famous book, *The Woman in White*, next.

"Nice job, Butch," Bertie said.

"I thought Lucy could use a hand," he said with a shy smile.

"You were a lifesaver," I said.

"Normally, I'm not in favor of the police threatening to arrest people for noncriminal activity," Steph said, "but I'll make an exception this one time."

We all laughed.

"Anyone for a drink?" Lucinda said. "All this book talk has made me thirsty."

"Sure," Ruth said, "but I need more than a drink. We didn't have dinner. How about that place we went Saturday night?"

"I'm good with that," Sheila said. "Ruth and I came with Louise Jane. Would you like to join us?"

"Sure," Louise Jane said.

"Bertie?"

"Not me, thanks. I'll drop you off at the restaurant, and you can catch a cab back to Mary-Sue's place. Is that okay?"

"A cab?" Lucinda said. "How much is that likely to cost?"

"I'll get my husband to come for us," Mary-Sue said.

"If he's sober," Lucinda mumbled.

"What was that, dear?" Mary-Sue said. "I missed it."

Lucinda gave her a radiant smile. "I said that would be nice of him."

Josie caught my eye and waggled her eyebrows. Butch and Steph stacked the chairs while Theodore collected empty dessert platters and carried them downstairs. Soon everyone had left the meeting room except for my cousin and me. We gathered the last of the glasses and the crumpled napkins and walked downstairs together as Charles ran on ahead, showing off his balancing prowess on the railings.

"I was sorry not to see Connor tonight," Josie said.

"He had a dinner meeting with some business group, which was called at the last minute, and he couldn't get out of it."

"How's everything going on that front?"

"Fine. Everything's going fine."

"Any updates you want to tell me about?"

I looked at her. "Updates? What sort of updates?"

"You two have been going out for almost a year now. It's none of my business, but I'm wondering if you're thinking of moving things up a level."

"Up a level?"

"Stop repeating everything I say."

"Repeating everything you say? I'm not."

She burst out laughing and I joined in. "If there's anything to tell, Josie, you'll be the first to hear, I promise."

We hugged goodnight at the door, and I made sure to lock up behind her. I turned off the main lights and made my way in the near dark to the alcove to switch on the light that would be left on all night. The police had returned most of the items from Charlene's and my historical display, and we'd reassembled it so our patrons could admire it. Some of the teenagers and kids were amazed that we'd been able to keep track of anything in those long-gone days BI—before internet.

I reached for the light switch. Charles vaulted onto the table and meowed at me. "It was a good night," I said. "I enjoyed the meeting once we finally got around to talking about the book. Butch put the fear of the law into anyone who'd come for no reason but to get the gossip."

Charles whined again.

I walked across the floor, heading for the stairs. It had been a good night—book club usually was—and I was ready for my bed. Charles did not follow. "Are you coming?" I said.

He sat down next to the pile of old books and studied me with his intense amber eyes.

"Bedtime," I said. "Yes, I know it's not even nine thirty yet, but I'm bushed."

He didn't move.

"Oh, for heaven's sake." I went back to the table and reached for him. As I picked him up, I glanced at the books.

The Celestine Prophecy was gone.

Chapter Fifteen

I couldn't be absolutely sure the book had been on the display table in the alcove when book club began. I'd stood at the door to greet our guests and then gone straight upstairs to start the meeting. I hadn't come into the alcove.

Someone might have taken the book out earlier, thinking it was available for circulation. But that book was no longer in our catalogue system; they wouldn't have been able to check it out in the normal way. Perhaps someone picked it up, read a few pages, and put it back in the wrong place.

While Charles watched, I went to the fiction section and searched under the "Rs." No sign of it. I tried the Religion and Spirituality shelves. Nothing.

I checked on the tabletops and in the magazine rack. I peeked under the table in the alcove, searched around all the chairs, and flicked through the books on the returns cart.

The Celestine Prophecy was nowhere to be seen.

I let out a puff of breath and dropped into a chair. I wouldn't normally give a thought—and certainly not at this time of night—to a missing book. It would turn up. They usually did. Someone had shelved it incorrectly, thinking they were helping us, or slipped it into their book bag without thinking, and would return it along with the rest of their books.

That book was nothing special. It wasn't rare or valuable, or of any particular interest to anyone. It had been removed from circulation when it got damaged.

The only thing that made it stand out was that it was the book that, apparently, Jeff Applewhite had checked out in the days surrounding the theft of the Blackstone necklace and his subsequent disappearance.

"Okay," I said to Charles. "It's gone. What do I do about it?"

Charles washed his whiskers.

I decided at this point in time to do nothing. I'd stood at the door, greeting book club members and guests (and those who'd barged into our meeting under false pretenses). Admittedly, I hadn't focused my eagle eye on what was going on in the main room, but I would have been aware (I should have been aware anyway) of what was happening. No one, as far as I knew, had browsed the shelves or gone into the alcove. All the book club members headed immediately upstairs when they arrived, most of them hoping Josie's goodies wouldn't have all been snatched up yet.

The only people who hadn't gone directly to the third-floor meeting room were Louise Jane and Sheila. Louise Jane had found the key to the gates and unlocked them. They'd gone to the upper levels, supposedly so Sheila could see the view from the very top. Louise Jane had come in shortly after to join the meeting, leaving Sheila alone. When Shelia joined us, she'd been holding her bag, a bag big enough to contain a regular-sized hardcover book. She'd fussed with that bag all evening but never opened it or took anything out of it.

Sheila, I was convinced, had taken the book.

Whatever for? was the question.

* * *

I didn't call Louise Jane and demand she put Shelia on the phone. I didn't go to Jake's Seafood Bar and track them down. I did nothing.

I decided to wait to see what Sheila wanted with *The Celestine Prophecy*.

Earlier in the summer, while doing much-needed renovations to the lighthouse foundation, we'd uncovered a code page and a hand-drawn map dating from the Civil War, hidden deep underground.

This, I thought, wasn't the same. Nothing at all was unusual about our copy of *The Celestine Prophecy*. It was a standard library copy of a mass-produced novel. It happened to have been taken out by a suspected thief around the time he disappeared, but I couldn't see what the book itself had to do with that. Theodore had checked into the provenance of our volume and found nothing at all out of the ordinary.

He might be wrong.

I might be wrong.

But I didn't think so.

I called to Charles and we went upstairs to bed. Sheila had some plan for the book, and I'd wait for her to reveal herself. She'd be back—and soon. I was sure of it.

* * *

I didn't have to wait for long.

Sheila strolled into the library as we were about to close on the afternoon following the book club meeting. Her canvas bag was tossed over her shoulder, and she was with Louise Jane.

They gave me such huge smiles I immediately knew something was up. "Are you here to return the book?" I said to Sheila.

"The book?" she asked innocently.

"The copy of *The Celestine Prophecy* you stole last night when you were pretending to be at the top of the lighthouse tower, watching the sun set over the mainland."

"I was watching the sun *beginning* to set over the mainland. I was too early, but it was still pretty up there."

"Okay. The book you stole after you watched the sun not quite set."

Sheila glanced at Louise Jane. Louise Jane shrugged and said, "Shelia borrowed a library book. You were busy, so she didn't want to bother you by asking to check it out officially."

"Another word for taking a book from a library without checking it out officially is *stealing*."

"Whatever." Sheila dug in her bag and produced the purloined volume with a flourish. "I've brought it back."

"Thank you."

"Is Bertie in?" Louise Jane asked.

"I am." Bertie stepped into the room, and Louise Jane and Sheila turned to her with their big smiles.

"Ladies and gentlemen," I said in a voice pitched to carry to every nook and cranny on the main floor, "the library is about to close. If you can bring your books to the circulation desk, I'll check them out for you. Thank you."

People popped out from the stacks. Mr. Snyder, who came almost every day to sit in the big wingback chair next to the magazine rack with Charles on his lap, got slowly to his feet after dislodging the reluctant cat.

As I checked out books and wished everyone a good night, out of one corner of my eye I watched Bertie with Louise Jane and Sheila. They were clearly arguing about something. Sheila was waving her arms around in the air, and Louise Jane was pointing a finger in Bertie's face. Bertie stood stiff and resolute, a rock firm against the constant battering of the waves. I thought she showed enormous restraint by not knocking Louise Jane's wagging finger out of the way.

"The book—" Louise Jane said.

"We can't waste any more time. Not if—" Sheila said.

"Absolutely not," Bertie said.

"Ready?" Connor McNeil said.

I let out a small cry and jumped.

"Sorry," he said. "Didn't you hear me come in?"

I allowed my heart to settle back into its regular rhythm. I looked at Connor and jerked my head toward the small group near the hallway. Louise Jane and Sheila were still waving fingers and hands and arguing. Bertie had stopped arguing and stood with her hands on her hips, shaking her head. Charles perched on the nearest bookshelf (Cooking and Gardening) and watched intently.

Connor went to join them. "Good evening, ladies."

Bertie smiled at him. Louise Jane grumbled, and Sheila threw up her hands. "You people don't know what you have here." She spun on her heels and marched out. Louise Jane ran after her. I realized Sheila hadn't given me the book. I called after her, but Louise Jane said, "Sorry, not now. We need it."

"What was all that about?" Connor asked.

"Louise Jane and her ghost hunting," Bertie said. "Although in this case I gather it wasn't Louise Jane's idea, but when Sheila suggested it, she couldn't say no and still save face."

"Suggested what?" I asked.

"Last night some fool suggested that maybe Jeff Applewhite has never left the library, and Shelia wants to have a séance in an attempt to talk to him and find out where the Blackstone necklace is. She has the book he supposedly took out and thinks that will help Louise Jane contact him. Stuff and nonsense."

"You know she stole the book, right?" I said.

"She did what?"

"Sheila took *The Celestine Prophecy* last night while we were upstairs, without bothering to ask if she could have it. That would have been before anyone mentioned Jeff or the necklace, so she got the idea into her head all by herself, maybe as a way of trying to contact Louise Jane's so-called spirits. When the meeting was over and everyone had left, and I was closing up, I noticed the book was missing. I figured Sheila had it. I also figured she'd be back with it sooner rather than later. Looks like I was right about that."

Connor shook his head. He'd come straight from the town hall and looked very handsome in a perfectly tailored blue suit, with a white shirt and a blue tie with thin pink threads running through it. Dark stubble was coming in thick on his jaw. He patted his jacket pocket. He was here to pick me up for dinner, as arranged. We had a standing date for Tuesday night, although we tried to get together at the end of the day as often as our schedules matched. I'm not much of a cook (boiling water is an adventure to me) and neither, so he told me, is Connor. We often order in pizza at his place or mine, or we throw together something using a supermarket-bought rotisserie chicken, but now and again we treat ourselves to a restaurant outing, and Connor had suggested that for tonight.

"I have to point out," I said, "that Sheila brought the book with her this afternoon but didn't give it back."

"Is it potentially worth something?" Connor asked.

"You mean monetarily? No, and it never was. It's a mass-produced book, unsigned, and it's badly damaged."

"Sheila seems to think it's worth something," Bertie said, "and I don't like what that something is one little bit. I told them there will be no séances in my library. Louise Jane tried to suggest they hold it in your apartment—"

I choked.

"—and considering the last time that happened you were not impressed, I said no. If you want to challenge that decision, it's up to you. Your apartment's your own space."

"I am most definitely not challenging that decision," I said.

"There was a séance in your apartment?" Connor said. "When was that? Did anything happen?"

"It was all much ado about nothing, as I tried to tell Louise Jane before she even started. It ended uneventfully."

That wasn't exactly true. The attempt at a séance ended when a thief broke into the library and was frightened away by Charles, and we ran downstairs to see what was going on. I never told Connor about any of that, but particularly I didn't tell him about the break-in and the attempted theft.

"Ready to go?" Connor said. "I'm starving."

Bertie smiled at him. She made no move to leave. Connor shifted from one foot to another. Finally he said, "Uh . . . Bertie would you like to join us? Nothing special, nothing special at all. Just dinner. We'll probably go to Jake's or Owen's. Unless Lucy wants to try someplace else. But it's nothing special. Really."

Bertie recovered herself and said, "No, but thank you, Connor. Sorry, I was trying to remember if I'd promised to meet Eddie tonight. He's not the only one getting absent-minded in his old age. Although, in Eddie's case he was absent-minded in his young age." She smiled at the memory. "You run along, Lucy. I'll close up."

"Won't say no to that," I said. Charlene had had the day off, and Ronald left after the final children's program. "Can you give me ten minutes?" I asked Connor.

"Sure. No hurry. I'll call to make sure we can have a table. Jake's or Owen's?"

"Owen's would be nice for a change." I ran upstairs and quickly changed out of my work clothes into something fresh to wear for dinner. It was nothing special, as Connor had said, but I always like to go to a bit of trouble. My mother's influence, I suspect.

I washed my face and reapplied a light touch of makeup and brushed my hair out and then tied it back again. I put on a black dress with a thin red belt and slipped my feet into red suede ballet slippers and added earrings made of red sea glass, while Charles watched. He likes to supervise my preparations for an evening out.

"Will this do?' I asked him.

He meowed, jumped off the bed, and preceded me out of the Lighthouse Aerie.

I stood at the bend in the stairs for a moment, watching Connor. Bertie had disappeared, and he was alone. He paced up and down in front of the magazine rack, patting his jacket pocket and mumbling under his breath. Charles wound himself around Connor's legs. Connor bent down and picked the big cat up. "You okay with this, buddy?" he said.

Charles meowed and rubbed his head into Connor's chest.

"Okay with what?" I asked.

Connor whirled around. "Lucy. I didn't see you there."

"Sorry. I didn't mean to sneak up on you. You and Charles were having a sweet little private moment there. What was it about?"

"Nothing!" Connor said. "I mean . . . nothing. Ready?"

"Yup," I said.

*   *   *

We had a lovely dinner. I told Connor about last night's book club meeting, and he said he was sorry to have missed it. His own meeting had been boring, repetitive, and totally nonproductive. He asked me if there'd been any developments in the Helena Sanchez murder, and I said I hadn't heard from Sam Watson or anyone in the police department today. The bill came, and Connor paid as he'd suggested the meal. We went to Connor's car, and he drove us out of town to the lighthouse.

We sat in the BMW for a few moments as the great first-order Fresnel lens flashed its beacon out to sea. "It's still early," I said. "Would you like to come in?"

He cleared his throat. "Actually, Lucy, I'd prefer a walk. How does that sound?"

"It sounds perfect."

"Is that Louise Jane's car over there?" He pointed to a rusty old van.

"It is. I wonder what she's doing here at this time of night."

"As long as she's not trying to break into the library once again, I don't really care."

"She came with Sheila earlier. Maybe they drove into town together and she left her van to pick up later."

We got out of the car. Connor took my hand in his, and we headed for the boardwalk. All was quiet. A light breeze blew from the east, bringing the taste of salt and the scent of the ocean. A half-moon hung high in the sky, throwing enough light to almost see by. Connor took out his phone and switched on the flashlight app. In the marsh, frogs croaked and insects chirped. A bat flew over-head. I took a deep breath of the salty air as we stepped onto the boardwalk, and the planks creaked beneath my feet. "I love it here."

"As do I," he said.

We walked toward the pier, holding hands, each of us wrapped in our own thoughts.

"So calm. So peaceful," I said. "So quiet. Most of the time anyway. Although I can't stop thinking about when I walked this way with Helena Sanchez on Friday night."

"Lucy . . ." Connor coughed.

"Still," I said, "we can't let that bother us, can we? The lighthouse has seen a lot of things over the years. Not all of them pleasant."

"No. But tonight, I'd like to think it's a good night for the lighthouse."

"It is," I said.

"What I mean is . . ." When we were about halfway to the waterfront, he stopped walking. He let go of my hand and I turned to see what he was doing. He turned off the flashlight, put it in his pocket and then put his hands on my arms. He stared into my face. The light from the moon threw deep shadows into the crevices of his handsome face. His sharp cheekbones looked as though they'd been carved by a knife, and his lovely blue eyes glimmered in the moonlight. "Lucy." He cleared his throat. "Lucy. I—"

A scream shattered the quiet of the night.

I yelped. Connor dropped my arms and whirled around. "Who's out there?" He fumbled for his phone and switched on the flashlight.

A woman screamed again. Footsteps pounded the boardwalk, coming from the pier, heading our way. Louise Jane burst into the small circle of light cast by Connor's phone. Behind her a brighter light broke the darkness of the marsh.

"What are you doing here?" Louise Jane shouted.

"What are *you* doing here?" Connor bellowed.

"What's going on?" I yelled.

Sheila arrived, preceded by a circle of bright light, breathing heavily.

"Get that light out of my face!" Connor snapped at her. "I can't see a blasted thing."

She did so, and our feet and lower legs were lit up.

"Louise Jane." Connor lowered his voice and his words came out slow and measured. "What is going on here?"

"I thought you were . . . it . . . him," Sheila said. "Why'd you turn off your light anyway? No one walks around out here in the dark unless they're up to no good."

I refrained from pointing out that we'd done just that last Friday when Louise Jane told us stories.

"I don't think I need to answer to you," Connor said.

"You have to leave, right now," Louise Jane said. "We can try to get him back."

"Get who back?" Connor asked.

My breathing slowly returned to normal. I recognized the object in Sheila's left hand. "That's our book! I don't believe it. You're out here, creeping around in the middle of the night trying to contact Jeff Applewhite."

"We can do what we want in the marsh, Lucy," Louise Jane said. "This isn't library property. We're not creeping. Besides, it's hardly the middle of the night. It's barely ten o'clock."

"That makes a big difference," Connor said. "Louise Jane, please."

"If I must," she said. "We're hoping we can use the book Jeff Applewhite took out of the library after he went missing, with or without the Blackstone necklace, to contact him."

"What I meant," Connor said, "is please go away. I didn't mean tell me your fool of a story."

"It was my idea," Sheila said. "When I found out what a powerful connection Louise Jane has with the spirit world, I knew we had to give it a try."

"You're assuming Jeff is . . . uh . . . hanging around out here," I said. "Why would he do that?"

"He took the necklace and he disappeared," Sheila said. "It's natural to assume he stole it for underworld figures, and they of course didn't want to leave any evidence behind or pay him his promised share. So they offed him and probably threw him in the marsh. Wearing a pair of cement shoes."

"They offed him, did they?" Connor said.

"Yes," Sheila said. "And if we can speak to the spirit of Jeff, he can tell us what happened to Helena."

"Why would he want to do that?" Connor asked.

"I don't see that whatever happened—or didn't—to Jeff has anything to do with Helena Sanchez," I said. "We've found no connection between Helena, and Jeff and the necklace."

"That," Sheila said triumphantly, "is what we're trying to determine." She put her hand on my shoulder. "Now that you're here, Lucy, we need to try again. Louise Jane was about to make contact when you disturbed us with your chatter."

"Sorry about that," Connor muttered.

"I had made contact," Louise Jane said. "*Appearances can be deceiving.*' That's what the spirits told me. I'm sure of it."

"This is all so exciting," Sheila said. "I have no psychic powers of my own, but I've been searching for someone who does, and Helena's death and the mystery around it is perfect for Louise Jane's abilities."

Louise Jane preened.

"I knew we had to act. Quickly now! Let's form a circle. Four people are more powerful than two." Sheila reached for Connor's hand. He jerked it away.

"I want no part of this. Lucy?" He held out his hand to me.

I took it. "Have a nice night," I called to Louise Jane and Sheila.

"Okay," Sheila said as we walked away. "Let them go. We don't need them."

"Once the link has been made and abruptly broken," Louise Jane told her, "it can be awful hard to get it back."

"We have to try!" Sheila insisted.

"Did you want to say something before we were interrupted?" I asked Connor once we were out of earshot.

He sighed. "It'll keep, Lucy. It'll keep."

Chapter Sixteen

"*Appearances can be deceiving.*"

I tossed and turned most of the night, the phrase running through my mind.

Why on earth I was letting Louise Jane's crazy fantasies interrupt a good night's sleep, I didn't know.

Leaving Louise Jane and Sheila chasing ghosts, Connor and I had walked back to his car. He'd kissed me long and hard before breaking away and studying my face, his expression dark and serious.

"What?" I said.

"There's never a dull moment with you, Lucy Richardson, is there?"

"Sometimes I think that's not necessarily a good thing."

He wrapped one of my curls around his index finger, gave it a gentle tug, and then he laughed. "Let's keep it interesting, shall we?"

"Yeah. Okay. I guess."

"Good night, Lucy."

"Good night."

He opened the car door, hesitated for a moment, and said, "How about we go away on Saturday evening? I mean really away. Someplace nice and quiet and secluded. My cousin has a vacation house in Rodanthe—nothing fancy, just an old weather-worn cabin near the beach. She's away at the moment, and anyone in the family's welcome to use it when she's not there. We can go up Saturday after you finish work, spend Sunday doing nothing much at all, and have you back Monday morning in time for opening."

"Sounds perfect," I said. "I'd like that a lot."

"Great." He kissed the top of my head and got in the car.

I walked up the path, knowing he'd be watching until I was safely inside. I hesitated before stepping into the circle of light cast by the lamp over the front door, and looked out over the marsh. I could see no trace of Louise Jane and Sheila's lights. I'd turned and waved to Connor and let myself into the lighthouse.

The idea of the quick little romantic getaway sounded marvelous. Rodanthe's a tiny, perfect seaside town of weathered houses on stilts, waves washing over the highway, sand blowing onto everything, and people who truly want to get away from it all. It's not far from Nags Head, but it seems as though it's in another world. I love living in the Lighthouse Aerie, but it does sometimes seem as though my personal life and my work life blend into each other more than can be good for me. I couldn't even go for an evening stroll with my boyfriend without tripping over library business. If the death of Helena Sanchez could be considered library business. And I suppose it could, as she died in the vicinity of the library, in the company of library staff and visitors, after an event at the library.

"Appearances can be deceiving."

A short break would be nice. Connor, I thought, could probably use it. He'd seemed on edge tonight. His mind had been elsewhere at dinner, and he'd kept patting his suit jacket pocket as if needing to confirm something was there. Important notes or the outline for a speech maybe. When Louise Jane interrupted us on our walk, he'd seemed genuinely angry rather than mildly amused, as he usually was by her antics.

Charles was curled against the small of my back, breathing softly, and I enjoyed his warmth through the sheet and light comforter. But I still couldn't sleep.

"Appearances can be deceiving."

They certainly could. I'd had a shock when I'd first seen Tina Ledbetter, thinking for a moment Helena had come back to life.

My eyes flew open and I sat up. Charles protested at being disturbed.

Was it possible Tina had pretended to be Helena the night of the party at the library? I'd mistaken her for her twin when I first saw her. The resemblance to her sister was so strong that when Tina had been watching Bertie's crowd at the hotel bar, she'd hidden her face under dark glasses and a ball cap so as not to be recognized.

I'd believed Tina couldn't have killed her sister because Helena had (as far as I knew) been killed by the letter opener, and the letter opener had been in the library alcove during the party. Charlene and I found it in the town hall in the dust-covered boxes of cast-off library supplies. I'd placed it on the table in the alcove as part of our historical display.

When exactly had I last seen it?

I struggled to bring images of Friday night to mind. The party, serving food and cleaning up. Keeping one eye on Charles. Chatting to Bertie's guests, everyone laughing about how much the world of libraries had changed. Everyone except Helena, who I hadn't heard laugh once all night.

The letter opener had been on the table when she'd been admiring the display. I was sure of it.

Well, almost sure anyway. If it had been missing when we were showing the exhibit to an important guest, I would have noticed. Charlene told Sam Watson it had been in place when she showed Helena the display, meaning the letter opener had been on the table when Helena saw the withdrawal slip with Jeff Applewhite's name written on it. She'd been shocked by something she'd seen or remembered and turned and walked away.

What had she done then? She'd moved into the crowd, and I lost track of her until it was time to leave for the walk, when the party was over and most of the guests had left.

Could there have been two Helena Sanchezes in the library that night? Might Tina have somehow slipped into the party? Helena had left from Tina's house, so Tina would have known what her sister was wearing. I hadn't seen anything striking or individual about the brown cape. It had been a warm night, the library heating up under the press of bodies, but Helena hadn't removed the cape. Was it her habit to keep her coat on indoors? Did she feel cold, never mind the weather? Did her twin sister know that?

The reunion group didn't know Helena well or at all. Even those who'd worked with her claimed not to have seen her in years. No one seemed to like her all that much, so no one other than Bertie sought out her company at the party.

I hadn't been paying a lot of attention to everyone; one or two of the women went outside now and again, presumably for a cigarette or some fresh air or to make a phone call. Had Tina come inside, dressed like her sister, taken the letter opener, and slipped out again?

If so, the question was why.

Not why Tina would want to kill her sister—she had a monetary reason to do that, never mind decades of resentment—but why go to the trouble of potentially being seen at the library and stealing the letter opener?

Unless the letter opener had some significance to Tina, the only reason she would do that would be if she wanted to frame one of the partygoers for the murder. One of the partygoers, or the library staff.

The police had asked Sheila, Ruth, Lucinda, and Mary-Sue not to leave Nags Head. Did that mean those four women were under suspicion? It must. What about Bertie herself? I knew Bertie hadn't killed anyone, but she'd had as much opportunity as the others did. Come to think of it, so had Louise Jane, Ronald, and me.

I threw off the covers and got out of bed, much to Charles's displeasure, but he made the most of it, and ran for his food bowl.

I sat at the kitchen table and thought.

I'd been assuming Helena's death was somehow related to the withdrawal slip and Jeff Applewhite's name. Which, considering the significance of the date he'd checked out the book, must have had something to do with the theft of the Blackstone necklace and Jeff's disappearance. Now, I had to consider that the killing had nothing at all to do with Jeff or Rachel's diamonds.

If Tina had killed Helena for her inheritance or in memory of past grievances, the necklace, the book, and Jeff were nothing but a coincidence.

If Tina had taken the letter opener to frame one of the reunion crowd, then, unless she was totally off her rocker, she had to have had a reason to do so.

I'd not considered that Tina might know one or more of Bertie's friends. I grabbed a pad of paper and a pen and wrote down the four women's names in one column, and then Tina's in another, and Helena's in a third. I drew lines to connect the four women to Helena, and another to join Helena and Tina.

And that was all. My page looked mighty empty.

If Tina had pretended to be Helena, could it be possible someone had killed Helena mistaking her for Tina?

Rachel Blackstone had known Tina, and she'd been aware of Helena, although, according to Rachel, they'd not been friends. If she suspected one or the other of the twins of stealing her family's necklace, might she have killed out of revenge? I wrote her name down and drew a strong line between it and "Tina" and then a light one to "Helena."

I scratched them out again.

Bertie, Charlene, Ronald, and I knew Rachel. If she'd come into the library during the party, one of us would have seen her. If Rachel wanted to kill Tina or Helena in revenge for the theft of the Blackstone necklace and the Rajipani Diamond, she'd had twenty-five years to do it and a great many better opportunities.

I leaned back with a groan.

My head was hurting.

If Tina had been hoping to frame someone, she wasn't doing a very good job of it. No other evidence, as far as I could see, had turned up to point to one of us. Perhaps all she wanted was to throw suspicion off herself. Helena died in the marsh, at night, in the presence of a limited circle of suspects, while Tina was apparently far away.

Tomorrow was Wednesday and I had the day off. I might take the opportunity to pay a call on some of the "suspects."

*   *   *

This time I thought it best to phone ahead. Sometimes people talk better in a neutral, comfortable environment. I fed Charles and let him out of the Lighthouse Aerie (Charles never got a day off from being the library cat), made a pot of coffee, and enjoyed it and my breakfast while reading the news from family and friends back in Boston. Then I checked for any updates on the police investigation into the murder of Helena Sanchez (of which there were none), showered, and dressed for the day. I was ready to make my first call.

"Hi," I said in my cheeriest voice. "It's Lucy Richardson here. From the Lighthouse Library?"

"Not you again," Tina Ledbetter said, in a not-cheery voice.

"Oh. Uh, yes, it's me."

"What do you want now?"

"As you're moving soon and we haven't had a chance to get to know each other, I was hoping to treat you to a mid-morning coffee break at Josie's Cozy Bakery."

"You're assuming I want to get to know you better."

"Uh. Yes. I guess I am."

"Yeah. Okay. I doubt you want to know anything about me, but you're interested in why someone would kill my sister. I told you we weren't exactly close, and I didn't know anything about her life. She might have had plenty of enemies I never knew about. I like the bakery and you're paying, so I'll bite. Pun intended."

"Ten thirty?"

"Might as well." She hung up.

*   *   *

Josie's Cozy Bakery could get mighty busy in the summer, even at mid-morning on a Wednesday, so I arrived early. The lineup for takeout drinks and pastries was long, but a few seats were free, so I snagged a table for two in a back corner. One of her staff must have told Josie I was here, because she came out of the back rubbing her hands on an apron with the bakery logo of a croissant curling around a lighthouse.

Josie had worked extremely hard to make this place a success, and I was thrilled at how well she'd succeeded. I don't have any sisters, being cursed with three older brothers, but Josie and I are as close as sisters. Closer than many sisters. Helena and Tina came to mind.

Josie had decorated her restaurant in "West Coast coffee culture meets Outer Banks fishing community." The counter area was all gleaming stainless steel, white subway tiles, glass display cases, and hissing espresso machines, whereas the chairs and stools in the dining area were covered in nautical blue and white, and some of the tables were made of reclaimed tea chests or ships' barrels. Framed prints of North Carolina lighthouses and ships at sea decorated the walls.

I jumped to my feet and gave my cousin a hug.

"Nice to see you," she said. "Day off?"

"Yes, I'm meeting Tina Ledbetter. Do you know her?"

"I do. She's a regular here. She likes my strawberry Danishes."

"Did you know she's Helena Sanchez's sister?"

"Is she? I didn't know that. Then again, I didn't know Helena."

"Can you take a break and join us?" I asked.

"I can. Breakfast rush is over. But why do you want me?"

"If she knows you, she might be more comfortable. Essentially, I am about to, discretely of course, ask her if she killed her sister."

Josie raised one eyebrow. "Discretely?"

"I can be discreet."

She smiled at me. Then she pulled off her hairnet (only Josie could still be beautiful in a hairnet) and shook out her long blonde hair. She grabbed an unoccupied chair from the next table and slid it over.

Blair, one of her assistants, appeared at our table so quickly he might have materialized in a puff of smoke. "Josie, can I get you something?"

"It's on me," I said. "We're waiting for one more person, and then I'll order at the counter."

"Thanks, Blair," Josie said. "I'm good for now."

He walked away.

"He's working out okay?" I asked.

Blair and Josie had clashed (to put it mildly) over the winter around the time of her wedding. Josie was a kind and generous woman, but she was also a small-business owner and boss.

She'd been about to fire Blair, but they came to an understanding in time. He realized this job was just about his last chance, and he dropped the hard-done-by attitude and promised to try harder to get on with Josie and the rest of the staff.

"He's coming along fine," she said. "I'm considering giving him the opportunity to work behind the register when Alison leaves next week for her sister's wedding in Rochester."

"Here's Tina now." I got to my feet and waved.

I had to remind myself that the woman approaching me was not Helena Sanchez.

Tina scowled at me, but she allowed herself the slightest of smiles when she saw Josie seated at our table.

"I hope you don't mind," I said. "Josie needs a break, so I asked her to join us."

"Don't mind at all." Tina sat down.

"What can I get you both?"

Tina asked for a strawberry Danish and a black coffee, and Josie ordered a bran muffin and coffee with cream. I went to the counter and joined the line. When it was my turn, I placed their order as well as one for a blueberry scone and a cup of hot tea for me. "We'll bring everything over for you, Lucy," Alison said.

"Thanks."

When I got back to our table, Tina was telling Josie about her upcoming move to Florida. "I'm not hanging around here any longer than I have to. The police are being cagey about when I can plan Helena's funeral." She looked at me as I slipped into my seat. "Do you know anything about that, Lucy?"

"About Helena's . . . uh . . . arrangements? Sorry, no."

"I thought you were in with the police."

We leaned back to allow Blair to place our food and drinks in front of us. "Thanks," I said to him.

"Always a pleasure, Lucy," he said with a smile.

They know how I take my tea here, and Blair had brought me a small jug of milk. Not cream. I poured a splash into the hot, fragrant liquid. "I wouldn't exactly say I'm *in* with the police. They don't tell me anything that's not for the general public."

"Whatever. If you are talking to them, you can tell them I didn't kill Helena."

I almost spat out my tea. I glanced at Josie. Her eyes were wide, and a slice of her muffin was frozen halfway to her mouth.

I'd been wondering how to gently ask Tina what she knew about her sister's death. Obviously I needn't have bothered.

She bit into her Danish. "The cops have been nosing around my house. Asking questions. Always questions about my relationship with Helena. They were interested when they found out I'm the only one mentioned in her will. I asked them how bad their family relationships are if they think leaving everything to your twin sister is suspicion for murder."

"Uh . . ."

"That went down about as well as you'd expect. That cop, the not-bad-looking older one, he doesn't have much of a sense of humor."

"You mean Detective Watson?"

"Yeah, him." She chewed and shrugged. "He wanted to know why my mother had left everything to Helena and how much that had been. I told him my family relationships were none of his business, but if he must know, my mother and I didn't get on. We never did. She always favored Helena over me. As for what sort of an inheritance that was, our mother had barely a cent left after her debts were paid. Let him ask his questions and poke around in my private affairs. What do I care? I didn't kill Helena, although at various times in our lives I might have wanted to, and now I'm off to Mount Dora as soon as I can go. I'm not going to wait until my house is sold. Do you want to buy a house?"

"Me? No."

"What about you?" she asked Josie.

"Not in the market at the moment, thanks."

"I know you didn't kill her"—I studied Tina's face carefully as I talked—"because you weren't in the library during the party."

"Right. I've never been in that library. I wasn't going to go there when Helena worked there, now was I? I've had no reason to go since. Besides, everyone knows Louise Jane McKaughnan has staked it out as her area of expertise."

"She has?"

Tina shrugged. "You can tell the police that."

She might be lying. She might not be.

"Someone killed your sister," I said.

"Helena and I never got on, as I told you. Our parents, our mother in particular, didn't like me much, for some reason I never understood. Helena was the one they fussed over. Helena was always the first, and sometimes the only." She finished her Danish in record time and began tearing the paper napkin into shreds. "But, despite that, I never wanted to see her dead. She was my sister, and since our parents' deaths, my only living relative."

She stared at the pile of paper on the table in front of her. I looked at Josie, and she shook her head, her big cornflower-blue eyes full of sadness. Neither of us would be able to understand what Tina and Helena had meant to each other. I have three brothers and several nieces and nephews. Neither of Josie's brothers are married, but her extended family is vast—as we discovered when trying to pare down her wedding guest list. Both sets of parents are alive and well and cheerfully interfering, or trying to, in our lives.

"I don't know why anyone would have wanted to kill Helena," Tina said at last. "I told the cops that. I don't know anything about her life. Funny, isn't it? I'm going to get the keys for her house and walk right into that life. If she knew I was coming, she'd have cleaned the place up. But she didn't know, did she?"

"No," Josie said.

"Your sister wasn't in the class of women who'd gathered for the reunion," I said, "but she knew several of them. Did she ever talk about them?"

"I don't think she knew who was going to be at that party. She said Bertie James invited her, and she wanted to see Bertie and check out how the library was doing. She liked Bertie—I knew that. She told me before she left for Mount Dora when she retired she was confident the library was in good hands."

"It is," I said.

She shrugged again. I was getting tired of that shrug. Tina obviously was getting equally tired of my company. She downed the last of her coffee and started making getting-up movements. Maybe all I'd learned was that Tina hadn't killed her sister and didn't know (or care) who had. I believed Tina. There had been a lot of anger in their family—hatred maybe—but the time for settling scores had long passed.

"I saw you at the Ocean Side Hotel on Saturday evening," I said.

Tina nodded. "What of it?"

"I was there with Bertie's college class."

"I saw you."

"Can I ask what you were doing there, watching us?"

"None of your business," Tina said.

"I know that. I'm only trying to understand what happened the night your sister died."

She hesitated. "Okay. It doesn't matter. A friend of mine works in the kitchen there. He'd heard that my sister died at the Lighthouse Library, and he called to tell me a bunch of library people were in the bar, laughing and having a great time. As though a woman hadn't died the day before."

"That's not entirely fair," I said. "Some of those women came a long way for their weekend, and Helena wasn't part of the reunion group. Most of them had never met her before Friday. I'd never met her before Friday."

Tina shrugged. "Fair enough. I didn't expect sackcloth and ashes and weeping and wailing. I thought I'd check them out, that's all, in case I recognized anyone. From Helena's past I mean. I didn't. No reason I should. I never met anyone she worked with."

"You didn't introduce yourself."

She looked genuinely surprised. "Why would I do that?"

"No reason."

"I have to go. I have packing to do."

"I've never been to Mount Dora," Josie said, "but I've heard it's nice. I hope you like it."

Tina picked her bag off the floor. "I'll like it well enough. I would have liked Hawaii better, but that didn't work out for her. Ha. I knew she was just blowing hot air with all that talk."

"Helena talked about moving to Hawaii?" I asked. "Why didn't she?"

"That plan ended as suddenly as it began. She was going to run away with some guy to live on a private island in Hawaii. I guess the guy decided to go without her. If there ever was a guy, which I doubt."

"Wait a minute," I said. "Back up. She told you she had these plans?"

"She bragged about it. I was having one of my not-so-good periods, and she came to check up on me. She probably made it up to make me feel even worse about my own life. Helena could be like that."

"When was this? Do you remember?"

Tina glanced between Josie and me. "Does it matter?"

"It might."

She leaned back in her chair. "As I said, it wasn't a good time for me. My husband walked out on me, leaving me with nothing but his bills, and I wasn't doing so good. Helena did me one favor in her life, and she found me a therapist and convinced me to see her. She, the therapist, helped me a lot, and things turned around for me because of that, so I sort of remember when Helena was talking about Hawaii. Spring of 1995."

I couldn't help sucking in a breath.

"What?" Tina said.

"She told you she was running away with some guy spring of 1995. Did she tell you anything about him. name? What he did or where he came from? How she him?"

"Her Prince Charming, she called him. Barf. As if any m with the money to buy a private island in Hawaii would ha the time of day for the likes of Helena Sanchez. She did say they met when he was working in the library, but that's all."

"Prince Charming. You told me earlier she settled down and forgot about her Prince Charming. I thought you were speaking in broad terms, not about a specific person."

"What of it?"

"You also told me you'd never heard of Jeff Applewhite. Is that still the case?"

"If I told you so, then that's the case. I don't lie." Tina laughed. "Unless I want to."

"Could Jeff have been Prince Charming?"

"Brad Pitt could have been Prince Charming, for all I know. Look, as interesting as all this is—*not*—I have to be going. I've a lot to do getting ready for the move."

"I have one last question. These plans Helena talked about. If it was spring 1995, it was around the time the Blackstone necklace disappeared. Can you think of any connection between your sister and the necklace?"

"No. I knew Rachel Blackstone. Not well, but we hung out sometimes. Helena wasn't ever a part of that scene. I told you the other day I didn't remember if I'd been at Rachel's house when the necklace was stolen, but that isn't right. I do remember, and I know I wasn't at Rachel's party that night because I'd just started to get some help. My therapist told me I had to

stop hanging with that crowd. I knew about the party—no one was ever invited: people just spread the word and showed up. I considered going despite what my therapist said, but at the last minute, I changed my mind. I've always been glad I wasn't there. The cops were asking questions about that party for a long time, and at that time of my life I didn't care for contact with the cops. Come to think of it, I still don't care for contact with the cops. Surely you can't possibly think Helena's death has anything to do with that party and the disappearing necklace? I always assumed Rachel gave it to someone and was afraid to tell her parents what she'd done, so she claimed it had been stolen."

"Rachel searched for it for a long time," Josie said. "She hired private detectives and all that."

Tina shrugged. "Whatever."

I was losing her. Tina was on the verge of getting up and walking away, so I spoke quickly, trying to express the urgency I felt. "Helena never told you what happened with Prince Charming and why they didn't go to Hawaii?"

"Helena stayed in Nags Head for another fifteen years, but I didn't speak to her again for a long time. My therapist wanted me to try to make friends with my sister; she said it was important for my progress, but when I called her, Helena hung up on me. I never tried again. I always figured she was too embarrassed to tell me her prince had skipped town without her. She continued working at the library. She retired. She moved to Mount Dora." Tina stood up. "And that's all I've got to say about it. Goodbye." She looked at Josie. "About the only thing I'm going to miss from these parts is this place."

"Good luck," Josie said.

We watched Tina weave her way through the tables and out the door.

"Wow!" Josie said. "I get mad at Noah and Aaron sometimes, but I've never not wanted to ever see my brothers again. What awful parents. Pitting one twin against the other."

"If that's what happened. Helena might have told a different story."

"True, but you have to admit that anyone who likes my Danishes can't be all bad."

I smiled at my cousin. "Tina's bitter, and I doubt she'll be any happier in Mount Dora. We take our problems with us wherever we go. But I do wish her well."

"What do you think about what she had to say about Helena and this prince of hers?"

"Prince Charming. I only met Helena once, and according to things I've been hearing, she changed a lot over the years, but I wouldn't have thought her the type to dream about finding Prince Charming." I dredged up what I know about *Snow White*, the fairy tale featuring the strangely named Prince Charming. "Apple."

"You want an apple Danish? I haven't made any lately."

"Snow White's given a poisoned apple by her wicked stepmother and falls into a coma. Prince Charming comes galloping along and saves her. Apple. Snow White. Applewhite."

"You think that was a reference to Jeff Applewhite? Seems a heck of a stretch."

"It is a heck of a stretch. But right now a stretch is all I have. The timing's right. Helena bragged to her sister about running away with some guy she called Prince Charming. The Blackstone necklace is stolen and Jeff Applewhite disappears.

Helena doesn't go with him, so we can assume he'd been spinning her a story. Then, all these years later, she sees his name on an old library card and is freaked out."

"I can buy that, if what you're saying is true. But why would someone kill her because of what happened so long ago?"

"Someone who was at the party must know something about Jeff that Helena did not. Not until Friday night."

Chapter Seventeen

I left Josie's and drove to the Nags Head police station in a flurry of excitement. I needed to talk to Sam Watson and tell him what I'd learned. I'd established a direct connection, although only speculative, between Jeff Applewhite and Helena Sanchez.

Watson wasn't in.

I walked back down the steps, unsure of what to do next.

If I should do anything next. I like to think I've helped the police with their cases before, but they never actually welcomed my help. More than once I'd been ordered to stay out of it.

"Hey, Lucy. What's up?" Butch Greenblatt was coming up the stairs, and he gave me a big grin.

I grinned back. "Hi. I wanted to talk to Sam, but he's not in. I don't suppose you know where he's gone and when he'll be back?"

"Nope. Sorry. Can I help?"

"I learned something about Helena Sanchez I think he'll be interested in."

"Call him and leave a message."

"I'll do that. Better to talk in person, but I guess we can do that later. No rush. Butch?"

"What?"

I hesitated. "Nothing. If you see him, tell him I'm looking for him, will you?"

"Sure. Catch you later, Lucy." He went into the police station, and I headed for my car.

I'd been about to ask Butch if he thought it would be okay if I asked some questions about what had happened all those years ago. I decided not to. Butch would be compelled to tell me not to interfere. I'd then go ahead and do what I wanted to do anyway, but I'd feel bad about it.

Sunday evening, after dinner at Aunt Ellen and Uncle Amos's, Rachel Blackstone had given me her number so I could contact her if I learned anything about the case. I got into my car and switched the engine on to get the air-conditioning going. Then I gave Rachel a call.

"Hello?" she said.

"Rachel, hi. It's Lucy Richardson. I've been doing some unofficial digging into the matter we talked about the other night, and I was wondering if I can come around and talk to you."

"I'm at home now. I'm working in the garden, but I'd enjoy taking a break. I've been out here since six, and it's starting to get hot." She gave me an address on a small street running parallel to the beach. "Come around the back. The gate's unlocked."

By Outer Banks beachfront standards, Rachel's house was fairly small, although multistoried and dotted with balconies, but it was beautiful, painted a soft blue with fresh white trim.

Two trucks from a landscaping company were parked in front of the house. Rachel's idea of working in the garden, I thought, wasn't mine.

I walked around the house and opened the side gate as instructed. I called out to Rachel, and she turned to greet me with a huge smile. I'd been wrong: Rachel had very much been working in the garden. She was dressed in dirt-encrusted khaki pants, heavy hiking shoes, and a once-white T-shirt. A big floppy-brimmed straw hat was on her head, and a streak of brown earth ran across her nose. She peeled off well-used gloves as she walked toward me and called over her shoulder, "I won't be long, Johnny."

Rachel's house was small, but the property was large. It's difficult to have a fabulous garden in grounds that are pretty much nothing but sand, but Rachel Blackstone managed. The gate through which I'd entered opened onto a flagstone path. Rather than an attempt at a lawn, pebbles and small stones surrounded the pathway which meandered gently through the property, eventually ending at a seagrasses-lined trail leading through the dunes to the beach beyond. Urns and pots of all sizes, overflowing with lush tropical plants and pale green succulents, bordered the flagstone path and were scattered around the yard. The central feature was a small pond with a gently splashing fountain and a stone statue of a graceful woman in the center. A single wooden chair sat next to the pond, making, I thought, the perfect place for morning contemplation with a cup of coffee and the newspaper, or for relaxing in the evening with a glass of wine and a good book. The white fence surrounding the turquoise pool was edged with small palms and ferns and pots of flowers.

One man was raking the pebbles while another trimmed foliage. The man Rachel had spoken to, Johnny, was on his knees digging a hole, surrounded by several small bushes still in their garden-store containers.

"Excuse the mess." Rachel took off her hat and brushed a lock of hair out of her eyes.

I held out my arms to encompass the splendor around me. "I don't see any mess. This looks fabulous. Beyond fabulous. What a marvelous oasis you've created here."

She beamed, clearly pleased at the praise. "I'm glad you think so. I love working in my garden, but I take a rather lackadaisical approach to it. After resisting for years, I'm opening it to the public on Saturday as part of the garden tour fundraiser for the Grandmothers Helping Grandmothers Anti-AIDS Campaign. I intended to do the work myself to get everything in tip-top shape, but I finally had to admit that's far beyond my capabilities, not to mention the time I have left, so I asked Johnny and his crew to give me a hand. Shall we have a seat?"

She led the way down the curving path and through a delightful iron gate, all swooping swirls and curlicues, to the pool area. The sparkling water looked so appealing I wished I'd bought my bathing suit. White wicker chairs cushioned in red fabric were placed around a table next to the house. Matching red umbrellas shaded the seats from the sun.

Rachel pulled off her gloves and tossed them and her hat onto the table. "I'm in need of a drink. Can I get you something? I've lemonade and tea in the fridge. Both made fresh this morning. Johnny and his gang work up a powerful thirst."

"Lemonade would be good. Thanks."

She slipped through the French doors into the house. I leaned back in my chair and admired the view. The ocean wasn't visible over the white fence, but I could hear the soft pounding of the surf and see brightly colored kites dipping and bobbing in the brilliant blue sky. Wrapped in appreciation of my setting, I started at the sound of the doors opening behind me.

Rachel came out carrying a tray with a pitcher of ice and lemonade and two plastic glasses. Store-bought cookies were arranged on a plate. She put the tray down, poured the drinks, and handed me mine.

"Thanks," I said.

She sat opposite me and studied me with her deep hazel eyes. "So, what did you want to ask me? I assume it's something about the necklace."

"I realize you've thought a lot about it over the years."

"That would be an understatement."

"Sometimes a new person asking fresh questions can help."

"Go ahead."

I took a sip of the lemonade. Far too sweet. Rachel slid the plate of cookies toward me. I accepted one and bit into it. I thought it dry and flavorless. I guess I've been spoiled by the plethora of homemade treats served at Josie's Cozy Bakery. "I've been thinking about the library withdrawal slip that seems to be at the heart of this. It has Jeff Applewhite's name on it, meaning he signed the book out of the library. You're the only person I've met who remembers him, but from what you've said he doesn't sound like a library user."

"One of the few things that sticks in my mind about Jeff, Lucy, is that that's precisely what he was. A reader, at any rate. He usually wore a baggy trench coat with lots of pockets. It was unseasonably hot the night of the party, but he kept that coat on. The police speculated that he'd put the necklace into a pocket and simply walked out the door with it. He always had a book with him, stuffed into a coat pocket. So, yes, he was a reader. I doubt he had much money; he was nothing but an unskilled construction worker, and in the days before cheap e-books, the library was the place to go for people who didn't have money to buy books."

"The library still is," I said firmly, "the place to go for people who don't have money to buy books, never mind electronic devices."

"Point taken." She took a cookie and chewed thoughtfully.

I let her think.

"He was a good-looking guy," she said at last. "Nothing special, I'm not talking movie-star quality, but in good shape, clean and always well groomed. I remember that about him too. Good bone structure and good teeth. Funny how it's all coming back."

That didn't sound like the Jeff in the picture I'd found online. In that one he looked like a street bum. Still, people can clean themselves up. When they want to.

"Did he have a girlfriend?" I asked. "Anyone he brought to your parties? Did you ever see him outside of your house?"

"Not that I remember." Her eyes opened wide and she slapped the side of her head. "There was something! Yes. Now it's coming back. One night, probably not the night the necklace was stolen, but another, people came over for dinner. I got a ton of Chinese food in because I didn't have any idea how many would show up. This girl—I never did get her name—was coming onto Jeff in a big way. He clearly wasn't interested, and another girl, again no name, told the first one she was wasting her time because Jeff went for the brainy sort. Jeff and the guys all laughed at that. I laughed too. I remember that now because she, the first girl, realized she'd been insulted, and she punched the second girl. They got into a real physical fight. We laughed even more. They broke an ornament. Hilarious. Mom was mad about that too."

"Did you tell the police about these women?"

"I did after the theft, but I don't know if they ever followed up. I told my private investigator, and I believe he tracked them down. I have his report, if you want the names. Clearly nothing came of it."

"I would like to know their names, thanks. But I don't want to take up too much of your time."

"You think one of these women had something to do with the recent murder?"

"I don't know what I think, but I've found that one question leads to another, and sometimes if you follow the trail of questions, you can finally arrive at the answer that matters."

Rachel stood up. "I'll pull out the report. It's no bother. I know exactly where it is."

She went into the house and returned with a thick file before I had time to sit back, sip my drink, and enjoy my surroundings. She sat down, opened the file, and flicked quickly through the pages until she found what she was looking for. "Here we are. I don't have pictures, but I have their information. The private investigator spoke to the women, and they claimed to have nothing to tell him. Neither of them were, so they said, at my house the night of the party in question. Jessica Raymond from Nags Head. Age seventeen in 1995. Elizabeth Correggio from Raleigh, aged twenty in 1995. At the time of this report, Jessica was a stay-at-home mother with one baby in Kill Devil Hills, and Elizabeth was working as a waitress in

Raleigh." Rachel looked at me. Her eyes shone with hope. After all these years, she was still hoping the necklace would be found.

I was sorry to disappoint her, but I had to. Jessica and Elizabeth were too young to have been one of the women at the library on Friday night, and I told her that. "Sorry," I said.

Rachel gave me a tight smile. She gathered up her hat and gardening gloves. "If you don't mind, Lucy . . ."

I jumped to my feet. "I'll let you get back to work. Thanks for this."

Her smile was tinged with sadness. "It would be nice to get my grandmother's necklace back, if only out of respect for her and my grandfather. But I've pretty much given up hope."

Chapter Eighteen

Where to go next?

I sat in my car in front of Rachel's house thinking it all over. That had been a dead end. This entire line of questioning was probably a dead end. I had to consider that Helena might not have been reacting to Jeff's name at all. Maybe she'd suddenly remembered something that upset her, and I had no chance of ever finding out what that had been.

Today was my day off. Another fabulous day on the Outer Banks. I could go to the beach. I could visit the Elizabethan gardens in Manteo, or take a hike on the dunes at Jockey's Ridge State Park. I could treat myself to a nice lunch out or go shopping for some badly needed new work clothes. I could just go home and relax in my apartment and read.

Instead, I found myself driving to the Ocean Side Hotel.

Sam Watson couldn't keep Bertie's friends in town forever. He'd have to let them go home soon if he didn't come up with something new.

I didn't have phone numbers for Ruth or Sheila, but I was in luck and found them by the hotel pool, wearing their bathing suits, stretched out on lounge chairs in the sun, icy glasses next to them.

"Hi," I said.

Ruth lowered her book and peered at me from behind a pair of enormous sunglasses. Sheila opened her eyes and squinted up at me. The sun was directly overhead, a ball of fire in a cloudless sky. I wondered if I should point out to Sheila that her chest was turning a bright pink. Instead, I said, "Nice day."

"It is," Ruth said. "I have to say I'm not entirely unhappy at being confined to this place." She glanced around the pool deck: sparkling water, splashing children, laughing parents, comfortable chairs. Even a waiter fetching fresh drinks and clearing away the used glasses. "When I told my boss I can't come in as I'm under police orders to remain in Nags Head, she insisted I give her the name of the officer in charge. She had to make sure I wasn't lying about something like that. The miserable old bat. My husband wasn't happy at having to cook his own dinners either." She lifted her arms and stretched. "Let him suffer for a change. I could get used to living like this."

"I'm not pleased." Sheila said. "My granddaughter's birthday party's on Sunday, and if I have to miss it, I'll be seriously angry."

"What can we do for you, Lucy?" Ruth asked.

I felt awkward looming above them, staring down, fully dressed while they looked up at me, shading their eyes with their hands. I dragged a lounge chair over and dropped into it.

"How'd it go last night?" I asked Sheila. "After Connor and I left?"

"What happened last night?" Ruth asked.

"You ruined the scene," Sheila said. "Totally and completely. Louise Jane tried to call them back, but everyone had fled."

"Call who back?" Ruth said. "I wondered where you'd gotten to last night."

"I was assisting Louise Jane," Sheila said, "while she attempted to contact the spirts of the marsh."

"Oh. Yeah. That." Ruth's eyes were concealed by dark glasses, but I was pretty sure she was rolling them.

"I keep trying to get a handle on Helena and I can't," I said. "Tell me about her."

"Not much to tell," Ruth said. "We worked together in Manteo for a few years in the early nineties. She was a competent librarian, pleasant enough. We were friendly at work but didn't socialize outside. I was married with young children and she wasn't, so we had nothing in common other than the job."

"If you don't mind my saying so, when you met her on Friday, she said you'd put on weight."

"So she did. And so I have. What of it? I have to admit, Lucy, the comment surprised me. I don't remember her being nasty."

"People change," Sheila said.

"Did you know Helena?" I asked.

"Never met her before in my life."

"Did you ever meet Helena's sister?" I asked Ruth. "Her name's Tina."

"No. I didn't know she had a sister. No reason I should know."

"Anything else you remember about her?"

"I don't remember Helena particularly well at all, Lucy. We meet so many people over our lives and our careers." She chuckled. "She had a terrible weakness for historical romances, I remember that. You know the sort, what they call bodice-rippers. Handsome pirates and beautiful aristocrats and der-ring-do on the high seas."

Sheila laughed. "Don't knock it. I had my romantic period too. Then I got married. That killed that fast enough."

An image of Connor McNeil flashed into my mind. *Was I having my romantic period in real life? Would it end some day?* I pulled myself back to the subject at hand. "Helena was a romantic?"

"Oh yeah," Ruth said. "Waiting for her Mr. Right. Poor thing. Looks like he never showed up."

Mr. Right. Prince Charming.

I stood up. "Thank you for your time."

Ruth settled back in her chair and reached for her book. "Anytime. Tell Detective Watson he can keep us here as long as needed. Another month might be nice."

"My husband had a few things to say about the cost," Sheila said. "He suggested I move to a budget motel, but I told him I'm sharing a room, so that mollified him a bit."

"At least we didn't have to move into Mary-Sue's place," Ruth said. "I bet Lucinda's having a ball of laughs. Not." She returned her attention to her book, and Sheila leaned back in her chair and closed her eyes.

"Sheila?" I said.

She opened her eyes, "Yes?"

"The sun can be strong at this time of day. You might want to be careful."

She glanced down at herself.

When I was back in the cool of the hotel lobby, I took out my phone and checked 411.com. Only one family named

Delamont lived in Nags Head and had a landline. I took a chance it was Mary-Sue, another chance she'd be home, and drove over there.

The house was small, with paint peeling off the window frames and the door, an unattended yard, and a weed-choked driveway. A recently washed beige SUV was parked outside.

I parked on the street and walked up the path. I glanced in the SUV as I passed and saw a stack of open house signs piled in the back. Mary-Sue, I remembered, was a realtor. This must be the place, and it must be her car. My luck was holding.

I rang the bell, and Mary-Sue opened the door. Her dark blue skirt suit, worn over a white blouse with a bow at the neck, and her stockings and pumps were too hot and formal for the day. Her gray hair was tied tightly back, and she blinked at me from under her thick glasses. Recognition crossed her face and she said, "Lucy? What can I do for you?"

"I'm hoping to take a few minutes of your time to talk to Lucinda and you about Helena Sanchez. Is that okay?"

"Not really." She glanced at her watch. "I have an appointment."

"Lighten up, Mary-Sue. Let the girl in." Lucinda appeared behind Mary-Sue, looming over the shorter woman.

Mary-Sue ducked her head and stepped back.

"I hope you're here to tell me I can go home," Lucinda said.

"You won't hear anything like that from me. Sorry."

"You might as well come on in anyway. Coffee's on, or we can get you something cold if you'd prefer."

"I'm fine, thank you." I glanced at Mary-Sue. It was her house and thus her place, not Lucinda's, to invite me in and offer refreshments.

"Never mind her," Lucinda said. "She doesn't really have an appointment. She's just wanting to get out of here and make me think she's busy."

"That's not true!" Mary-Sue said. "It's open house day for realtors. Some promising properties are coming onto the market."

"If you say so." Lucinda took my arm and gave me a broad wink. She didn't try to be subtle about it either, and Mary-Sue noticed. She flushed.

Lucinda almost dragged me down the hallway to the kitchen. The kitchen was spotless but seriously in need of some updating. The floor was brick-patterned linoleum, the counter-tops brown laminate, the fridge and stove yellowing white, and the tiles on the backsplash behind the sink showed Dutch windmills and fields of tulips.

"Have a seat." Lucinda gestured to the chipped and scarred pine table as she opened the fridge and stuck her head in. She pulled out a bottle. "There's some wine left. How about that?"

"No, thank you."

"You shouldn't be drinking at this time of day." Mary-Sue's tone was highly disapproving.

"Maybe not, but as I don't have to go anywhere today, I'll suit myself if I want to." Lucinda put the bottle back and took out a can of Diet Coke. "You sure I can't get you one, Lucy?"

"No. Thank you."

Lucinda sat down. Mary-Sue hesitated and then did the same. They looked at me.

"As I said, I've been thinking a lot about Helena and wanting to know more. You both worked with her, didn't you?"

"We were never at the same library." Lucinda popped the tab on the can. "But we met at conferences, regional librarian meetings, that sort of thing. I can't tell you much about her, Lucy. I scarcely remember her."

"She seems to have remembered you," I said.

Lucinda peeked at me from under her false eyelashes in a gesture that was far too girly for a woman of her age. It was midday in a beach town in the summer, she was staying at the home of a friend who didn't want her there, and Lucida was made up as though she was about to step in front of the cameras for her close-up. "I like to think I'm memorable. Even after all these years."

Mary-Sue snorted.

"You knew her better," I said to Mary-Sue.

"Yeah, I knew her. She worked in Manteo for a number of years."

"When Ruth was there."

"That's right. She moved to the Lighthouse Library when she got the director position. I was working there, and she became my boss."

"When was that?"

"January 1995. We didn't work together for long. She fired me for absolutely no reason."

"When?"

"May 1995. Okay, so I took some days off and lied about why, and I left early without asking a couple of times when'd she'd gone into town or something, thinking she wouldn't be back. But what of it? Everyone does that sort of thing. Roger was sick and we were having money troubles, and I had a lot of things to worry about."

I said nothing and tried to keep my face expressionless. The events of the spring of 1995, I was convinced, were key to this case. "It wasn't my fault," Mary-Sue said. "The work in her office was getting on Helena's nerves, and she took it out on the person who happened to be a suitable target at the time. Me."

"What do you mean work in her office? Was someone else using her office at the same time?"

"Not that kind of work. Some renovations were being done inside the library, and the director's office got a refresh. A new paint job, some minor cracks in the walls were repaired, new windows put in. A whole new floor was the major part of it. All the dust and noise and interference that means."

"We've all had horrible bosses," Lucinda said. "I could tell you stories of things that happen in Hollywood that would curl your hair." She glanced at my out-of-control mop of frizzy black curls and burst out laughing. "Bad joke. Sorry."

"We're not talking about Hollywood," Mary-Sue snapped. "Although I thank you once again for reminding us that you work there."

Lucinda glanced at me, lightly slapped her hand, and rolled her eyes. I pretended not to notice.

"Helena wasn't so bad at first," Mary-Sue said. "Tough, yes, but fair. I can't say I ever liked her; she wasn't one for getting on with the staff on a personal level, but she was an okay boss. Then, out of the blue, she turned on me. Come to think of it, she probably did me a favor. It was time to move on." Judging by the expression on her face, even Mary-Sue didn't believe that. "My colleagues said the place wasn't the same without me. Helena must have needed me more than I knew. She went off the rails after I left, people said. The Lighthouse Library wasn't a nice place to work anymore. I'm glad to hear it's back the way I remember it, now Bertie's in charge."

Lucinda put her hand on top of mine. Her eyelashes fluttered and she stared deeply into my eyes. I shifted in my seat. "I hope you're not making something out of nothing, Lucy. Helena hadn't lived in Nags Head for a long time. She would have had time to make plenty more enemies since then. Someone must have followed her to the library and took the chance to rid themselves of her. Unpleasant, I know, but so is life sometimes." She sighed theatrically and lifted the soda can to her mouth.

"I suppose." I said nothing about the possible murder weapon—the letter opener removed from our display. "Did either of you ever meet her sister?"

Lucinda shook her head, and Mary-Sue said, "I didn't know she had a sister."

"Her name's Tina Ledbetter. She lives in Nags Head."

The women exchanged glances and then shook their heads again.

My luck might be in when it came to finding the people I wanted to talk to, but not as regards the information I needed. This was nothing but another wasted trip. I stood up. "Thank you for your time."

"Time," Lucinda said, "is about all I have right now, seeing as to how I'm stuck in this place. I told the cops I expect them to pay for my flight home. It costs a lot to rebook you know." She glanced at big round clock on the wall. "It's almost two. Wine time!"

Mary-Sue walked me to the door as Lucinda headed for the fridge.

"You really know nothing about when they'll be allowed to leave?" Mary-Sue kept her voice low.

"Sorry, no."

"I don't know how much longer I can put up with her in my house. It's bad enough having to listen to her brag about her Hollywood exploits and all the stars she's best friends with, but she's mistaken me for a hotel maid and my husband for her chauffer and wine supplier." Mary-Sue tugged at her hair. "It's a nightmare."

"Why don't you tell her to go to a hotel? The police won't care—not if she lets them know where she'll be."

Mary-Sue looked shocked at the very idea. "I can't do that, Lucy. She's my friend. We were in college together. We roomed together one year. She came to my wedding. Despite her bragging, it's obvious she can't afford to go to a hotel."

"Thanks for your time."

"If you're ever in the market for a home, you'll think of me, right?"

I briefly considered mentioning to Mary-Sue that Tina was putting her house up for sale. Then I decided not to interfere. Mary-Sue might not care for Tina any more than she'd liked Helena.

"Sure," I said.

Chapter Nineteen

I love my Lighthouse Aerie. I love the tiny apartment, I love the view, I love the lighthouse, and I love the commute.

But, as I've said, living above the library was erasing the boundaries between work and home, and that was probably not a good thing.

I wanted to stop worrying about Helena Sanchez and who'd killed her. I wanted to go home, grab my bathing suit and towel, and head to the beach to enjoy the rest of my day off. I could stop into Josie's for a sandwich and a treat to take with me. I'd eat and swim and read and sunbathe.

I've been living in the Lighthouse Aerie for a year now. Maybe it would soon be time to start thinking about looking for a proper apartment.

Then again, maybe not. I did love my cozy apartment. It had the best view in the Outer Banks. Although the cell phone coverage could be a lot better.

I hoped I'd be able to sneak into the library, get upstairs, grab my stuff, and sneak out again.

Unfortunately, the Lighthouse Aerie doesn't have its own entrance. I have to walk all the way through the main room to get to the stairs, then tiptoe past the children's library and sneak by Charlene's office on the third floor, all the while hoping no one will stop me with a question that has to be answered *right now.*

My aunt Ellen was at the circulation desk today, chatting to a group of women while she checked out their books. Charles perched on the returns cart, listening to the conversation. I caught something about the upcoming garden tour as I dashed past. Aunt Ellen gave me a wave, and Charles twitched one ear, but I didn't stop. I hit the stairs and ran up. A babble of excited, high-pitched voices came from behind the door of the children's library. I opened the gate, and took the next flight of stairs two at a time. On the third floor the door to Charlene's office was closed. I ran on.

I unlocked my apartment, let myself in, and slammed the door behind me. Made it!

Seeing Rachel's lovely garden had inspired me, and as I don't even have a window box in my apartment, I decided that rather than go to the beach, today would be a good day to pay a visit to the Elizabethan Gardens in Manteo. I'd have a walk around, admire the plants, maybe pick up a birthday gift for my mother, and treat myself to a late lunch/early dinner in a nice restaurant overlooking Roanoke Sound. If I was going to eat by myself, I needed my book to keep me company.

But first, something Lucinda and Mary-Sue said had caught my attention and I wanted to check a detail with someone. I signed onto the staff area of the library's website, accessed the Friends of the Library list, found the number I needed, and made a call.

"Hello?" said a woman's voice.

"Hi, I'm looking for Glenda Covington?"

"This is she. Lucy, is that you?"

"Yes, it is. Hi. I hope you don't mind my calling, but I have a quick question. I've been thinking about something you said the other day."

"I'd be happy to help if I can."

"It's about Helena Sanchez."

"Oh yes. So sad. What about her?"

"You said many people didn't get on with her, but you always had a soft spot for her. Can you tell me more about that? From what I've heard she was . . . 'difficult' might be the word."

"We lived in Manteo for a few years. I taught fifth grade at the public school there. I knew Helena when she was at the Manteo Library. She was a highly efficient librarian, perhaps a bit on the stern side. I knew the children didn't like her, but she was always pleasant to me, to everyone, whether staff or patrons. I was pleased for her when she got a promotion and went to the Lighthouse Library. A few years after that I was transferred to a school in Nags Head and we moved house, so I started going to the Lighthouse Library. Helena had . . . changed, I thought."

"Changed. In what way?"

A long pause came down the line. I let Glenda think.

"She wasn't . . . nice any longer. Still efficient, still strict, but she didn't even attempt to get along with people. She'd never been the friendly sort, the sort to make friends easily or to even to want to make friends. She didn't associate with the patrons, except to do her job, but when she did she'd always been pleasant enough. At the Lighthouse Library, she was . . . different. That's about all I can say, Lucy. Some people speculated that she was experiencing pain and didn't want to show weakness, but I didn't see signs of that. I wondered if she'd had some crushing disappointment, a betrayal so great it changed her view of people and the world, or perhaps reinforced her inclinations, but I never knew what that might have been. It certainly wasn't something I could ask her. I continued to get on with her, maybe because I sensed her underlying sadness, but not a lot of people did. While she was the director, I was about the only member of the Friends of the Library who stayed any length of time. When she retired, I don't think the staff even had a party for her. I was genuinely sorry to hear she died. I wish I'd known she was visiting Nags Head, but I never heard from her after she retired and moved away."

"Thank you for telling me."

"Am I helping, Lucy? Do you know who killed her?"

"No, I don't. I'm sorry."

"You take care, dear," she said and hung up.

I grabbed my book off the night table, stuffed it into my bag, and headed out, ready to enjoy the rest of the day without worrying about the death of Helena Sanchez.

When I got to the second floor, children's story hour was letting out, and I descended the rest of the steps surrounded by a pack of excited kids as well as an excited cat. Charles leaped onto the railing and walked down next to me.

Bertie had come out of her office and was standing by the front door, waving goodbye to the children and chatting to their parents. A long line of kids gripping their books waited for Aunt Ellen to check them out. I ducked my head and ran for the door.

"Lucy!" Mrs. Peterson popped out from behind the stacks. "There you are. Ronald told me you were off today. Never mind. I won't take much of your time. I've been thinking about programming for teenagers. As you know, my Charity is fifteen now, and getting too old for the children's library, as excellent a librarian as Ronald is. It's time that she . . ."

Curses! Foiled again!

I shifted from foot to foot, my smile straining my face. Mrs. Peterson had five daughters. In charitable moods, I considered her to be stalwart of the library in general and the children's library in particular. In less charitable moods, I thought she was a pest. She had social ambitions for her daughters that her family's financial situation simply couldn't accommodate. Therefore, as she couldn't afford a private library and librarian for her children, she simply decided to treat the Bodie Island Lighthouse Library and Ronald as such.

And now, it seemed, she had designs on me.

"As the youngest librarian here, I thought you'd be the best one to get the program going. You can have visiting professionals. Scientists, doctors—people like that—talking to the young people about their work. I would, of course, leave everything up to you, but if you wanted my help . . ."

I searched for an opening in the stream of words, but nothing presented itself. If I didn't get out of here in the next minute, I'd spend an hour listening to Mrs. Peterson's idea. She'd probably order me to start working on a position paper while she stood over my shoulder and dictated.

Bertie must have caught sight of my stricken face. "Lucy, there you are. I'm so dreadfully sorry, Mrs. Peterson, but something vitally important has come up and I need Lucy."

"Won't be a minute, Bertie," Mrs. Peterson said. "Now, once you've got the lineup set, then we can—"

"Did I see Primrose outside chatting to the Burke boy? Such a nice young man, isn't he?" Bertie said.

"Primrose? With Brian Burke! So sorry, Lucy. I have to run. We'll talk later. Phoebe! Where's Phoebe? Put down that book, we have to go."

"But—" seven-year-old Phoebe said.

"No 'buts,'" her mother said. "Now."

We watched Mrs. Peterson charge out the door, trailed by a bewildered Phoebe.

"That was mean," I said with a laugh. Primrose was thirteen. Mrs. Peterson had already lost control of her oldest daughter, Charity, and was determined not to let Primrose have any interest in boys.

"Mean, perhaps," Bertie said. "But true. Primrose is indeed outside chatting to the Burke boy. Although it's ten-year-old Kyle, not his older brother Brian."

"Mrs. Peterson," I said, "is in for a rough few years."

"She is indeed. I had a call from Ruth earlier, wanting to meet for a drink later. She told me you'd been at the Ocean Side."

"Just asking questions. The more questions I ask, the more questions I have."

"We shouldn't talk here," Bertie said. She led the way down the hallway and into her office. She left the door open. "You're not getting anywhere?"

"Nope. Every time I decide what happened to Helena must go back to the spring of 1995, to the theft of the Blackstone necklace and the disappearance of Jeff Applewhite, I then decide that's nothing but a coincidence. I've found nothing at all to link Helena to Jeff and Rachel except Tina, who knew them both. But Tina never introduced her sister to them. She wouldn't have because they didn't exactly get on, as we know. Anyway, I've decided to forget about it. I've done all I can."

"That's all anyone can ask of you."

I smiled at her. "Thanks for saying so. I know I get like a dog with a bone, but I also know when it's time for me to move on. And right now, I'm moving on to the Elizabethan Gardens for the rest of the afternoon."

"Enjoy," she said. "I love it there, but I haven't been for ages."

"Knock knock," said a deep voice from behind me. I turned to see Sam Watson standing at the door.

"Come in," Bertie said.

"Hope I'm not interrupting," Watson said. Charles slipped into the room between his legs. Charles always liked to be kept up to date on police activities. He sprang onto the top of the filing cabinet and settled down to listen while he washed his whiskers.

"Not at all," Bertie said, "Lucy was telling me about her plans for the rest of the day. What can I do for you, Sam?"

"Nothing really. I just popped in with an update."

Elizabethan Gardens forgotten, I made no move to leave.

"I wanted to take another look at the boardwalk and the marsh. Sometimes, it helps to go back to the scene, clear my mind, try and imagine how things went down."

"And did it?" I asked.

"No," he said. "I've been in contact with the Mount Dora police, and they have nothing important to tell me about Helena Sanchez. She had no police record, and her neighbors say she was a quiet woman who kept to herself. She volunteered at the local library twice a week. The officer who spoke to the library director got the impression Helena wasn't popular there, but the director wouldn't come out and say so. She said Helena worked best when she was left alone, so they often put her to work designing posters to advertise visiting authors or other special events."

"That sounds like Helena," I said. "She didn't get on with a lot of people. Aunt Ellen quit the Friends of the Library group here because of Helena."

"All of which might be true, but that's not usually grounds for killing someone. As far as the Mount Dora police have been able to tell, there's no reason anyone would have followed Helena here with the intention of killing her."

"I've been hearing conflicting stories about her," I said. "Ruth told me she was friendly enough on a professional level when they worked together in Manteo, but Mary-Sue hated her when she was at the Lighthouse Library. I'd put that down to the usual personal conflicts except that, as I said, Aunt Ellen couldn't work with Helena either. Aunt Ellen likes most people, but she doesn't suffer fools gladly. Not that Helena was a fool, but you know what I mean."

"Not everyone is liked by everyone," Bertie pointed out. "I can think of a few popular people I'd cross the street to avoid. Personalities clash."

"True. But I'm thinking it's more than that."

"More in what way?" Watson asked.

"The Helena I met on Friday was, to put it mildly, out-and-out rude and nasty."

"You think she changed at some point?" Bertie said.

"I do. Glenda Covington in particular knew Helena when she was in Manteo and then later when she was the director here. She told me Helena changed considerably over those years, although she didn't know what might have happened. I think whatever happened to Helena happened in the spring of '95."

"The time of the Blackstone necklace and Applewhite's disappearance," Bertie said.

"They have to be connected."

"No, they don't," Watson said. "Anything could have happened—if anything did—to Helena that spring."

"But Jeff Applewhite's signature was on that withdrawal card."

"So were other signatures. The necklace and Applewhite disappeared twenty-five years ago. That's a long time, Lucy. If—and I'm not saying I agree with you—that had something to do with Helena's death, we might never get to the bottom of it."

"I've never heard you be pessimistic about a case before, Sam," Bertie said.

He rubbed at the stubble on his jaw. The shadows beneath his eyes were deep and dark. "Maybe I'm just tired. I've been running in circles with this one. Except for that letter opener, I'd think this was a random attack. Although, I have to point out, we have no proof the opener found in the marsh is the same one taken from here or even the one used in the murder. The ocean washed it clean."

"The coincidence of it not being the same one would be too much to believe," I said.

"I need proof, above all, to take to court, Lucy," he said.

"Which is why I can help you," I said. "I go where my instincts take me and don't worry about court."

"Which is why," he said with a twinkle in his eye that belied his words and lifted some of the darkness from his face, "I don't ask for your help."

"I assume you've been checking into the backgrounds of the women who were on the walk with Helena?" Bertie asked. "Who, I hate to remind you, are my friends."

"I have. Again, nothing comes up that might indicate a life of crime or an overwhelming need for revenge against someone who might have wronged them years ago. Your friends are, Bertie, more or less what they appear to be. Although Lucinda Lorca isn't quite the showrunner's personal assistant she says she is. More like the part-time helper to the second sub-assistant of the assistant to the showrunner."

Charles snorted.

"I won't even try to work that relationship out," Bertie said. "But I suggest you not read anything into that. We all try to impress our friends at reunions. I suspect Mary-Sue's success in the real estate business isn't quite what she says it is. I've seen a few of her signs around town advertising homes for sale. I don't think I've ever seen one with a sold sticker slapped on it."

I thought of Mary-Sue's run-down house and her air of desperation. Watson wiggled his eyebrows, but he also said nothing.

Then again, was I making all this far more complicated than it needed to be? Was I seeking patterns where none existed because of some hidden desire to show off my sleuthing skills rather than come to the simplest and most obvious conclusion?

"Tina Ledbetter and Helena had a difficult relationship," I said. "Tina has clearly benefited from her sister's death, as she's

Helena's heir. Maybe all this other stuff is nothing but a coincidence, and Tina finally decided it was time to get revenge on her sister for what she sees as a life of wrongs, and inherit at the same time. She's anxious to get to Florida and start her new life. Maybe she followed Helena here and hid outside in the dark, waiting for her chance, and followed us to the pier." *And just happened to have a Nags Head anniversary letter opener in her pocket.* I didn't say that last part out loud. "She knew Helena was dead before you told her."

"All of which would have had me taking her down to the station for some in-depth questions," Watson said, "except for the fact that Tina has an alibi. A good one."

"Oh," I said. "You didn't tell me that."

"Believe it or not, Lucy, I don't tell you everything."

"Uh, right."

"At quarter of ten last Friday evening, Tina was threatening to call the police on her neighbors, who were having a barbeque in the backyard and playing their music, according to Tina, too loud. It's not the first time they've clashed and threats have been made. Tina stuck her head over the fence to yell at them, so she can be positivity identified, and they're confident of the time, as the homeowner checked his watch and told Tina that at that time of the evening noise bylaws don't apply. Tina went back inside. It's about a fifteen-minute drive to the lighthouse from her house, so she would not have had time to get her car, drive here, sneak up on Helena and kill her, and be back home by one minute past ten when she again yelled at the neighbors."

"Oh," I said.

"For what it's worth, lest you believe the neighbors are some sort of biker gang or the type of hard-rock fans who can be bribed into lying to the police, they're in their seventies and had gathered like-minded friends to enjoy a cello recital by Yo-Yo Ma over their vegan burgers and quinoa salads."

"Not everyone," Bertie said, "is a fan of classical music."

"True. The police have been called more than once to Tina's complaints about her neighbors. And vice versa. The neighbors were, they told me, overjoyed when they saw a "For Sale" sign go up on her lawn. After I leave here, I'm going to call Lucinda, Ruth, and Sheila, and tell them they can leave Dare County tomorrow, pending no new developments. I'll also be lifting restrictions on Mary-Sue Delamont's movements." He wished us a good day and left.

"So that's that," I said.

"Not necessarily," Bertie said. "Sam will keep digging. You know he will."

"Yes, but he's got other cases on his plate, and once the women are gone, it'll be harder for him to talk to them." *And I won't be able to either,* I thought, but didn't say out loud. "Tell me about them, please. I know you haven't seen most of them in a long time, but what do you remember?"

"I remember," Bertie said, "good times. We were young and free, passionate about our courses, loving college, loving being away from home, stretching our wings. I shared a dorm with Lucinda, Sheila, Mary-Sue, and Ruth our freshman year. I stayed in touch with them more than the other women in our class mainly because we all settled in eastern North Carolina, and we'd get together occasionally as a group when one of us organized something. But sometimes even the closest of friends drift apart. And that's the way it should be, Lucy. People grow and change."

From his post, Charles nodded sagely.

"Ruth, Sheila, and I remained librarians, but Lucinda moved to California, and Mary-Sue went into real estate. Ruth, Sheila, and Mary-Sue married and had children. Lucinda married and divorced twice, and I never did."

A bell went off in my head. And I realized I'd been missing something all along. "When did Lucinda go to California?"

"I don't know."

"She was working as a librarian somewhere in this area, and she knew Helena. Then she quit and went to California to work in television. She told me when that was, but I don't remember. Can you find out when she actually left?"

"You think it matters?"

"I don't know what matters until I know."

"You could ask her."

"She might not tell me the truth."

"Margaret Hurley is our class record keeper. She kept track of us as much as she could, wanting our contact information to organize events and keep us in touch. She might know."

"Can you ask her, please?"

Bertie reached for her phone. She scrolled through her contact list, gave me a nod, and then made the call. I could hear the tinny voice on the other end that indicated she'd reached a recording. "Hi, Margaret. It's Bertie James here. I have a question for you about our class. Give me a call when you get a chance. Bye."

"Let me know what she has to say," I said. "As for me, I'm off to the gardens."

"Enjoy," Bertie said.

I turned around and collided with Louise Jane. I let out a screech, and Louise Jane threw up her hands.

"For heaven's sake," I said, "don't sneak up on people like that."

Charles jumped off the filing cabinet and landed on the edge of Bertie's desk. Louise Jane stroked him, and he purred happily. The traitor.

Louise Jane made a poor attempt to hide her smirk. "Sneak up? I'd hardly call walking down a corridor in a public building in the middle of the day, sneaking up. What are you two talking about anyway? More developments on the case? Isn't today your day off, Lucy?"

"I was just leaving."

"You shouldn't spend so much time here. I've been reading up on the importance of a proper work–life balance. You're not married, Lucy, so your job is just about all you have in your life, but . . ."

"I have a perfectly fine work–life balance, thank you, and a good group of friends. Bertie and I were discussing . . . non-library business." Too late, I realized I'd once again snatched the bait.

Louise Jane reeled in her catch. "My point exactly. You need a larger group of friends. Now to the purpose of my visit. Sheila and I put our heads together, and we've come up with a plan to help Lucy get to the bottom of the murder."

"Help me?"

"Everyone knows you've been asking questions all over town Lucy. If you want to be a detective, you need to be more discreet."

"I'm not going undercover!"

"Louise Jane," Bertie said. "I doubt very much I want to hear what you and Shelia have decided, but you'll tell me whether I want to hear it or not, so you might as well go ahead."

Louise Jane dipped her head. "Thank you, Bertie. After our adventure in the marsh on Tuesday night—"

"What adventure?" Bertie said.

"That doesn't matter now. We had no luck summoning anyone except for a couple of young lovers who didn't seem at all happy at being summoned."

"What lovers?" Bertie asked. She must have read my face, which wouldn't have been hard as I'd turned a bright scarlet, and she quickly added, "Oh. Never mind."

"The police are going to allow Sheila and the others to go home tomorrow—"

"How do you know that?" I asked. "Watson left here a few minutes ago. He hasn't told them." I snapped my mouth shut as I realized, too late as usual, that I'd just confirmed what was probably only a guess on the part of Louise Jane.

She smirked. "Haven't you figured out by now, Lucy, honey, that I have my sources? The police station is a modern building, but the ground on which it stands has been occupied for a long, long time."

More likely than an unworldly informant, I thought, Louise Jane has a friend or a distant cousin working for the police who keeps her up to date about goings-on there.

"Anyway," she went on, "as they will be leaving, we have one night, and one night only, to attempt a re-creation."

"I hope you noticed," I said, "that I haven't asked what you meant about 'summoning.' I don't want to know."

"And I don't want to know what 're-creation' you're talking about," Bertie said.

"Sure you do." Louise Jane gave Charles a final pat. He strolled across Bertie's desk and settled on the computer keyboard for a nap.

"Tonight, we'll gather together the people who went on the walk on Friday to reenact the events of that night. Including you,

Bertie, plus Lucy and Ronald. My cousin Jolene is about the same age and height as Helena, although quite a bit heavier come to think of it. Never mind, it'll be dark. Jolene will play Helena. I, of course, will be on high alert, prepared to speak to any of the marsh spirts who want to help us understand what happened."

"Why would they want to do that?" I asked.

"Do what?"

"Help us understand."

"Because I'll ask nicely, Lucy, honey. Now, you tell Ronald, and I'll get Sheila to call Lucinda, Mary-Sue, and Ruth. We won't tell them what's happening, of course. We'll say it's a farewell party. Hmm, come to think of it, you'd better make the call, Bertie."

"I'm not tricking my friends into participating in one of your wild fantasies," Bertie said. "And that is that."

"I suppose you're right. Besides, women of"—she coughed and avoided looking at Bertie—"a certain age don't usually start parties after nine. It'll be better coming from Sheila anyway. She'll invite them to join her on a pleasant evening stroll on the library grounds. No one can object to that."

"I don't know . . ." Bertie said.

"Fortunately," Louise Jane said, "I do. What harm can it do? If nothing happens, we'll all drive into town for a farewell drink at the Ocean Side."

"Very well." Bertie reached for her phone.

"Who are you calling?" Louise Jane asked.

"Sam, of course. He can send a couple of officers to hide in the shadows and arrest anyone, if that becomes necessary."

"Not a good idea," Louise Jane said. "More people will disrupt the atmosphere I need. We have to enact events as closely as possible as they happened on Friday night, and we didn't have a bunch of cops tramping around in their big boots, frightening the birds and yelling at each other. I checked the weather forecast for tonight, and the conditions will be much the same as they were on Friday. Weather exerts a powerful influence over the spirt world."

"Do they not like going out in the rain?" I asked. Louise Jane ignored me.

"We can't—" Bertie began, but she stopped when I gave her a jerk of my head. Louise Jane's back was to me, as she faced Bertie, feet apart, hands on hips, ready to argue her point to the death. I nodded at Bertie and lightly tapped the side of my head, indicating that I had an idea.

"I guess," Bertie continued, "it can't do any harm. Except to the reputation of this library. As library director, I suppose I'll have to assume responsibility for that."

"I knew you'd agree, Bertie. You can always be counted on to see reason." Louise Jane turned and beamed at me. "You're always so negative, Lucy. You need to get some control over that."

"Me?"

"I'm off. We don't have much time. I'll call Shelia now and fill her in on the plan. Bertie, you speak to Ronald."

"He might have plans for after work," Bertie said.

"He can change them. Tell him to be here at nine thirty. We left at quarter of ten on Friday, and we'll do the same tonight."

"You're filling Sheila in on your plan?" Bertie said. "What if she's the killer? Won't you have tipped her off?"

"Sheila's not the killer," Louise Jane said.

"How can you be so sure?"

"She's as eager as I am to contact the spirits and ask what really happened that night. She wouldn't be, would she, if she'd killed Helena? Try to dress in the same clothes you were wearing that night. That will help with the accuracy of the re-creation."

Louise Jane left.

Charles lifted his head and looked from Bertie to me. I decided not to point out to Bertie that the document on her computer screen was filled with rows of "e's".

"What," Bertie said, "have I agreed to?"

I tiptoed to the door, listened, and then quickly stuck my head out. I looked up and down the hallway. Neither Louise Jane nor anyone else was lurking in the shadows, listening.

Nevertheless, I closed the door, approached Bertie's desk, and spoke in a low voice. "Louise Jane's invisible friends aren't going to reveal themselves to us tonight or any other night. And they're certainly not going to point skeletal fingers at the guilty party. And that guilty party, whoever it might be, is hardly going to reenact her steps up to the point of attempting to kill the fake Helena, also known as Louise Jane's chubby cousin."

"Agreed. So why are we doing this?"

"Because I have an idea. It might not be much of an idea, but, as Louise Jane said, if it doesn't work, we can all go to the hotel and have a laugh about it over a drink."

Charles leaned closer in order to hear better.

Chapter Twenty

I never did get to the Elizabethan Gardens. Instead, I took my phone into the marsh, where I could be sure of not being overheard, and made a call.

I then put my head down and charged through the library, determined not to get trapped into making polite conversion or answering questions, and ran upstairs to my apartment. Once safely locked inside, I took out a pad of paper, a pen, and several different-colored highlighters, made a pot of coffee, got my iPad, and sat at the small table in the kitchen. I wrote down everything I knew about the four women: Lucinda, Sheila, Ruth, Mary-Sue. Unlike Louise Jane, I wasn't ready to remove Sheila from the suspect list. People outside of the reunion friends, Rachel and Tina among them, might have had reason to kill Helena, but they had not been inside the library during the party, and thus they had not stolen the letter opener. It was possible, as Watson had said, that the opener the police divers dredged up from the bottom of the marsh was not the one taken from the library and not the weapon that had killed Helena, but I decided to apply Occam's Razor.

The theory of Occam's Razor maintains that the simplest explanation is most often the right one, meaning: don't complicate things unnecessarily.

I was good with not complicating things. I set to making notes.

Facts—things I knew for sure because I'd seen or learned them for myself, or someone I trusted completely had told me—were highlighted in blue.

Probable facts—what more than one person had told me—were marked green.

Speculation—what I guessed—was colored pink.

False or probably false, including what I'd been told but didn't believe, was underlined in black ink.

The landline in my apartment rang once. I answered, listened, thanked the caller, and recolored a line from pink to blue, giving it a nice purple shade.

I checked a few details on the internet.

At last, I drew a circle around one name. I leaned back in my chair with a sigh.

I knew who'd killed Helena. I could guess why.

I had nothing I could take to Sam Watson, and absolutely no idea how I was going to prove it.

I got up to answer a scratch and whine at my door. I opened the door and looked down. Charles's little face peered up at me. All was quiet below, and I checked my watch.

It was after seven o'clock. I'd been working for hours.

Charles sauntered into the kitchen area and checked his bowl. Empty. He turned and gave me a glare of disapproval.

"Sorry." I shut the door. "I've had a lot on my mind. Did you have a nice day?"

He didn't answer. I filled the bowl with kibble and added a couple of spoonfuls of canned cat food, and he dug in without so much as a pause to say, "Thank you, Lucy."

The suspects were gathering, if all went according to Louise Jane's plan, at nine thirty, and we'd head into the marsh at quarter to ten. My special guest should be here at nine fifteen.

I changed into the clothes I'd been wearing that night: black slacks and a black shirt. For Bertie's party it had been suitable attire for being a waitress. Tonight it was perfect for creeping about the marsh on a moonless night.

I went back to the table, intending to go over all my notes again, and found loose sheets of paper scattered around the kitchen. "Okay," I said, "you got your revenge for a late dinner. Now we're even."

Charles raised one eyebrow as if to say, "I'll decide when we're even."

I crawled under the table, reached beneath the fridge, and gathered up the pages. While Charles napped on the bed— being petted and adored all day is a tiring job—I reread my notes and checked a few more details on the internet, but I was too nervous to keep my mind focused on the task, and I kept checking the time.

At nine o'clock, I went downstairs. I had to do some nimble footwork to get out the door without a suddenly attentive Charles. I did not want to have to worry about keeping an eye on a big Himalayan while laying a trap for a murderer.

I ran lightly down the spiral iron stairs. All was dark and quiet. A light burned in the alcove and another in the hallway. The computers were switched off, the books lined up neatly on their shelves. I love being in a library at night, surrounded by millions upon millions of words of literature, history, and science. I believe books love to be read. I believe books need to be read, and I like to believe that when the library's closed, they're waiting eagerly for tomorrow, when once again people stream through our doors, wanting to take the books home with them. When my imagination runs away with me, I imagine the characters climbing out from between their pages after everyone has gone, and getting to know each other. I hope Lizzy Bennet would like what Seth Grahame-Smith did in *Pride and Prejudice and Zombies*; or that Sergeant Cuff of *The Moonstone* would enjoy the exploits of his modern counterparts, James and Kincaid, in Deborah Crombie's series; or that Sherlock Holmes wouldn't mind *too much* being re-created as a modern young woman in Vicki Delany's Sherlock Holmes Bookshop series.

Tonight, I was far too nervous to imagine dreaming books or literary characters exchanging news and gossip. I went outside and paced up and down the path. I checked my watch so often the minute hand scarcely seemed to be moving.

The warm night was a close replication of Friday's weather. Heavy cloud cover hid the moon and stars, and the wind was still. The occasional bat flew overhead, and insects were on the hunt.

At long last, lights lit up the row of red pines, and a car approached. My heart sped up. It settled back down when I recognized Ronald's car. I ran to greet him.

"What on earth is going on?" he said the moment he had one foot on the pavement. "Bertie told me we're going to try to reenact Friday night. Are you sure that's wise, Lucy?"

"I'm not sure in the least, but it's worth a shot. Just be on alert, please, and watch what's going on."

"I can do that. Here comes Bertie. She told me to wear the same clothes I had on that night." Like me, Ronald was all in black, but, unlike mine, his outfit was accented by the yellow polka-dot bow tie.

Our boss's car pulled up. "Mary-Sue's bringing Lucinda," Bertie told us, "and Louise Jane and her cousin will pick up Sheila and Ruth. Did you . . . uh . . . make the other arrangement?"

"What other arrangement?" Ronald asked.

"Better you don't know," I said. "Yes, I did, and I hope she hurries up." I checked my watch. "She's late. I said quarter after nine. It's twenty-five past now. If the timing's wrong, everything will be ruined."

"I'm not asking what will be ruined," Ronald said before clamping his lips firmly together.

"I did as you asked, Lucy," Bertie said.

"Good." I spotted the lights of another car turning into the lane. "I hope this is her now. It must be. I told her to park on the far side of the lot. You two wait here for the women. I'll get everything in place." I ran across the lawn to greet the newest arrival.

Tina Ledbetter killed the engine, switched off her headlights, and got out of her car. She waved when she saw me jogging her way. She was dressed in brown pants and a calf-length brown cloak and had twisted her gray hair into a tight knot at the back of her head. Tonight, the resemblance to Helena was truly striking.

I stared at the cloak. "Is that . . ."

"You said to wear a dark coat. So I did." She gave a bark of laughter. "You should see your face. If you're thinking this belonged to Helena, it didn't. The police haven't returned her things to me yet. Not that I want them. I've had this for a long time."

The cloak was almost identical to the one Helena had been wearing when she died. I'd heard that sometimes identical twins act much alike and often have the same habits and tastes, even when they're adults and live far apart.

I swallowed and said, "Thank you for coming."

"Glad to be of help. What do you want me to do?"

"Come with me, but hurry. The others will be arriving any minute. I have a light for you." I pressed a small flashlight, one I'd taken off my keychain, into her hand. "Please don't use it until the last minute if you don't have to."

"It's mighty dark out here."

"We can move in sync with the lighthouse." I waited until the light finished its dormancy and then said, "Okay, let's go."

I led the way across the lawn, around the back of the lighthouse, toward the boardwalk. It was a jerky walk, as we had to keep stopping to move in conjunction with flashes of light from above. The regular bursts of illumination breaking the darkness completely destroyed any night vision we might have otherwise had. Tina said not a word. She walked silently as her cloak floated around her.

When we reached the boardwalk, I said. "Okay, you wait here. Keep quiet, don't use the light, and wait for my signal."

"The police said Helena was found in the water." Tina's voice came from the darkness. "We're not near the water yet. I don't need to wait here. I'm not going to fall in. I'm not a total fool. Unlike my sister."

I thought that rather unkind considering how Helena hadn't exactly tripped, but had been pushed into the water by her killer, but I said nothing. The time for Tina and Helena to reconcile had long passed. "Someone followed her down to the pier, and they aren't going to do that this time, are they?"

"I guess not," she admitted. "Okay, I'll wait here."

"You know what to do?"

"Yes."

As Tina and I had crept through the shadows of the solid bulk of the old building and across the lawn, I'd heard the sound of car engines approaching and then being turned off, doors slamming, and voices calling. When I returned to the library, I found everyone gathered inside. Other than Sheila, Louise Jane, and a woman I'd never seen before, who must be her cousin, no one looked particularly happy. They had not taken seats.

"Ridiculous," Ruth was saying as I came in.

"I thought we were having a farewell drink," Lucinda said. "Isn't that it? You're not exactly set up for a party here, Bertie."

"That's what Sheila told me," Mary-Sue said. "I pointed out that the hotel would be a lot more comfortable, but Lucinda would be happier to come here as she wouldn't have to pay for her drinks."

"Hey," Lucinda said. "I resent that. I can pay for a drink, thank you very much. I don't like being tricked, that's all." She turned around and headed for the door. "I'm outta here. You can have your little party without me."

"You're welcome to leave," Louise Jane said, "but you don't have a car." Louise Jane had worn her maid outfit. I figured that alone should have told the women they weren't gathering for a farewell drink.

"I'll call a cab," Lucinda said.

"Suit yourself," Bertie said.

Lucinda hesitated.

"I thought," Sheila said, "as we're leaving tomorrow and are unlikely to all be together again, it would be nice to have a walk in the marsh and say farewell to Helena."

"I thought you didn't know Helena," Mary-Sue said.

"I hadn't met her before Friday, but I spoke to her then."

"Lucky you," Mary-Sue said. "I have nothing to say to Helena, dead or otherwise. She ruined my life. Let her be."

"Ruined your life?" Lucinda snapped. "It seems to me that you have a roof over your head, you have children and grand-children, and a good job. You have a husband, although I'll admit he's not much of a catch."

Mary-Sue burst into tears. "A good job! You mean that horrible real estate gig? Running to and fro at all hours of the day and night, at the beck and call of people who have no intention of buying but want to wander around the inside of beach houses. I work so hard, but I haven't sold a house in over a year. We're up to our eyeballs in debt. I loved being a librar-ian. All I ever wanted to be was a librarian, and *she* took it away from me."

Bertie patted Mary-Sue's shoulder awkwardly. Lucinda edged back into the room.

"I hope you're not implying that those of us who stayed in the library field are rolling in dough," Ruth said. "It's not exactly a lucrative occupation. At my library, the cutbacks have been so heavy that—"

We had to get moving. My plan threatened to fall apart if all the women wanted to do was stand around inside and tell the others how unfairly life had treated them. I threw a look at Louise Jane.

"As pleasant as this is," Louise Jane said, "I have to admit you're right. Sheila brought you here under false pretenses."

"Hey," Sheila said. "Don't blame me. It was your idea."

"No, it wasn't. I distinctly remember you saying—"

"We're all here now," Ronald said. "Even me, who has better things to do tonight. What's up, Louise Jane?"

"Louise Jane believes she can contact the spirts of the marsh, and they'll tell us what happened to Helena," Sheila said. "They must have seen it all. Under the proper circumstances, they'll reveal what they saw. Isn't that right, Louise Jane?"

"Oh, for heaven's sake," Ruth said. "Sheila, you always were too gullible for your own good. I remember the time in junior year when Leslie Connolly convinced you to write her paper for her. You were almost kicked out of school."

"It wasn't Leslie," Ruth said. "Wasn't it—"

"Under the right circumstances," Louise Jane said, "the spirits might be persuaded to reveal themselves. I myself have seen them on more than one occasion."

"See!" Sheila said. "Told you so."

I remembered one incidence of Louise Jane creeping about in the marsh while on the phone to her great-grandmother, asking what to do next. For her pains she ended up cold and wet, pretending not to be discouraged.

I didn't bother to point that out to the group. Instead I said, "Great idea. It's almost ten. We have to get going if it's going to be as close as possible to the time we left on Friday."

Ronald gave me a look.

"Whatever," Ruth said. "I've nothing better to do tonight."

"Nothing better than getting a good night's sleep," Mary-Sue mumbled.

Ronald opened the desk drawer and reached for the Maglite.

Louise Jane said, "We don't want that."

"Why not? I had it on Friday."

"That's the one thing we'll have to do without. The light's too strong. The spirits won't like it."

"I'm not wandering around in the dark without a light," Mary-Sue said.

"We'll have small flashlights and cell phone lights," Louise Jane said. "Just not that one."

Ronald closed the drawer with a shrug.

"Okay, but if we're reenacting Friday, then who the heck are you?" Lucinda pointed to Louise Jane's cousin, who so far hadn't said a word. I couldn't help but notice that she didn't bear the slightest resemblance to Helena. She wore a long black winter coat, way too heavy for this warm night.

"Her name doesn't matter," Louise Jane said. "She'll play Helena."

The cousin smiled and waved.

"Can this get any more ridiculous?" Ruth muttered.

"I bet it can," Ronald grumbled under his breath in return.

"Now remember, everyone," Louise Jane said. "Try to stick as closely to the path you took on Friday as you can remember. Helena, you keep to yourself and stay out of the light."

"What do I do?" the cousin asked.

"You're pretending you're Helena, and I just told you what to do."

"Oh, right. Sorry. Stay out of the light. Got it."

"Ready?" Louise Jane asked. She didn't wait for anyone to reply before saying, "Let's go then. Now remember, do what you did on Friday. I'll be on high alert for any paranormal presence, but if you sense something, give me a shout."

"I sense," Mary-Sue said, "that it's past my bedtime."

"I sense," Ruth said, "a drink at the hotel bar calling my name."

Louise Jane threw open the door.

Connor McNeil stood there, his hand raised to knock. He blinked in surprise.

Louise Jane stifled a yip of shock but recovered quickly. "Sorry, Connor. We're busy. Private party. Women only."

Connor spotted Ronald waving at him from the back of the crowd and raised one eyebrow.

"Women and librarians," Ronald said, "I'm sure we can make an exception in His Honor's case."

"No, we cannot," Louise Jane said. "If Connor tags along, it'll spoil the atmosphere."

"What's happening?" Connor asked me. "This doesn't look like much of a party." He was dressed in a sharp suit, crisp white shirt, and silk tie; his unruly hair was combed flat, he was freshly shaven, and he'd applied too much aftershave.

"None of your business," Louise Jane said.

I gave him an apologetic shrug as Bertie stepped forward. "Actually, as the library's owned by the town, and as Connor's the mayor of our town, it *is* his business. He can stay."

For a moment Louise Jane looked as though she was about to argue, but recognizing that time was quickly passing, she gave in. "Okay. You can come. Be quiet and unobtrusive." She marched out of the library. The line of women followed her. Ronald followed them. Bertie and I were last.

"I wasn't expecting you tonight," I said to Connor. "Is something wrong?"

"Wrong? No, nothing wrong. I was hoping to find you in, and I was surprised to see all those cars." He took a deep breath and then spoke as though the words desperately wanted to be said. "As I haven't had much luck in saying what I need to say, Lucy, I hoped to find you here alone and we could . . . talk. I guess this isn't going to be the time either." He patted his jacket pocket.

"Come with us," I said, grabbing his hand. "We can talk later."

"Somehow, I don't think the mood will be right later."

Bertie gave him a huge grin. "Never give up, Connor, never give up. The prize is worth the effort."

"What on earth are you two talking about?" I said. "Never mind. We have to catch up with the others."

Chapter
Twenty-One

We trooped across the lawn to the boardwalk in a tight group. Some people seemed to be taking this more seriously than others. Ruth told everyone she was disappointed when the police told her she could leave: she'd been enjoying the enforced vacation. Sheila bubbled excitedly as she walked next to Louise Jane, constantly asking if Louise Jane sensed anything yet. Louise Jane finally snapped at her to be quiet. Mary-Sue asked Bertie if she'd ever thought about selling her house.

"What do I do now?" Fake Helena asked.

"You do nothing and keep quiet, as I told you," an exasperated Louise Jane said.

"Okay. Sure is hot out here tonight. Do I have to keep this coat on?"

"Yes!"

Fake Helena stepped in a hole and pitched forward. She gave a startled yell and would have hit the ground face first had Ruth not grabbed her by the arm with a cry of "Watch it there."

Louise Jane muttered something impolite.

Lucinda kept up with the rest, but she had nothing to say.

As a reenactment of the events of last Friday, this wasn't working very well. That night, people had spread out almost immediately on leaving the library. Some walked faster than others, some strolled and chatted or enjoyed the evening, some stopped to admire their surroundings. Tonight, the group kept close together. Everyone, except perhaps Louise Jane, was frightened and wary. Lucinda didn't try to flirt with Ronald, Sheila didn't beg Louise Jane to tell a story, and Bertie and Ruth didn't talk about the birds and wildlife of the marsh. Ronald hadn't brought the Maglite, and I was definitely not enjoying the peace and quiet.

When the great 1000-watt bulb overhead went off, I couldn't see a thing beyond the range of our few weak flashlights. The people around me were nothing but dark shapes drifting through the expanse of darkness. I was glad of the strong, solid warmth of Connor's hand in mine and the steady sound of his footsteps on the ground and his regular breathing. He said nothing, just gripped my hand tightly.

The boardwalk appeared up ahead. "Step back," Louise Jane said to her cousin. "Like I told you."

Silently, Fake Helena slipped out of the circle of light and disappeared.

She must be, I thought, *braver than she seems.*

As one, the group stepped onto the boardwalk.

"It was here," Louise Jane said, "that we turned out the lights."

"Lucinda," Bertie said, "by the time we reached the boardwalk, hadn't you gone back to the library?"

"I'm not wandering off by myself tonight," Lucinda replied. "This is creepy."

"I'll walk back with you," I said. "Connor, why don't you stay with Bertie and the rest? You always love listening to Louise Jane's stories."

"I do?"

"Yes. You do."

"I sure do," he said.

It was an effort, but I managed to let go of his hand. I shone my little flashlight on the ground in front of Lucinda. She turned and walked away, and I followed her, focusing my light on the other woman's feet.

Behind us Louise Jane began to speak. "Lights out, everyone." One by one the flashlights were switched off. My eyes struggled to find their night vision. "Imagine it's 1611, and after months of journeying across storm-tossed seas, the coast of North America has appeared at last." Tonight, Louise Jane's voice was different than it had been on Friday. Not strong, confident, self-assured, this one came across as hesitant and unsure. It quavered with nervousness. "You can smell land, but you can't see it. No lights guide the way."

After I'd taken about ten steps, I took a deep breath, steadied my shaking nerves, and turned off my flashlight. I'd timed it to coincide with the beginning of the lighthouse light's dormant period, and the entire area was plunged into total and complete darkness. Louise Jane's voice came out of the void: "Is that a light you see in the distance? Yes. Friend or foe is the question."

Lucinda stumbled and she began to protest. The words died in her throat as something swayed a few feet in front us, coming our way. I was expecting it, but even I stifled a scream.

A shape began to take form out of the dark. The shape was that of a human, but it was faint, unworldly, without boundaries or edges. A thin waving light glowed from within. Brown cloth and long, loose gray hair, like tendrils of seaweed, shuddered in the slight wind. The face was nothing but deep hollows, yellow shadows, and huge accusing eyes.

Helena Sanchez stood before us. She said nothing; she did nothing. She stared at Lucinda.

Lucinda screamed. I almost screamed myself.

"What's happening?" Ruth yelled.

"They're here," Sheila bellowed. "Be quiet, people."

"Everyone stay calm," Ronald said.

"Lucy?" Connor called. "Are you okay out there?"

I managed to force the words out. "Yes. Stay where you are."

Lucinda was frozen to the spot, staring at the apparition in front of her. I didn't make a move. I knew what was happening; I'd set it up, yet even I was terrified.

Was it possible Louise Jane truly had summoned something?

Helena lifted one arm and pointed directly at Lucinda. Her cloak fell back. "Why?" the deep voice said. "Why? After all these years."

Lucinda stepped backward, trying to take herself out of the range of that accusing finger. "I'm sorry. I didn't mean to do it. I just . . . I just . . . I'm sorry. Go away, please—go away!"

Louise Jane had stopped talking. No one moved. No one breathed.

"Why?" Helena said again.

"You know why! Jeff lied to me. He told me I was the one he loved. He told me we'd be together always. But it was all a lie. He never meant to go with me. He wanted you. You! Not me. I couldn't live with that. He had to die. I had to kill him. It was all his fault!"

"Why?" Helena repeated.

"When you saw the withdrawal slip, you knew what happened all those years ago. I couldn't let you tell anyone else."

"Tell them what, Lucinda?" I was amazed at how calm my voice was.

I doubt she even heard me. With a screech of pure rage, Lucinda sprang forward and fell on Tina Ledbetter, screaming, "Why couldn't you stay dead!"

Chapter
Twenty-Two

Lucinda moved before I could react. She knocked Tina to the ground and jumped on top of her. Tina fell hard, and the light hidden beneath her cloak went out. I heard the sickening sound of fists hitting flesh and ran blindly toward the thrashing figures. Someone had, thank goodness, switched on a light, illuminating the scene so I could see Lucinda on top of Tina, raining blows on the other woman's face and body. I grabbed Lucinda around the chest and tried to pull her away, but I didn't have the strength, and my feet couldn't get a solid grip on the wet, muddy grass. Lucinda was like a mad thing, fighting me while screaming and pounding Tina and shouting over and over, "You're dead. You're dead!" Tina got one arm loose and managed to land a solid punch on Lucinda's right cheek. Lucinda recoiled, and I pulled her backward as hard as I could, but it wasn't enough to get her off Tina. I was aware of people yelling all around me, but for the longest of moments it was as though the three of us were alone in the marsh, engaged in a desperate fight to the death. Or, as Lucinda saw it, a fight past death.

I've been threatened, and I've had to run for my life in the past, but I've never actually been in a physical fight before.

Tina pushed and punched, and I pulled and slipped, and still Lucinda pounded and scratched and screamed.

I felt strong arms around my waist, and I was yanked away from the screaming women and tossed unceremoniously to one side. "I've got her," Connor said. "Whoa there." He grunted as he pulled Lucinda off Tina. They fell backward and Connor's grip broke. Lucinda rolled onto her front and sprang to her feet with an agility that belied her age. She took a swing at Connor, who'd also gotten to his feet. Her punch hit him full in the face, and he staggered, but he didn't fall. He lifted his fists but hesitated, clearly not wanting to hit an older woman.

"My sister was a darned fool," Tina Ledbetter, still on the ground, shouted. "But not nearly as much of a fool as you." She reached out and grabbed Lucinda's ankle with both hands and twisted. Lucinda dropped like a stone as Tina rolled away from her.

Then, as though night had suddenly turned into day, I was blinded by light. Pain shot through my eyes, and I lifted my hands to shield them. A deep voice broke the silence. "Lucinda Lorca, I am arresting you for the murder of Helena Sanchez. Anything you say—"

"What? You can't arrest me. Those people attacked me. It was three against one. I didn't—"

Butch Greenblatt pulled Lucinda to her feet, and Holly Rankin snapped handcuffs on her as Sam Watson continued giving the warning. At an unseen signal, blue and red lights flashed, and sirens screamed through the row of trees as police cars sped to the scene.

Lucinda recovered her wits quicker than I would have expected her to. "It was a trick," she yelled. "They wanted to play at having their silly séance, and I decided to play along so we could get this nonsense over with and go back to town. You have to believe me, Detective. I knew that woman wasn't Helena's ghost. I'm not that stupid."

"We'll sort it all out downtown," Watson said.

Tina stepped in front of Lucinda. Holly Rankin braced herself to intervene. Tina's lip was cut, her face battered, her nose bleeding, and she'd have a couple of impressive black eyes tomorrow, but she gave the other woman a big grin. Lucinda made no move toward her, but simply studied Tina's face for a long time before saying, "You're Helena's sister."

"Identical twin. When we were kids we had great fun pretending to be each other. Our parents hated that."

Butch hustled Lucinda, still proclaiming her innocence, across the lawn to a police car discreetly parked in a copse of trees in the loop at the end of the laneway. More uniformed officers ran up.

"What took you so long?" Bertie said to Sam Watson. "Lucinda turned into a mad woman. Tina might have been killed. Lucy might have been killed. We couldn't see a blasted thing."

"Sorry," Watson said. "We must have gotten turned around in the dark. We were at the other end of the boardwalk when we heard the screaming."

"Nice diversion, Louise Jane," Tina said. "If I didn't know you were an old fraud, I'd have almost thought you were onto something with this 'summoning the spirits' stuff."

Louise Jane sputtered, but she decided she had other people to be angrier at than Tina. "Sam, what are you and your lot doing here? Bertie, this is all your fault. I told you not to involve the police."

"It was more my doing," I said. "Of course I involved the police. Didn't you hear? The rest of us did. Lucinda confessed to murdering Helena."

Louise Jane took a step toward me. The look on her face was positively murderous, and I was glad Connor stood next to me and we were surrounded by police officers. "You have completely ruined the mood. They were here. I know they were. I felt them. They were coming. They wanted to talk to me. For once, just once, the marsh spirits wanted to talk to *me*!"

"That was the entire point, Louise Jane," Bertie said calmly. "It was your idea originally, and Lucy and I ran with it. We knew Lucinda would be scared of contact with *real* spirits and thus ready to be frightened when she thought the ghost of Helena was confronting her. We considered going ahead with your plan to let the spirits tell us what happened, but I pointed out to Lucy that Sam could never take that to court."

"Got that one right," Holly Rankin muttered under her breath.

Louise Jane huffed, but some of the anger faded from her eyes. "You could have told me what you were up to."

"I considered doing that," Bertie said, "but we needed your total concentration to ensure the mood was absolutely perfect."

"Natural enough, I guess," Louise Jane said. "I'm always happy to be of help."

"To create a distraction anyway," Tina said, "while others do the real work."

"You are not helping," Ronald said.

"Not trying to," Tina replied.

"The resemblance is uncanny." Shelia stepped in front of Tina and peered into the woman's face. "I'll admit that, but I wouldn't have been fooled so easily."

"Okay, Lucy, you're forgiven," Louise Jane said. "The energy here tonight is awful powerful, and I'm sure I can do something to salvage it. Sam, you've got what you need. Get your people out of here and move those lights. Turn off the sirens too, will you? I'm going to try again. I can't leave things like this. The spirts don't like to think they've been tricked. Everyone, resume your positions."

"Are you kidding me?" Mary-Sue said. "I scarcely know what's happened here, but whatever it is, I've had enough of it."

"That goes for me as well," Ruth said. "Do you need me any more tonight, Detective?"

"I'll have to take your statements before you leave," Watson replied. "Bertie can we use the library?"

"Of course," she said.

Connor groaned.

"What brings you here tonight anyway?" Watson asked him. "When Lucy called me, she said they were going to attempt to reenact the events of Friday, but you weren't part of this group originally."

"I wanted to talk to Lucy."

"What about?" I asked.

"It's private," Connor said.

"Can it wait?"

"It'll have to," he said, "although I'm starting to give up hope that the right time will ever present itself."

Louise Jane threw up her arms. "Oh for heaven's sake, Connor. Just come out with it and ask her to marry you and get it over with. We'll all pretend not to be listening."

Louise Jane and her stupid, inappropriate jokes.

I looked at Connor, ready to laugh along with him. Instead, the look on his face had my jaw dropping and my heart fluttering.

He took both my hands in his. He stared into my eyes.

My heart stopped. I stared back.

"Lucy." He cleared his throat. "Lucille Richardson, you've been the light of my life since I was fifteen years old. Even over all those years we were apart, I always knew you'd come back some day, and I kept a place in my heart ready for you. Lucy. My love. Will you marry me?"

My heart started again. It didn't just start. It leaped. It summersaulted. It did cartwheels.

I had no hesitation whatsoever. "Yes, Connor. Yes, I will marry you."

Police officers, employees of the Bodie Island Lighthouse Library, librarians and ex-librarians, one spook-hunter, and one twin sister burst into cheers and applause. Connor swept me into his arms and we kissed, long and deep.

"Can I come out now, Louise Jane?" called a voice from beyond the circle of light. "My foot's gone to sleep."

Chapter Twenty-Three

When at last Bertie's friends, Louise Jane's cousin, and Tina Ledbetter had given their statements and left, the police had finished whatever police do, Bertie and Ronald had headed home, and Louise Jane had finally—finally—been persuaded that Connor and I really—really—did not want to go back to the marsh to once again try to contact the sprits, Connor and I were alone in the library.

Alone, that is, except for Charles, who was only too keen to stay up and help us celebrate our engagement.

Our engagement. At the moment I was nothing but a tumble of conflicting emotions. I was slowly coming down from the terror of the moments on the marsh and the fight in the dark, followed by watching the police going about their business and then the long tedium of waiting to give Sam my statement and for everyone to leave, combined with the overwhelming joy of knowing Connor's love for me was real.

I smiled at Connor—my fiancé.

At the moment my fiancé didn't look too good. Lucinda had landed a solid punch on his jaw, and the skin was turning all sorts of shades of purple and bluish-gray.

He'd gone to the washroom to clean up, and when he came out he said, "The citizens of Nags Head will not be impressed. But never mind my political reputation: I hope it never gets out that a sixty-year-old woman did this to me." He dropped into a chair.

"The rage," I said, "the pure rage that must have built up in that woman's mind over the past twenty-five years. Not only that she'd kill Helena once but then try to kill her again!"

"Humiliation is a powerful emotion. Some people are able to get over it. Some never can. I don't quite understand what happened earlier. I heard Lucinda say something about *him*, and *him* wanting Helena, not her. But other than that . . ."

"Jeff Applewhite and the Blackstone necklace, but that's still only speculation on my part. Let's wait until we hear what she has to say to Sam."

Connor rose to his feet. "The ring. I forgot all about the ring." He'd taken off his jacket and put it over the back of a chair. He fumbled in the pocket and bought out a small blue box. "This isn't a real stone, Lucy, just something temporary. I want you to come with me so we can pick out the right ring together, but I got this imitation one so I could ask you to marry me properly. That didn't exactly work out as planned."

I smiled at him. He opened the box, took out a thin band with a small white stone and slipped it on my left hand. I liked the way it looked there. We both admired it for a moment, and then he slapped his forehead. "The champagne. I forgot that too. I put a bottle of champagne in a cooler in my car, on the off chance that you'd say yes."

"And I did say yes. In front of half the population of Nags Head, North Carolina. I guess I can't take it back. By now the other half will be informed via the grapevine."

"If you want—"

"I do not want to take it back." I stretched on my tippy-toes and kissed him. "Not now. Not ever. And as nice as a glass of chilled champagne sounds, I suggest we not open it tonight. You got a blow to the head, and I had my teeth, not to mention my brains, rattled. We have the rest of our lives to have champagne."

He stared down at me. His lovely blue eyes were very wet. "Do you know that I love you?"

"I'm beginning to get the impression," I said.

We only separated when Charles jumped onto the shelf behind Connor and began scratching at his right shoulder. "What on earth do you want?" he asked the big cat.

Charles yawned. *Bedtime.* He was clearly unimpressed at our news. I suspect he'd known all along that Connor's and my fate was to be together.

"My folks are out of town right now," Connor said, "but they'll be back on the weekend. I'd like to invite them around to my place for dinner one night, and we can give them the news?"

"I'd enjoy that." I liked Connor's parents very much, and I knew they'd make great in-laws.

"We can make plans for the wedding later. I want to marry you tomorrow, but I suspect our mothers might want some input."

"Mine will," I said. "I'd like to tell her in person, but, as you said, the news will soon be all over town, which means my aunt will know by tomorrow. If Aunt Ellen knows before Mom, my mother will not be pleased."

Connor chuckled and folded me into his arms.

Charles headed for the staircase.

Chapter
Twenty-Four

It was the early hours when Connor left. Too late to call my parents. I went to sleep with a warm, happy glow, and I awoke before the sun, still warm, still happy.

My mom was an early riser, and I knew she had a regular doubles tennis game every Thursday in the summer at seven. I made the call without even getting out of bed. Charles clearly didn't approve: my first task of the day was always to check his water and food bowls. "Just this once," I said to him as the phone rang at the other end, "you can wait."

He pouted.

"Lucy!" my mother said. "Is everything all right? It's early for you to be calling."

"Couldn't be better, Mom."

"This is rather sudden," she said when I'd given her my news. "You've only known him for a year."

"A year's a long time, Mom. Didn't you and Dad know each other for all of six weeks before you decided to get married?"

"That was different."

"It sure was. I'm thirty-three. You were seventeen."

A long silence came down the phone line. I waited. I often wondered if Mom regretted her sudden, impulsive, too-young marriage. I'm the youngest of their four children, and for all the years I'd been growing up, my parents' marriage had not been a good one. They didn't fight—at least not in front of the children. Neither of them ever stormed out or threatened a divorce, but they barely spoke to each other and rarely went anywhere together unless it was to an event for Dad's law firm or a party at the country club where they were members. Things had come to a head last summer, and they'd been on the verge of separating, but they'd worked things out and agreed to give it another try. When I'd last seen my parents in February at Josie's wedding, they'd seemed genuinely happy in each other's company.

"You're right, dear, as you usually are," Mom said at last. "If this is what you want, and if this is the man for you, I wish you both all the happiness in the world. Now, when are you coming to Boston? You'll be married at the club, of course. I'll call today and have them pencil in a suitable date, and then you and I can meet with the wedding planner."

Josie's wedding had been in danger of being taken over by strong-willed relatives. I was determined that was not going to happen to me. Which meant, I knew, I had to nip Mom's plans for a big Boston country club wedding with all her friends (and some of her enemies) as guests in the bud.

"Connor's family's in Nags Head," I said. "My friends are here, and my coworkers, plus Aunt Ellen, Uncle Amos, and Josie. This is where I live now, Mom. We're having the wedding in Nags Head."

She hesitated and then she said, "An excellent idea, dear. A beach wedding would be nice, but you know what's best for you. Your father and I will want to come down as soon as possible to give you and Connor our congratulations in person. Will you let me know what a good time would be?"

"Thanks, Mom," I said.

* * *

Sam Watson came into the library shortly before closing. I guessed he was here to let us know what he'd learned from Lucinda, and I could barely contain my impatience as I finished showing an elderly man how he could take out books on the e-reader that had been a birthday present from his grandchildren. I helped the last of the day's patrons check out their books, listened to Mrs. Peterson's complaints about the summer science camp she'd sent Dallas to (*"Not up to our standards, Lucy"*), and tried not to tap my foot while Mr. Snyder untangled Charles from his lap. At last they were gone. I slammed the door and firmly locked it.

Charlene, Ronald, Charles, and I followed Watson into Bertie's office. First thing this morning, Ronald had told Charlene, in great dramatic detail, about the events of last night, and she'd proclaimed herself highly disappointed to have missed it. Bertie leaned back in her chair, Charlene took the visitor's seat, and Ronald and I stood against the walls. Charles assumed his favorite position on top of the filing cabinet. His intelligent amber eyes narrowed, his ears stood at attention, his tail flicked slowly back and forth.

"First things first," the detective said when he had our attention. Which hadn't been hard to get. "My congratulations, Lucy."

I blushed, twisted the ring on my finger, and said, "Thank you."

"Lucinda Lorca," he went on, "has been assigned a lawyer. The lawyer advised her not to say anything to us, but she has chosen to disregard that advice. Perhaps she needs some soul cleansing, but that's not up to me to say. In April 1995, she had a boyfriend by the name of Jeff Applewhite."

"So I was right," I said.

He smiled at me. "As you so often are, Lucy. Applewhite was a drifter, younger than her by a couple of years. He did odd, unskilled jobs on small construction sites or at home renovations, stayed in one place for a while, and then moved on. She was a librarian. Her first marriage had recently ended, and she was bored and restless. She was afraid, she says now, of getting old without having had any adventure in her life."

"Tell us about the necklace," I blurted out, "What happened to the necklace?"

"All in due time, Lucy. All in due time. Now remember, what I have to tell you is what she told me. We have a heck of a lot of digging to do to get to the truth of what happened."

"Understood," Bertie said.

Ronald, Charlene, and I murmured our agreement. Charles flicked his tail.

"Applewhite got the idea in his head to steal the Blackstone necklace. Where that idea might have come from, I can only speculate. Lucinda had gone with him to at least one of the parties at Rachel's house. She'd heard about the necklace. She would have had some idea of its value. She told me that night at Rachel's was one of the best nights of her life. All those people simply having fun without worrying about tomorrow. No serious jobs, no families, no responsibilities. Rachel herself with all that money and nothing to spend it on other than having a good time."

"That's sad," Bertie said. "Rachel was lucky: she found out in time that, despite appearances, that's no life."

"Whether taking the necklace was Lucinda's idea or Jeff's doesn't matter. They planned to steal it at the first opportunity and run off . . . somewhere. Which is what happened. The first part anyway. Jeff stole the necklace. Lucinda didn't go with him to the Blackstone home that night; she wanted a plausible alibi, I believe, in case the police came calling before the two of them could get out of town."

"What does any of this have to do with Helena?" Ronald asked.

"Jeff planned to make off with the necklace," I said. "Not accompanied by Lucinda, but Helena."

"Yes," Watson said. "Jeff figured it would be a couple of days, probably more, before Rachel realized the necklace was missing. He told Lucinda it would look suspicious if he suddenly left town, as he was in the middle of a job. Lucinda came to realize that in reality he was waiting for Helena. He finally told her, Lucinda, quite bluntly—and very foolishly in my opinion—he was in love with another woman, and they were leaving town together. With the Blackstone necklace. As Lucinda remembers it, he laughed at her, threw the other woman in her face. She followed him here, to the Lighthouse Library, when he came to fetch Helena on the night of May 2. Somehow Lucinda persuaded him to go for a walk with her before he talked to Helena. He might have been young and charming, but I suspect Jeff Applewhite wasn't all that bright. Lucinda killed him."

"Oh my gosh," Charlene said.

That was what I'd suspected, but even so I was still shocked. Lucinda had initially told me she left North Carolina in 1993. Margaret Hurley had checked her records of their class and discovered that Lucinda had actually left in May of 1995. That might have been a simple mistake of the sort anyone would make, but Lucinda's lie started me down the path of wondering what else she might be lying about.

"She killed him and dumped his body in the marsh. Probably not all that far from here," Watson said.

"All the more reason," I said, "for Lucinda to be susceptible to the idea that last night Helena rose from her own watery grave."

"All these years, Helena thought Jeff had left without her," Bertie said.

"Believing that turned her bitter," I said. "Bitter, angry, betrayed, untrusting. Feelings that only grew and festered when she never heard from him again. I heard different accounts of Helena's personality from different people, and when I realized it was around a particular time that she changed, I started wondering what might have happened. She'd never gotten on with her parents or her sister, so it couldn't have been that. She told Tina she'd met a man and she was quitting her job and going with him to Hawaii. She never went to Hawaii, and a couple of weeks after the theft of the necklace and the disappearance of Jeff Applewhite, she turned on Mary-Sue and fired her. Mary-Sue, I suspect, was nothing but an outlet for Helena's rage when she finally accepted the fact that, as she thought, Jeff had run out on her, taking the Rajipani Diamond and the other jewels with him."

"Was Helena aware he had the necklace?" Charlene asked. "Did she know he planned to steal it and had done so?"

"I don't know," Watson said. "We probably never will. It's likely he told her he was coming into some money, so she could afford to quit her job."

"She knew," I said. "Helena was a romantic, but not a total fool. She told Tina she and her Prince Charming were going to live on a private island in the South Pacific. She would have had some basis for believing they'd have the means to do that. Tina laughed at her. All the more reason Helena never confided to Tina or anyone else that she believed Jeff had run out on her. If she'd gone to the police when he and the necklace disappeared, Tina would have mocked her relentlessly."

"That all makes a twisted sort of sense," Charlene said, "but what does any of it have to do with *The Celestine Prophecy* and the withdrawal slip?"

Watson grinned. "Oh yes. That. Two days after Lucinda murdered Jeff, she came back to the Lighthouse Library. To gloat over what she'd done perhaps, or maybe out of regret. Maybe to see Helena, her rival. Probably a combination of all three. She took out a book and signed it "Jeff Applewhite." If the police began searching for the necklace, she wanted to leave some evidence that Jeff had been alive and in Nags Head on May the fourth."

"*Star Wars* Day," Ronald said.

"What?" we chorused.

He pointed to today's tie featuring colorful drawings of the robots R2D2 and C3PO. "May fourth is *Star Wars* Day. May the fourth be with you." His voice trailed off. "Sorry. Please continue, Detective."

"What was the significance of *The Celestine Prophecy* itself?" Charlene asked.

"I don't know," Watson said. "Never thought to ask."

"That book was hugely popular in its day, particularly among those who liked the idea of abandoning their mundane lives and rushing off to seek enlightenment," Bertie said. "I'd hazard a guess that Jeff Applewhite strung Lucinda along, probably telling her how meaningful the message of that book had been to him. Perhaps taking it out, in his name, was her final message to him."

"Easy to seek enlightenment when you're in possession of a twenty-five-million-dollar necklace," I said.

"I've sometimes wondered why we're so impressed by lumps of carbonated crystals," Charlene said.

"In *The Moonstone*, the jewel everyone's after is a holy relic," Bertie said. "Oh, sorry, Sam. All that's somewhat off topic. Please continue. What happened then?"

"At some point, Lucinda drove Jeff's truck to the bus station in Elizabeth City and left it there. The police found the truck when they started searching for Jeff. It was in pretty bad shape, and they speculated he'd dumped it and caught a bus out of North Carolina, escaping with his ill-gotten gains. As for the copy of *The Celestine Prophecy* she'd taken out under Jeff's name, Lucinda dropped it in the returns box at another library and it was sent back here. Ironically, no one noticed Jeff's name or gave it a single thought."

"Until last Friday." I said.

"Until last Friday. Helena must have recognized Jeff's name right away. We'll never know exactly what she thought, but she would have realized he wouldn't have come into her library two

276

days after they'd been supposed to leave together, just to take out a book. Maybe she knew the handwriting wasn't his." Watson shook his head. "We'll never know for sure, but we do know Lucinda saw the moment Helena realized what she was looking at. Lucinda's saying Helena gave her what she calls an 'evil eye.' Which might be nothing but her guilt talking."

"Helena knew, at that moment, Jeff hadn't willingly left without her," I said. "I'm sure of it. And I'm glad. I don't think she suspected Lucinda of having something to do with his death. She didn't react more negatively toward Lucinda than to anyone else that night. But as we've seen before, 'The guilty run when no one pursues.'"

"So true," Ronald said.

"And so sad," Bertie said.

Charles and Charlene said nothing.

"Helena might have paid no attention to Lucinda," I said, "but Lucinda was horrified when she first saw Helena at the party. I'd forgotten that until I started putting things together and then I realized how over-the-top her reaction had been."

"Lucinda believed she had to kill Helena before Helena could do anything about what she suspected happened all those years ago," Watson said. "If, when the police first started looking for Jeff, Helena had told them he was supposed to meet her the night in question at the library, Lucinda might have been caught. Instead, Helena believed she'd been betrayed and was too humiliated to say anything, even when word got out that the police were looking for Jeff Applewhite."

"I suspect," I said, "she feared the mocking of her twin sister above all."

"So sad," Bertie repeated.

"The police assumed Jeff had left with the necklace. A natural enough assumption to make. Lucinda quit her job and moved to California not long after, wisely not wanting to be around if they did come to wonder if Jeff had left Nags Head. As for the necklace, Lucinda went to California, but she never showed signs of having anything in the way of money, so she didn't have it. Jeff never showed it to her, she says, so it's even possible he wasn't the one who stole it. If he was, perhaps he had it on him when she pushed his body into the waters of the marsh. And there it lies."

We were all silent for a few moments.

"In several hundred years," Charlene said, "the sands will shift as the sea level rises and the tides move, and the necklace might be exposed once again. And everyone will wonder how such a precious thing came to be at the bottom of the ocean. Books will be written about it."

"What happens now, Sam?" Bertie asked.

"Lucinda Lorca has been charged with the murder of Helena Sanchez. I've started gathering evidence for that, which means I need to talk to you at length, Lucy."

"Happy to help," I said.

"I'm also reopening the investigation into the disappearance of Jeff Applewhite. Lucinda confessed that she killed him, but a confession means little in court without evidence, particularly in the absence of a body. We've got divers back in the marsh. The tides are strong around here, and it's been a long time, but his body might have snagged on a root or something and still be here."

"Please, please, do not tell Louise Jane that," Bertie begged. "I do not want her trying to make contact."

Watson laughed. "Believe me, I don't want her help either."

I said nothing. Louise Jane had said the marsh spirits told her, "Appearances can be deceiving." That phrase put the idea in my head of using Tina pretending to be Helena to frighten the killer into confessing. Had the spirits truly been trying to send us a message?

Of course not. I'd simply taken my inspiration from Louise Jane's attempt to make herself sound important.

"About that, Sam," Ronald said, "you might be too late. Before I came down, I spotted Louise Jane and her binoculars heading for the boardwalk at a rapid pace."

Chapter
Twenty-Five

Connor had a council meeting that night, but he called me when it ended. We decided to postpone the trip to Rodanthe until next weekend so we could look at engagement rings tomorrow after work and then have a special dinner to toast each other on the beginning of our life together. He'd invited his parents to his house for dinner on Saturday without telling them why.

I hoped they'd be delighted at the news. We'd decided to have our wedding next autumn. It seemed so far away, but I knew the time would pass quickly. We talked for a long time, and I turned out the light and snuggled under the covers with a warm, happy feeling.

I should have dreamed about weddings on the beach and beautiful dresses and the man I loved, but instead my night was full of the work that had been done earlier this year on the lighthouse foundations. Shoring up the historic building had been a major, not to mention expensive, job but it had gone well and we expected the lighthouse to stand tall and proud in the face of storms for many decades, hopefully centuries, to come. In my dream, the job hadn't finished, and I was frantically running to and fro with piles of shovels cradled in my arms, trying to convince people to come and help me dig.

I woke in a sweat and a tumble of bed clothes. Charles snoozed peacefully beside me. I stared up at the ceiling, wondering why I'd been dreaming about the restoration.

And then I knew.

I checked the time. Quarter past four. Far, far too early to call Bertie.

I tried to get back to sleep, but sleep wouldn't come. I got up at five, made coffee, showered and dressed for the day, and then paced up and down until six. Bertie was part-owner and instructor at a yoga studio in Nags Head, and she often led classes before coming into work. I hoped today wasn't one of those days.

"Lucy," she said when she picked up the phone. "Is something the matter? It's quite early."

"Everything's fine. What's the earliest you can get here?"

"I don't have a class this morning, so I was planning a walk on the beach and then popping into Josie's for a leisurely breakfast before work. Do you need me?"

"I think so, yes." I told her what was on my mind.

"I'll be there in twenty minutes," she said. "Twenty-five with a stop at Josie's."

"I'll have a latte," I said.

Next I called Connor.

"Checking to see if I've changed my mind?" he said when he answered. But his voice was light, the tone joking, so I replied, "Not yet, but I did have a restless night. Bertie's on her way. If you've got the time, I'd like you to join us."

"I have time," he said, "my first meeting isn't until the afternoon."

"Good. Oh, one thing: Do you have anything lying around that would be suitable for prying up floorboards?"

"I won't ask why you need such a thing, but I'm sure I can find something."

* * *

Charles and I were pacing in the main room when Bertie came in, followed by Connor, carrying a tire iron.

"Bertie handed me a take-out cup. "Sorry, Connor, I would have gotten you something but Lucy didn't tell me you were coming."

"We can share," I said, and he grinned at me.

We went into Bertie's office.

"You sure you want me to do this?" Connor gripped the tire iron tightly.

Bertie glanced at me, her face forming a question.

"If I'm wrong," I said, "I'll pay for the damage. I'll probably have to pay for the damage even if I'm right. We know Jeff Applewhite did odd jobs working as an unskilled laborer for contractors, and his last job was with Reynolds Renovations, which isn't in business anymore. Aunt Ellen told me Reynolds did some work at the library, modernizing the interior, although she didn't say exactly what or where they'd done this. Mary-Sue told me the work was getting on Helena's nerves, and that probably pushed her over the edge into firing Mary-Sue. A new floor was laid in the director's office and the other work was mostly cosmetic, fresh paint job, new windows and such."

"Do you know for sure Jeff was working here, at the library? I remember Reynolds Renovations. They were a big firm; they did work all over the Outer Banks." Connor hadn't dressed for the mayor's office this morning, but he'd come in jeans and a T-shirt. His hair was still damp from the shower, his chin and cheeks were smooth, and he smelled of good soap and spicy aftershave. I almost wanted to ask Bertie to give us a few minutes alone. My wild plan could wait.

I swallowed and said, "No, I don't. But he had to have met Helena somewhere, and they didn't seem the sort to move in the same social circles. Yes, he was a library user and a reader, but the library director doesn't usually have much, if anything, to do with casual patrons."

"Which I regret," Bertie said, "but go on."

"Tina told me Helena met her Prince Charming when he was working at the library. I know this library didn't have any male employees back then, so I assumed that by working, she meant working on a research project or something, but now I think Jeff was working in here. Meaning in this office. For Reynolds Renovations."

Connor and Bertie glanced around the room.

"Jeff Applewhite stole a multimillion-dollar diamond. He couldn't carry it around with him. Even though the necklace hadn't been reported missing, his lifestyle made him the sort that could get stopped by the police at any time. He might have kept it in his truck or in his room, but Rachel said he was a drifter. It's possible he didn't consider his room to be safe from prying eyes and vehicles can always be stolen. The night he planned to leave Nags Head he came to the Lighthouse Library where he was confronted and killed by Lucinda. Lucinda believed he was here to get Helena. Which might have been the case, but was he also here to get the necklace he'd earlier hidden under the floorboards? He could have hidden it anyplace in the library where they were doing work, but Helena's office would have been the most logical if he wanted to retrieve it quickly and easily on the night he came to get her."

"Only one way to find out." Connor thrust the end of the tire iron under a board and yanked. The boards screamed in protest.

Ripping up a floor turns out to be a heck of a lot of work. First Bertie, Connor, and I carried out Bertie's desk, the computer, chairs, and her potted plants, then we took the drawers out of the filling cabinet and dumped them and the cabinet into the hallway, before Connor got to work wrenching up the boards. Bertie found a hammer and used one end to loosen the nails, and I carried the boards away and stacked them in the hallway out of the way.

"What on earth is going on here?" Ronald said.

I wiped sweat and dust out of my eyes and explained.

"Let me at it," he said. "Connor, you need a hand. Be right back." He soon was, carrying an axe.

"You just happened to have that in your car?" I said.

"Nan and I went to a Christmas tree farm to cut down our own tree. I never got around to putting this thing away. Let me at it."

"I declare," Charlene said when she arrived. "Do we have an infestation of giant mice?"

"An infestation of treasure-hunting librarians," I said. "You take over from Bertie. She could use a break."

Bertie came out of the office with a grimace on her face, sweat in her eyes, and one hand pressed into the small of her back. "Not quite as young as I once was." Bertie always complains that her office is too small. Today, we were glad of it.

When the floorboards were all stacked in the hallway and in the staff break room, we gathered in the office, standing on the support beams, staring down into the dark hole of our own making.

"I don't see anything," Charlene said.

Bertie produced a flashlight and swept it around the space. We saw plenty of cobwebs and evidence that mice had recently been in residence. We saw no twenty-five-million-dollar diamond.

My heart had sunk into my stomach. I'd guessed Jeff had hidden the necklace under the floor because that was the major change made to the office. But it might have gone into the window frames or even a hole in the wall that was patched before being painted. I didn't know if we could completely destroy this room.

"Did they do any other work at the time?" Connor asked. "Apart from the director's office?"

"I don't know," I admitted. "I suppose they might have."

"We can't tear down the entire place," Charlene said.

I became aware of a loud banging noise coming from the front door.

"It's nine twenty-two," Ronald said. "We're late opening."

"Will you take care of that, please," Bertie asked him. "Don't let anyone into the hallway."

When Ronald had left Bertie surveyed the damage. "I have absolutely no idea how we're going to put this all back together."

"I'm so sorry. This was obviously an incredibly stupid idea." I was crushingly disappointed. Because of a stupid dream, I'd dragged my boss away from a rare leisurely morning; I'd ruined the morning after our engagement for my fiancé as well as me; and I'd caused the destruction of the entire office floor.

Charles, who'd been watching the activity with a confused expression on his face and getting in everyone's way, jumped into the hole.

"Get him out of there," Bertie said, "He'll start digging around and we'll never find him."

I fell to my knees and stretched out flat on my stomach. I stuck my arms under the supporting beams calling for the cat and feeling for the thick fur. "Come on Charles, this isn't a playground. I'm not in the mood to play."

Bertie shone a flashlight onto the spot where Charles had disappeared.

"Charles," I said, "if you don't come right now, I'm cutting off your tinned food for a week."

The tips of his ears appeared, and then his entire head. Something was in his mouth. He leaped out of the hole in one smooth movement and dropped what he was carrying next to me. I jumped to my feet with a shriek. He'd given me a dead mouse.

"Oh my goodness," Charlene said.

"Can it be?" Bertie said.

Not a dead mouse. A dust-encrusted black velvet bag tied with a black drawstring which I'd mistaken in my panic for a rodent's tail. The black bag had blended so completely into the dark of the hole, we hadn't seen it even with our flashlights.

We stood in a circle staring at it.

Charles swatted the bag.

"Lucy," Bertie said at last. "I think you'd better check that."

I bent over and took the bag in my hands. The contents shifted as I lifted it up. The drawstring was tattered and frail and the knot had been chewed away. I looked at Connor. He gave me a nod. Scarcely daring to breathe, slowly and carefully I opened the bag, turned it over, and held out my hand. The contents poured into it like liquid fire.

It was as though the sun had come inside. The enormous, multifaceted diamond caught the lights of Bertie's office, reflected and magnified them many times over and threw the rays at us. The smaller jewels—deep red rubies, glowing green sapphires, diamonds made of pure light—sparkled and danced as though delighted to see the light of day after all these years trapped underground.

"The Rajipani Diamond," I said, "and the Blackstone necklace."

Chapter
Twenty-Six

O nce we'd recovered some of our wits, Bertie marched into the main room, announced that the library would be closed for the rest of the day, and unceremoniously hustled confused patrons out the door. When they'd gone she used the phone on the circulation desk (because the one in her office was balanced on a support beam) to call first Rachel Blackstone and then Sam Watson.

Bertie put the necklace on the circulation desk and we all gathered around, staring at it. When Rachel saw it, having simply pulled a track suit on over her pajamas, she took one look and burst into tears.

We went outside, letting her spend some time alone with the necklace and her thoughts.

"I hope you won't have to take it into evidence, Sam," Bertie said to the detective when he arrived.

"Believe me, Bertie, I do not want anything like that in my possession for a moment longer than necessary. I'll take it to the station and have it photographed and get a jewelry expert in ASAP. Rachel can stay with me the entire time, if she wants, and then take it home. She can call a jeweler of her own to verity it's the original."

He checked his watch, decided she'd had enough private time, and went inside.

Butch had come with the detective. "I hear congratulations are in order." He gave Connor a hearty handshake and me a hug that had me fearing for the state of my ribs.

Rachel and Watson came out of the library moments later. Rachel carried the bag and Sam Watson stayed very close to her.

"Detective Watson says it was you who guessed where it was," Rachel said to me. "I don't know what to say. Except thank you."

"It's my pleasure," I said.

"He also tells me you've been busy lately. You got engaged. Congratulations to you both."

Connor put his arm around my shoulder and pulled me to him.

Rachel smiled at him. "Your Honor, will you call me later? I have a proposition for you."

"Sure," Connor said.

"You can drive with us, Ms. Blackstone," Watson said, "I'll send someone to get your car."

They walked away. Butch followed, his hand on the butt of his gun and his eyes checking out everything around him as though expecting international jewel thieves to leap out of the marsh grasses and accost them at any moment.

"Maybe she wants to make a donation to the town or the library in thanks for the recovery of the necklace," Charlene said when police car had disappeared. "That's nice of her."

* * *

Rachel Blackstone did contribute handsomely to the library, but that wasn't what she wanted to talk to Connor privately about.

"Do you want to accept?" he said to me later that night as we sipped champagne and toasted our future in the quiet of my Lighthouse Aerie. Charles had inspected my glass, decided the bubbles that hit his nose were not to his liking and settled himself onto the cushions on the window seat to wash his paws.

I thought for a long time. "I think I do. Not because of the value, but because the offer is truly coming from her heart."

Rachel had told Connor she intended to have the necklace broken up. She'd keep a chain with a small diamond for herself, in memory of her grandparents, but the rest she wanted to sell in order to donate the proceeds to adult literacy and organizations promoting girls' education in the US and in Africa.

She'd sell the rest, except for one flawless two carat diamond which she wanted to give to Connor to have set into my engagement ring.

"I think it's suitable." Connor lifted his glass in a toast to me. "That we start our journey through life together with a memory of the latest of your wild escapades. By the way, Rachel has offered to pay to have Bertie's floor replaced. I accepted on the library's behalf." He put his glass down and stood up. He walked toward me and plucked my glass out of my hands. Then he lifted me to my feet and wrapped me in his arms. "I've said it before, and I'll say it again. Lucy Richardson, life with you will not be boring."

"Sometimes," I said, "I could use a bit of boredom."

He chuckled. "What do you want to do about living arrangements? This apartment is nice and all, but it is a bit . . . uh . . . small for two people."

"Why don't we start looking for a house together? We're in no hurry, so we have time to find the perfect place."

"Exactly what I was thinking." He put his glass down, took mine out of my hand and placed it next to his, and gathered me into his arms.

* * *

I'd been living in the Lighthouse Aerie for more than a year, and I loved it here, but it was time to move on. I knew that with Connor beside me, I was ready for whatever life threw my way.

As I settled into Connor's kiss, I heard Charles yawn.

Author's Note

The Bodie Island Lighthouse is a real historic lighthouse, located in Cape Hatteras National Seashore on the Outer Banks of North Carolina. It is still a working lighthouse, protecting ships from the Graveyard of the Atlantic, and the public is invited to tour it and climb the 214 steps to the top. The view from up there is well worth the trip. But the lighthouse does not contain a library, nor is it large enough to house a collection of books, offices, staff rooms, two staircases, and even an apartment.

Within these books, the interior of the lighthouse is the product of my imagination. I like to think of it as my version of the TARDIS, from the TV show Doctor Who, or Hermione Granger's beaded handbag: far larger inside than it appears from the outside.

I hope it is large enough for your imagination also.

Acknowledgments

Since the publication of the first Lighthouse Library novel, *By Book or By Crook*, I've been overwhelmed by the support and enthusiasm of the cozy-reading community. Your encouragement has kept this series going and I am sincerely grateful.

Thanks to Kim Lionetti and Linda Wiken for tossing ideas around with me over a delicious breakfast somewhere in the wilds of Pennsylvania. Sometimes all a book needs is a spark.

Thanks also to the team at Crooked Lane Books and my marvelous agent Kim Lionetti from Bookends, without whom Lucy, Charles, and the gang wouldn't be able to get into so much trouble.

Shelagh Mathers made the winning bid at auction as part of the Women Killing It Authors Festival to have a character in this book named after her mother. And thus we have Margaret Hurley, librarian. I hope you like my Margaret, Shelagh.